THE CLARKS OF WILLSBOROUGH POINT

A JOURNEY THROUGH CHILDHOOD

Darcey Hale

TBR Books
Brooklyn, New York

TBR Books is a program of the Center for the Advancement of Languages, Education, and Communities. We publish researchers and practitioners who seek to engage diverse communities on topics related to education, languages, cultural history, and social initiatives.

TBR Books

146 Norman Avenue

Brooklyn, New York

www.tbr-books.org | contact@tbr-books.org

Front Cover Illustration: Willsboro Point © Philip Hall

Cover Design © Nathalie Charles

Back Cover Illustration: Darcey Hale © Nancie Battaglia

Inside Illustrations: © Philip Hall, Bruce Hale, Ashley Ahrent, Erwin H. Austin

ISBN 978-1-947626-28-7 (paperback)

ISBN 978-1-947626-29-4 (eBook)

Library of Congress Control Number: 2019945162

A tribute to Jared Van Wagenen, Jr. who in *The Golden Age of Homespun* collected and recorded the lore and the methods by which our forebears in Northern New York lived upon their land.

DEDICATION

Throughout my research and writing I have continued to receive immeasurable advice and support from the four amazing people who were at my side through thick and thin when I wrote *The Long Trek North*. You shared your knowledge and expertise time and time again, and when I was stumbling, off track, or just plain wrong you were there to help me over the hurdle. Without you I would never have been able to bring to life yet another chapter in the lives of the Clarks of Willsboro Point. Thank you one and all!

Ron, the Town Historian, I relied upon you to ensure that the historical facts about Willsboro that I cited were accurate. I cannot begin to count the number of times I looked to you for information and watched you retrieve it from the depths of your memory with such ease. Thank you for sharing your time and knowledge so generously.

Morris, the consummate researcher, once again I have you to thank for all of the interpretive work that you did over the past twenty years as we tackled what sometimes seemed to be an insurmountable mountain. You were correct. The Clark Collection was the gift that would not stop giving, and it continues to be just that.

Philip, my eldest son, where would I have been without you? As always, you stood beside me when I needed advice and counsel on a seemingly infinite variety of topics, and you were patient beyond belief as I encountered one computer problem (or should I say challenge) over and over again.

Fabrice, you believed that I had a story to tell. Without your pushing me hard, and then providing much needed assistance, I would never have embarked upon my current writing escapade. Thank you for believing that this octogenarian could write not one, but two, books.

I cannot close without formally thanking my husband, Bruce, for his support in such countless ways. You were infinitely patient when our lives had to be set aside once again because of THE BOOK. As if that was not enough, at the eleventh hour I asked you to do one last edit of the manuscript before it went to the publisher. This required two days of almost non-stop reading at a speed that an engineer does not usually exhibit. Your edits were superb, and your recommendations were right on target.

ACKNOWLEDGMENTS

It is an honor to recognize the individuals and organizations that continue to share their wisdom, expertise and experience with me so generously. Without their support I would not have had the courage or the fortitude to embark upon sharing the story of the Clarks of Willsborough Point with others – a journey that has taken me through *The Long Trek North*, now this book, and hopefully, three others to come.

Thanks to the commitment of its Board of Directors the Hale Historical Research Foundation has fulfilled its mission. Each and every board member participated in the effort to secure a permanent home for the Clark Collection that would meet the criteria that the foundation had established. All 51,000 paper documents now reside at the New York State Library where they are being catalogued in preparation for digitization. The almost 6,000 photographs will be on their way there soon. Thank you, Art Cohn, Jim Fuller, Cory Gilliland, Morris Glenn, Bruce Hale, Nick Muller, Patty Paine, Teresa Sayward, Lorilee Sheehan and Caroline Welsh. Kudos and farewell to the Foundation!

Peter Nastasi, Director of Manuscripts and Special Collections at the New York State Library, has been unfailing in his recognition of the importance of the Clark Collection as an outstanding representation of life in the Champlain Valley of New York in the 19th Century. Thank you for your care and support. A portion of the Clark Collection of textiles and clothing is now in safe keeping at the New York State Museum. Thank you Cornelia Frisbie Houde for giving these personal and household articles a permanent home.

Thank you, Hallie Bond for continuing to be an excellent tutor as I have tried to develop an understanding of quilts and quilting from a historic and craftsmanship point of view. Thank you, Ted Comstock and Jane Mackintosh for continuing to be available to me for advice and counsel when I have sought it. Thank you, Bill Krattinger for providing wisdom and insights regarding the former Clark property as a National Historic District.

I cannot end the acknowledgments of gratitude without including John Bingham Rinda Foster, Linda Hacker, Joyce Lindemann, Nick Muller, and my ever-patient husband, for your careful editing and advice with regard to punctuation, grammar and, most important, meaning of the text. There is a piece of each of you in this book.

THE ILLUSTRATIONS

After I wrote my first book, *The Long Trek North,* several people asked me why there were no pictures. I hastened to explain that photography did not exist at the time of this story and the lives of George and Lydia Clark certainly did not warrant portraiture or paintings. When I began to work on *A Journey through Childhood* a friend loaned me a book that her grandfather had written many years ago. *The Golden Age of Homespun* by Jared Van Wagenen, Jr. turned out to be one of those rare treasures that come to you by sheer coincidence. The addition of the delightful, simple line drawings done by Erwin H. Austin greatly enhanced the charm of the book.

As I began planning the layout of *A Journey through Childhood,* I thought that the inclusion of a drawing in each chapter would add a nice flavor to the book. Cornell University Press, the original publisher of all three editions (the last was in 1960) heartily endorsed my using any of the illustrations in *The Golden Age of Homespun* that would fit with the text. Mr. Van Wagenen's daughter and granddaughter were equally delighted to see this happen. In order to have enough pictures in addition to those of Mr. Austin I called upon Ashley Ahrent, a local college art student, my son, Philip, and my husband, Bruce, to fill in the gaps. Although they are all using the same medium for their illustrations you will note some individual stylistic differences. It has been a true cooperative endeavor which we are happy to share with you.

LIST OF ILLUSTRATIONS

TABLE OF CONTENTS

FOREWORD

Darcey Hale, and her husband, Bruce, built a house on Ligonier Point in Willsboro, New York. Their property also included two historic houses. Old Elm, a large classic revival stone farm house with some of its outbuildings still standing sits facing east on Point Road that connects the long peninsula jutting into Lake Champlain, commonly called "The Point," with the village of Willsborough Directly opposite Old Elm a road runs east down Ligonier Point passing the other historic house called Scragwood.

In the late 18th and early 19th century the men and women whose story she tells migrated from New England to "the Point" and shaped never before settled land into homes and farms where they lived and worked, experienced the joy of creating families and the satisfaction of seeing the fruits of their hard work emerge, confronting the anguish of the death of loved ones, and dealing with the imposition of the world beyond with commercial dislocations, the second war with the British, and the fighting on the lake and in the settlements that surrounded them. The foundation of this story emerged from the historic buildings that for generations served as the homes and workplaces of the Clark family. The Clarks did not "downsize." Instead they gave meaning to the old New England adage of "no string too short not to save." As the Hale's explored Old Elm and Scragwood and their outbuildings, they discovered huge numbers of historical records and documents, books shelved two deep, material culture, tools and implements, furnishings, decorative arts, costumes, letters and diaries, and other items, all of museum quality. For a decade Darcey with help, particularly from Morris Glenn, long a seasonal resident of nearby Essex, an indefatigable researcher who had catalogued and organized the fruits of his labors and written and published books and reports on the history of the area. Darcey lived with the evidence that described the lives of men, women and children who spent their days where she now lived. She took responsibility for that rich and textured record, and it gradually developed its own hold on her.

She devoted a decade to retrieving the vast collections including, some discovered in a hidey hole in the basement of Scragwood, providing professional quality conservation and storage, cataloging and archiving the materials and records and documents, all of which the Hale's donated to the New York State Library's Manuscripts and Special Collections section. Many of the textiles and costumes have gone to the New York State Museum. She developed a bond with men and women she had never met who had bequeathed the evidence of their lives to her. She felt the responsibility to treat it with care and compassion and to preserve their record for generations yet unborn.

A Journey through Childhood expresses her tenderness for men and women she had come to know intimately through the magazines books and catalogues they read, the letters they wrote and received, business and farm records they preserved, the chairs they sat on, the instruments they played, the tools they used (and often fashioned themselves), the clothes they wore, and by mid-century the imagery that depicted them. She felt compelled to tell their story in an intimate, granular fashion in a portrayal constructed on a solid foundation of evidence of their lives. She explores the creation of a farm and family, the importance of traditional and deep commitment to religious beliefs, the making of a larger community with shared responsibilities, including maintaining the Point road that connected them to the village of Willsborough and to the larger and often dangerous world beyond.

Her story centers on three major characters, Billy Blinn, his wife Rhoda, and their son, Orrin Clark, who they informally "adopted" through indenture at the age of eight. Her closeness to the vast collections lends her the confidence to project the thoughts and emotions of the Blinn's and others who populate *A Journey through Childhood*. More join the cast as Rhoda births children and other families settle nearby on the Point. But the story remains focused on the Blinn family and Orrin's growth from a difficult early childhood into the steady, accomplished young man that prepared him to become the progenitor of the Clark clan.

The written records and the material culture Darcey and Bruce discovered and conserved, allowed her to compose a detailed and intimate account of constructing a cabin from available materials and adding to it as the family grew. She explores the slow backbreaking process of removing the trees and stones to create fields and the planting of crops after plowing and harrowing. Billy adopts a new design for an improved plow that he and Orrin and their oxen learned to use. She describes scything hay and grain with homemade tools including one Billy fashioned in a small size that Orrin could use and emulate his "father." Rhoda created a garden that Darcey recognizes as a necessity for survival, but also as a retreat to escape the unrelenting drudgery of housework and the constant demand of childcare. Darcey understands how Rhoda designed her garden and where she planted and tended the herbs for seasoning and medicinal purposes and where in the garden, she raised vegetables for food and preserving for the long winter and spring until the next summer's crop. She details the work and the pleasure of tending and using horses and oxen, taking care of cows, pigs and fowl and the repetitive rhythm of daily chores necessary to sustain life. She explores knowingly relationships between siblings as the family grew. She sketches the myriad of other details of living on Willsborough Point in the first decades of the nineteenth century, all described with a love and interest and a gentle certainty of a writer intimately familiar with her subject and the people who lived it.

Not everything traveled on a clear path to a congenial future. The Blinn's unlike some of their friends and neighbors survived "1816 and froze to death," when the volcanic ash from the eruption Mt. Tambora in the Dutch East Indies weakened the sunlight and brought snow and skim ice every month of the spring and summer stunting crops, gardens and livestock. They did not escape death of an infant. Darcey writes evocatively about those crises. An investor, with a ubiquitous lawyer in tow, who had purchased a pre-Revolutionary patent of land granted to a British officer arrived on the Point and claimed legal ownership to the land Billy, Rhoda and Orrin through their labor and love had built into a thriving farm. Billy could not dispute the claim. Careful and frugal and wise without the trappings of sophistication, Billy decided to settle with the investor and slowly bought the property and clear title with a mortgage-like scheme he paid fully over time. The Blinn's and Orrin Clark and his families would live on and added to that land for generations.

Written as a sequel to Darcey's first book (*The Long Trek North*), *A Journey through Childhood* might well become a "prequel" to a third volume in the saga of the Clark family. Her readers will welcome this second book about the Clarks and they will also welcome, if not demand, a third one to meet new characters and their endeavors, challenges, and triumphs all lovingly and skillfully described by Darcey Hale from the trove that family bequeathed to her and to posterity.

H. Nicholas Muller III, Ph.D., historian.

PREFACE

OUR JOURNEY CONTINUES BEYOND THE LONG TREK NORTH

On a warm, sunny day in late July I wended my way south to the depot in Westport and prepared for the usual interminable wait for the train that is always late. Much to my surprise my reveries were soon broken by the faint sound of the train's whistle as it rumbled along the rail toward me, bringing our "French Son" with it. This was to be his usual August visit to a quiet place where he could work on his latest book. Within seconds of alighting onto the platform and exchanging the usual two cheek kisses, Fabrice announced in a commanding tone of voice that he and I had lots of work to do during his stay. I naively assumed that, once again, I would serve as his American editor. Not so! This time the spotlight was on me. I was to publish a book—my first, at age 85!

For several years I had intermittently attempted to bring the story of the Clarks—a family I had grown to know intimately through their diaries, correspondence and countless other records. Friends kept asking, "When are you going to finally put it to paper," to which I would simply reply, "Someday." With fierce determination Fabrice would accept no excuses and drew a line in the sand by pronouncing that he would not leave Willsboro until my book was ready for publication. Thereafter, my days and nights were filled with writing, rewriting, clarifying, editing, and then editing some more. Surprisingly quickly I found myself plunged into a world of which I knew virtually nothing as ISBN numbers floated by, summaries were complied, endnotes and an index were created, endorsements sought, pictures taken, Amazon and Barnes and Nobles pieces prepared, a cover designed, and on

1

and on. At last *The Long Trek North* was on its way to the printer. Whew! My life had changed forever as The Clarks of Willsborough Point came into being. Fate had intervened!

With my first writing endeavor of this scope completed, I heaved a sigh of relief and prepared to sit back for a while. But not so, my generous readers clamored for another book since I had left the first with a cliffhanger—an unsolved mystery. As much as I might try to deny it, I forgot about the hard work and endless hours I had spent on my first book. Positive reinforcement from my readers led me to accept the challenge and move forward onto Book Two. The writing bug had bitten me, and I had to admit that I loved what I was doing. I was eager to continue telling the Clark's story. So here we are once again.

With some sadness we must now leave behind young George and Lydia, and their offspring, who were the centerpiece of Book One. Now, we will turn the spotlight onto their eldest son, Orrin, whose life will change dramatically as, at age eight, he is separated from his family. With imaginary binoculars in hand we will see him become an integral part of yet another family—one that will accept him with love and care as he develops into a devoted son and brother. As he matures, we will watch him grow into a tall, strong, healthy, and energetic adolescent who is rapidly learning the craft of one who tills the land, just as his father had done in his early years.

In Book One, *The Long Trek North*, with the exception of the introductory chapter that sets the scene, my writing fell into the category of historical fiction, periodically interspersed with primary source information. Since factual and personal information about the lives of the Clarks was largely conjectural in nature, I had to rely upon research that would assist me in portraying the lives of a typical, early 19th Century rural family in the Champlain Valley. I quickly discovered that our North Country is closely akin to the northern New England states and bears little resemblance to the New York areas to the south or west of Willsboro. As a result, I drew upon research sources across the lake in Vermont. Local family records and lore were also very helpful in this regard. Although the amount of primary source materials has increased to some extent this book could also be deemed to be historical fiction. As I said before, "Whether you are a historian, researcher or someone who is just plain interested in history and the people who created it, I hope you will join me as this part of my story unfolds.

With young Orrin as our centerpiece we move northward from the Village of Willsborough to Willsborough Point. "The Point", as it is commonly called, is a peninsula, surrounded by the waters of Lake Champlain on three sides. It runs roughly north and south, is six miles long, only spans a mile and a half at its widest and is attached to the rest of Willsborough by a narrow neck of land. Its eastern shore looks over one of the widest parts of Lake Champlain toward Vermont and the Green Mountains. Its western shore runs along Willsborough Bay and faces a range of mountains rising from steep cliffs. For the most part The Point's terrain is gently rolling, although a small height of land is set back from the western shore of The Bay. It was once heavily forested, but over time much of the land was converted to agriculture. Today, only a few farms remain, many of the trees have come back, and much of the land is populated by seasonal and year-around residents. (Note: The town's original name was Willsborough, in honor William Gilliland, its founder. The United States Postal Service shortened it to Willsboro in the early 20th century. At the same time the nomenclature for Willsborough Bay was also shortened. We will use the 19th century spelling for both throughout this book.)

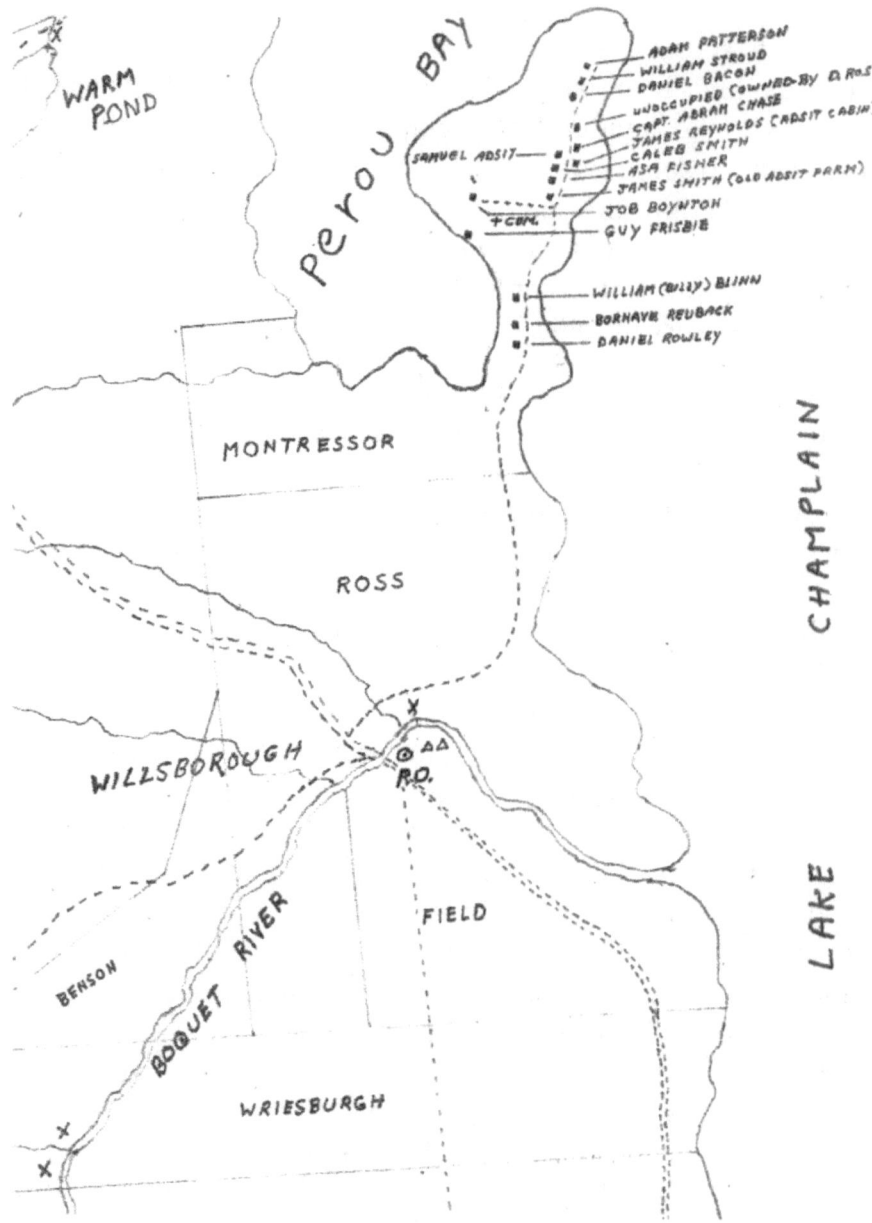

Figure 1 Map of Willsborough Point. Willsboro Heritage Society Collection

When seen from above several bays punctuate The Point's outline. The most notable of these is Willsborough Bay, a sizeable body of water that stretches from the northernmost tip of The Point to its southern end, and is noted for its enormous depth, in some places exceeding 400 feet. This geologically amazing body of water went through several name changes. In 1667 it was called Corlear's Bay, after a Dutchman who drowned there. By 1760 it was named Baye de Pichon (Bay of Fish), and then, for some reason, in 1820 it became Perou, and next Peru Bay. In 1885 it was dubbed Willsborough Bay.[1] Now it is simply referred to as "The Bay".

Until the latter part of the 18th century, The Point lay in isolated splendor. It is said that Samuel de Champlain paid it a brief visit, and other adventurers and explorers may well have followed suit. Upon occasion Native Americans, who were passing from one hunting and fishing locale to another, also stopped there, but no permanent settlement was established. It was also visited briefly General Burgoyne on his retreat to Canada after his disastrous defeat at Saratoga.

The land remained heavily forested just as time and nature had created it. Then, as the 18th century was coming to a close, its silence was broken as settlers began moving north from the Village of Willsborough in search of land to develop and live upon. The earliest permanent settlers on The Point claimed land that they deemed to be their own, having no knowledge that they had no rightful or legal claim to it. This caused considerable difficulties in later years, as we will see. The labyrinth of promises, events, and even intrigue, that led up to this fascinating bit of history is often untold yet is truly worthy of mention. As the French and Indian War came to a conclusion in 1763, King George III authorized the colonial governors to issue grants of land to those who had served in the British Army, and he gave special preference to those who had served in the recent Canadian campaigns.[2] Unbeknownst to them, prior to the war, France had also granted patents, often for lands that were now part of England's holdings.[3] The complications and confusion that resulted from the varying grants, known as patents, took many years to reconcile, and some never achieved this end.

One patent, in particular, is important to our story. On June 6, 1765, John Montresor, Frances Mee and Robert Wallace received a grant for substantial acreage in recognition of their military contributions to the British Crown during the previous war. The so-called Montresor Patent was described as "situate between Peru Bay and Lake Champlain and extending southerly including 3,000 acres." It extended as far east as the offshore islands known as Les Isles de Quatre Vents (Islands of the Four Winds, and now Four Brothers Islands), and at one time included Schuyler Island. [4] At that time what is now called Willsboro Point was referred to as Ligonier Point. The origin of this name is a bit uncertain, but it has been conjectured that it might have been to honor Sir John Ligonier who was the commander-in chief of the British Army during the French and Indian War.[5] Ligonier never actually came to North America.[6] Like most of the grantees, Montresor lived in England and never crossed the Atlantic Ocean to claim his rights as patentee. However, he was connected to America in a different and rather interesting way. Story has it that Ethan Allen's second wife, Fanny, was the illegitimate child of John Montresor.

So, one can ask, "Why is any of this worthy of inclusion in our story?" It all goes back to William Gilliland, the first white settler in Willsborough who, as we know from Book One, *The Long Trek North*, established a rather grand domain or manor near the Boquet River. [7] As a shrewd businessman he planned to lease portions of his land to others for a fee.[8] Later he made seven additional claims which, together, gave him about 15,000 acres. He established his claim and created a settlement along the banks of the Boquet River, which possibly was named for a British general in the French Wars.[9] Sadly, as we saw earlier, the British destroyed his settlement during the War of Independence. Gilliland's life from then on was tragic, and on Feb. 2, 1796, he lost his way back from Vermont on foot and died on Split Rock Mountain.[10]

Now we can see how complicated the situation was. We have land claims granted to individuals by both Great Britain and France and, then later, people like Gilliland laid claim to lands that had never been formalized legally by the original grantees. Issues of ownership continued to become even more complicated as the years went on, and other enterprising individuals made claims that were legitimate in their own eyes. Samuel Barney was granted a piece of land by the American government in recognition of his prior military service in the Revolutionary War.[11] It happened to be the same land that Gilliland had claimed when he came to Willsborough in 1765. Barney and Gilliland, as well as any undefined French grantees, each believed that they had legitimate claims. Barney had an obvious advantage since he was already there and had a far better chance of exercising his ownership than the Montresor patentees who lived thousands of miles away. None of the parties knew that they were all claiming the same land for themselves.

As the numbers of settlers coming into the Willsborough area continued to grow, those who were most recent had to choose a place to live that was farther from the village. Many went south to an area that was soon to split from Willsborough and become Essex. There was nothing to the east but the broad expanse of Lake Champlain. A few hardy souls ventured west onto Willsborough Mountain, but it was deeply forested, with significant areas that were very rocky and not conducive to farming. Timbering was the primary use of this land. Others began to head north in pursuit of land that they could turn into productive farms and, of course, The Point was an obvious place for many of these early settlers to go.

According to the April 3, 1796 Town of Willsborough Highway Records there were seventeen settlers on The Point at that time. They were listed as: William Doty; Rufus Perrigo; Samuel Adsit; John Crum; Smith Hadley; Isaac Dow; Peter Waterbury; Samuel Hadley Jr., Samuel Hadley Sr., Silas Pratt; Peter Payne Jr., Joshua Shearer; Caleb Smith; B. Roback; Abijah Stow; Jos. Powers; and, Aaron Fairchild. John Crum, and his son William, established themselves at the end of The Point and Samuel and Phoebe Adsit chose a piece of land midway along it.[12] Not know anything about the claims on the land that already existed, these settlers believed that they had a legitimate claim to the land upon which they settled. They had no idea that they were merely "squatters".

Now let us turn to our story—a story that will focus on the intertwined lives of Billy Blinn and Orrin Clark.

CHAPTER ONE

NEW LIFE ON THE POINT

Before we introduce Orrin Clark, whose life and family we will be tracing for the next century, we must acquaint you with Billy Blinn, who will assume a significant role in Orrin's early years. His legal name was William Billy Hurlburt Blinn, but he was always called Billy. He was born in Canaan, Connecticut on December 31, 1782, the eldest son of William Stillman Blinn and Hannah Hurlburt Blinn.[13] (Yet again, there is a link with those in our story who also hailed from Canaan, including George and Lydia Clark, Levi and Chloe Higby, and Charles and Thankful McNeil.) Billy spent his early years in Canaan and then, sometime before 1790 his parents made the decision to move north in search of better land, and more opportunities.[14] His father, William Blinn chose to settle on a parcel of land just outside Shelburne, Vermont, a small, rural village with a population of 389 in 1790.[15]

William, and his son, often came into the village itself and, there, Billy met Rhoda Saxton, the second daughter of Frederick and Rhoda Saxton and in 1805 Billy took the hand of Rhoda who was five years his junior. They decided to set up housekeeping across the lake where they had heard there was an abundance of land waiting to be settled out on Willsborough Point. The plot of land that Billy chose lays on the west side of the narrow road, which led all the way out to the end of The Point. Prior to relocating his wife, who was great with their first child, Nelson who was born on July 25, 1806. Billy moved across the lake and built a very small shanty in which he could live temporarily while he built a more permanent log cabin. He also constructed a small, enclosed structure for the mare that he would bring with him. With the energy and vigor of a young man, he was determined to harness the energy and beauty of "his" land, and to bring it to its full potential.

Life for Billy was very crude. His shanty had no windows so the only light that reached him came from the door to the outside, in which he had cut a few openings for air and a bit of light. He always kept a candle close by, in case he had to move around in the shanty or go outside during the night. For a bed he had laid a layer of logs that he had squared to raise him above the dirt floor. He covered these with a pile of old blankets that Rhoda had given him. His only furniture was a couple of rough three-legged stools, and a small table that he had made previously. He drew his water from the nearby lake and did his very simple cooking over the small fire pit that he had dug near his simple abode.

When he did not need the assistance of his mare, she spent her days roaming freely and foraging for whatever bits of edible grass she could find. This made it very simple for Billy to get her ready for work. He did not fear for her safety when it was light outside. She never ventured far and seemed to feel called to keep a close eye on her owner, who she adored. Toward day's end, he led her into her enclosure, replenished her water supply, and gave her a quick rubbing on her nose, and behind her ears. She nuzzled him happily in return for this attention. Wolves, bears, and all manner of other wild animals roamed freely after dark, and he feared that they might make a delicious dinner of her. Just as he had done with his shack, he had constructed a heavy wood door for her protection. At first the mare seemed a bit indignant to be enclosed in such a small space, but she soon adapted to her quarters, and always greeted him with a nuzzle when he came to feed her and let her out of her "prison" in the mornings.

Day after day, Billy worked until late into the evening when the light began to dwindle to a point where he could no longer see well. Sometimes, he would try to prepare a real meal for himself on the iron grate that fit over the fire pit but, more often, he simply resorted to eating the bread that he had made previously in a cast iron pot with a tight lid.[16] It was delicious when he lavishly spread each piece with Rhoda's jam. Then he would wearily curl up on his makeshift bed and sink into the arms of Morpheus.

As the first light of dawn cast out the gloom of the shack, Billy rose from his bed, stretched his back, and hastily pulled on his clothes. If he had time, he would prepare a rough porridge. Otherwise, he would simply resort to bread once again. With axe in hand, and great resolve, he set forth to begin the laborious process of creating an opening in the seemingly impenetrable forest. As he went about felling tree after tree, he realized that this was a painstaking and grueling endeavor, to say the least. While he was working, he kept an eye out for very old growth trees that had few knots where limbs had been, and were straight up and down, and not tapered. He would use these logs for the cabin he would soon build. He had already laid out its size and had decided upon a structure that was sixteen feet on a side, so he sought trees that were tall enough to give logs of this length. Fortunately, he had an abundance of very old pine trees from which to select.[17] For what seemed to be days on end, he repeated the regimen of selecting, and then cutting down, tree after tree. Once felled, he quickly stripped away the remaining limbs, and then left the tree trunks where they fell, until he had enough to construct his cabin.[18]

Because everything was so new to him, Billy was not certain how long it would be before he and his family could move into a more permanent domicile. For now, the cabin he was going to build was be sufficient. When he needed additional space in the future, he anticipated that rather than building a new structure he would probably wind up building around his cabin and using it as the core for the bigger structure. With this in mind, he decided to put a cellar under his cabin. He knew that this would be a perfect place for storing root vegetables, and other foodstuffs, that needed to be placed in a cool, dark place.

Digging the hole was a bigger job than he had anticipated because he kept hitting stones, and some of them were huge. Billy needed the assistance of his mare to remove them from the hole so he tied a rope around each stone as best he could and attached it to the ring on her work saddle. He then coaxed her gently forward until the stone rolled out, and onto the ground surrounding the cellar hole. Later, he planned to use the biggest stones as the anchor stones that he would place under each corner of the cabin. He selected a large, but rather flat stone to use for the threshold outside the doorway. Then he piled up the other stones. He would place these between the sill plates and the ground. They would keep the wood above the damp ground, or the snow in winter.

Finally, he was ready to begin actual construction of the cabin and he prepared his mare for work by placing a leather work collar around her neck. The horse's work reins were then attached to the crude sledge that he had put together. He planned to use this means to move and set the stones that he had selected to the building site. After his first try with the rig that he had constructed he realized that the mare was simply not going to be able to haul stones of the size that he needed for the foundation of his cabin.

Fortunately, Samuel Adsit and Asa Frisbie, both of whom were neighbors, had been stopping by periodically to see how he was progressing, and to lend a hand, when needed. Billy explained that he knew moving the logs would be a particularly challenging endeavor because they were almost twenty feet long. They all agreed that this project would require the brute force of several men. The next day Samuel arrived with a yoke of oxen that he thought could make fast work of the project. He quickly hitched them to the sledge while Asa and Billy used an iron peavey to roll the logs onto the sledge. Then, while Samuel guided his oxen, Asa and Billy walked on either end of the logs and made adjustments when they were needed.[19] By the end of the day, all of the logs were in place by the cellar hole and ready for use the next day.

Early the following morning, with the logs safely placed along what would be the four walls of the cabin, the men turned their attention to the stones. They rolled each huge stone onto a stone boat which Samuel had brought with him.[20] The massive beasts of burden then lugged the corner stones into position. With three of them working, they soon had the stones in place, and the logs that would serve as the sills anchored on top of each of them. [21] Their next job was to create notches in the ends of each log.[22] An adze was the perfect tool for this.[23] By the end of the day the men had accomplished far more than Billy had ever imagined. All was in readiness for actual construction of the walls. Samuel and Asa returned to their homes to attend to their evening chores but promised that they would return at sunrise the next day.

True to their word, they arrived as the sun peeked over the Green Mountains of Vermont and made a path across the broad lake toward them. Soon thereafter, a few other men appeared, fully prepared to join the group. There was excitement in the air, and even the mare and the team seemed to sense it. Everyone was in readiness. The first thing that they did was lay the floor joist logs on top of the sill a foot apart.[24] This was a fairly quick and undemanding job and the group turned their attention to building the walls.

Together, the men lifted the first layer of logs into place, with the front and back logs laid first, and the notched side logs fitted into place at right angles to them, with the aid of a broad axe.[25] The men stood back to admire their work and to be certain that what they had put in place was as squared as they could make it, and that the gap between the logs and the sills was as small as possible. This would remain critically important as they moved along, because a small gap required less chinking and daub later and allowed for minimal intrusion of cold winter air once the cabin was completed. By the end of the day they had put layers of logs in place as far up as they could reach. Weary from the lifting and fitting that they had been doing all day, the men stepped back to admire their work. The two of them promised to return on the morrow, if the weather was fair.

Their prayers were answered, and the day dawned clear and bright. The men placed several planks along each side of the cabin. They would use these to roll the logs that were above their reach into place. Billy attached ropes to each end of a log and Asa and Samuel climbed up their ladders with the ropes in hand, pulled the wall logs up along the planks, and swung them into place.[26] Fortunately they only had to do this for the last three rows. Meanwhile, Billy and two other men cut notches in what would be the top row of the log walls. They did exactly what they had done for the first row of logs by cutting notches into the wood at specified intervals with an adze. They would butt the floor joist logs for the loft into these notches and Billy would actually lay the floor later.[27] When all of the wall logs were in place, the men agreed to stop and return in the morning to begin to work on a roof.

On "raise the roof" day, the weather remained cooperative, for which the five men were very grateful. Today's work would be exacting and would demand sheer brute strength and agility. The first thing that they had to do was to construct the rafters for each end of the cabin. Because the roof would have to span sixteen feet, as well as carry the weight of snow and ice in the winter, they determined that they should exercise prudence and install rafters at one-foot intervals. They had decided to run the roof from north to south, with the back of the cabin abutting the woods that would block the worst winter winds. The front, which would have a door and a window, would open to the south. Positioning the roof this way would also prevent rain and snow from flowing down the roof and onto these apertures. In order to distribute the weight of the snow as much as possible, and to make the roofing easier to handle, they opted to construct a low-pitched roof.

All five of them went to work building the rafter sets on the ground. There were to be seventeen of them. The men selected strong timbers that were long enough to meet at what would be the top of the roof and allow for foot long rafter tails where the timber met the log walls. These tails would keep rainwater from running down the sides of the cabin, thereby causing leaks and rot. Billy sawed off one end of each sidepiece on a diagonal so that they would fit together at the top. When a set was completed it was basically a triangle with a brace joining the two pieces of wood. This would give it added strength. The ridgepole would rest between these rafter sets when they were all in place. They left a space in the rafters through which the chimney would come at a later date.[28]

With this done, the men placed rough logs along the joists on which they could walk. Then Billy attached a rope to each rafter set. The men, who would put them in place, used this means to get the rafters up to their level and ready to install. Now, with two men on each side they maneuvered the rafter set into the notches in the top log. Finally, the weary group of men put the ridgepole in place atop the rafters.[29] As they descended from their aerial work, they heaved a sigh of relief. Although they were physically spent, they glowed with satisfaction when they looked up at their day's work. They had done what they could to be helpful to their good friend and neighbor, and he could do the rest of the work by himself, or with a helping hand from time to time.

Figure 2 Building a Log Cabin. Ashley Ahrent

During the months ahead, Billy continued to work diligently on his cabin. The first thing that he did was to finish the roof. He spent almost a week splitting cedar logs with a frow and cutting the pieces into the correct size and shape for roof shakes.[30] Mercifully, it had been a relatively dry summer and he was able to get all of the shakes installed before a summer storm came his way. Now that he had a roof over his head, he could turn to putting the finishing touches on the cabin. Earlier, when he had dug the cellar hole, he had carefully not disturbed a portion of earth that would be inside the west wall. It was big enough to support the weight of the stone fireplace he was about to build. He dragged stones into the cabin from his pile outside and laid them on the logs that he was using as temporary flooring. Little by little, he carefully laid up layer upon layer of stone, with the largest ones at the bottom to support the structure above. He made sure that the chimney was high enough above the roof that it would draw well, and any sparks would be less likely to set the roof on fire. As he stepped back to view his work, he could not help feeling a bit proud. After all, he had never done anything with stone before and, as a result, he had had to rely upon information from others to guide him.

Next, he had to cut two holes in the log wall on the south side of the cabin—one for a door, and the other for a small window. With a chisel and hammer in hand, he carefully made openings through the logs. He had to be very careful that there was a full-length log above each aperture. Otherwise, the hole would collapse.[31] When the openings were rough-cut, he used a small saw to smooth the edges, and then chinked and daubed any holes that appeared. He made a sturdy board door that swung on iron hinges that the blacksmith in the village had made for him and inserted several round openings that he made with an auger.[32] These would let in light but keep animals out. Finally, he installed a string latch. He inserted a few bars made of thin sapling in the window to keep animals out and left it open. Then he added a one-piece wood shutter that he had made to cover the opening in winter. It was hinged at one side so would be relatively easy to shut when that time came. With this done, he turned to cutting a small window on the east and west sides of the cabin. These would let in light and air and make the interior of the cabin seem less gloomy.

When the days were fair, Billy spent them outdoors, where he patiently filled in every nook and cranny in the walls that he could find. He chinked the larger holes with small stones as tightly as possible, and then packed sand, mud and clay within them as deeply as he could.[33] On a bright, sunny day he walked along the walls, and inspected each log section to be certain that no holes remained. If he found one, he simply repeated the process he used before. This was painstakingly slow work, but he knew that sealing every possible opening was critical to the health and wellbeing of his family during the long, cold winter. When he was satisfied with his work outside, he turned to the inside, where he also filled every nook and cranny that he could find.

Now, there were a few last things to do before he could bring his wife and baby son, Nelson, across the lake. He needed to install puncheon floors that were smoothed on one side in both the main living area and the loft. He also had to make a few—very rough—pieces of furniture to supplement the two stools and small table that he had in the shack. Once more, he turned to his pile of logs, and selected the ones that he thought would meet his flooring requirements best. He spent considerable time making logs into flooring. First, he stripped the bark off the log with a broad axe. Then he cut away the surface of one side of the log to flatten it with his adze. This was the hardest part of the process. When he had enough flooring, he hauled it into the house, and laid the logs, flat side up, until the joists were all covered, except for the hole to gain entrance to the cellar below by means of a ladder.[34]

By early autumn, 1806, Billy had put the finishing touches to his cabin, and completed construction of a couple of very rustic enclosures for the livestock and fowl that he intended to purchase before winter set in. He had installed the fireplace trammel that the blacksmith had made for him, acquired a few cooking implements to hang on it, and set up a nice pile of wood and placed a few buckets outside the door. He would use these for fetching water from the lake, and he thought that this would do until he could dig a well, which he hoped to do before winter set in. He had even found time to build a rough eating table and benches, a settle and cots for Nelson, himself and Rhoda.[35]

After a year of endless hours of hard work, he was ready to bring Rhoda and the baby to their new home.[36] Exhausted, but filled with pride, Billy crossed the lake to participate in Nelson's baptism in the Congregational meetinghouse in Charlotte. Following this important event, the young couple prepared for the move in the fall of 1806. Rhoda had been carefully putting things aside for months. When all was in readiness, Billy packed the wagon that he had built, and hitched his faithful mare to it. Together, they made their way south to Charles McNeil's ferry, crossed the lake to Essex, and then proceeded through Willsborough, and out onto Willsborough Point.

As they approached Billy's land, she caught sight of the cabin, and its outbuildings, and, with tears in her eyes, clapped her hands with joy. Even a wisp of smoke curled from the chimney as a sign of welcome. As the mare came to rest before the door, Billy turned to his side and embraced his wife tenderly. At last they would be together again, and, this time, it would be in their own home. As he helped his wife and child down from the wagon, he silently offered a prayer of thanksgiving.

CHAPTER TWO

YOUNG ORRIN'S FUTURE

Following the mysterious disappearance of Lydia's husband, George, many Willsborough citizens stepped forward to provide whatever assistance they could to Lydia and her offspring. Among them was Billy Blinn. Upon the occasions when he came into the village on an errand he tried to stop by the Clark home to see if he could provide help with some of the chores that Lydia and her young brood could not manage on their own. As yet, he only had his wife, Rhoda, and infant son, Nelson, to feed, so he was also able to provide some foodstuffs that would supplement what Lydia could grow in her small garden. As Billy grew to know the family better he could see how hard Lydia was struggling to meet the emotional and physical needs of her family. At times she seemed to be completely and utterly overwhelmed. She continued to be baffled by George's precipitous disappearance, and steadfastly refused to think that he would not magically appear on their doorstep one day. She was also perplexed and daunted by the notion that her father continued to be unwilling to welcome her and his grandchildren into his own home in Stillwater.

One day Billy stepped forward, and told Lydia that he and his wife, Rhoda, had discussed the plight of the young Clark family, and they had both agreed that God was calling them to step forward and give than more than assistance with the occasional small job and food. He offered to give her 10-year-old eldest son, Orrin, the opportunity to come to live with he and his family until he reached his majority at age 21. (At that time, it was not uncommon for a family that was not able to take care of its children to "bind out", or indenture, one or more of them to someone who was in a position to assume responsibility for their upbringing.) He promised her that they would provide Orrin with a place to live, as well as food and clothing. More importantly, Billy noted that he would welcome the child into the family as if he were one of his own offspring. In return, Billy also promised that he would teach Orrin the necessary skills to become a farmer on his own when he reached his majority.

Although sad and grief stricken that life circumstances gave her no other recourse, Lydia was very grateful that Orrin would be with a family that she knew because they shared a common heritage in Canaan. She and George had known Billy to be an honest, hard-working and caring person. Even more importantly, she had grown to trust and respect Billy during the times that he had been so helpful. She felt certain that George would have approved of her decision to have his son become part of Billy's family. She was also greatly relieved that Billy had assured her that as long as she remained in Willsborough, she and her other children would be able to see Orrin when he came into the village. In the end, Lydia was immeasurably relieved and grateful for the opportunity that her son was being given.

The scene is now set for Orrin's indenture to Billy Blinn to commence. Early in the fall of 1808 the day came for Orrin's departure from the home that had been his since he was three years old arrived. Lydia had packed his small trunk with his clothing and some reminders of his life in the village, and his older sister, Polly, had added a few special treats to help him on his way. All was in readiness. As the eldest son in the family Orrin had grown particularly close to his mother after his father's disappearance, and he knew that he would sorely miss the hustle and bustle of his former home, as well as his six siblings, especially Polly. Even though he was not moving far from the village where he had grown up, he still felt sad that he would be leaving behind all that he had ever known.

When Billy and Rhoda reached the Clark home everyone was gathered outside awaiting their arrival. Billy dropped the horse's reins, and he and Rhoda climbed down, and stood quietly beside their cart while the farewells and hugs were being exchanged. First, Orrin hugged his brother George, then Sally, Lucy Mira, Calvin, and little Lydia, who was too young to understand the emotionally charged events of the day. Then he turned to say one of the most difficult farewells of all. He knew that he would desperately miss Polly. They had been so close since he was born, and she was always there for him when he needed her. As he did so, he fought hard to keep the tears back. Then, last, came the hardest farewell of all. Parting from his mother was almost unbearably painful for him, despite her assurance that they would see one another from time to time. Orrin could no longer hold back his emotions, and the tears rolled down his cheeks uncontrollably.

The time came when the boy's departure could not be delayed any longer. Billy pulled his horse and cart forward, quietly stowed the boy's belongings in the back of the cart, and then helped his new "son" climb onto the seat. He placed him alongside Rhoda, who gently wrapped her arms around him and let his floods of tears flow forth. Billy climbed up and placed himself on the other side of the crying child. He gave Orrin a reassuring pat on the knee and, then, with a slap of the reins, he moved the cart forward as the boy turned to wave a final farewell to his assembled family members. Soon they crossed the bridge over the Boquet River, and began the steep climb that took them up and out of the village. As they reached the end of their ascent the road flattened out and forked. Billy explained that, if they continued on as they were going, they would be heading up and over Willsborough Mountain. Today they were going to take the fork to the right that put them on the well-trodden, relatively flat track to The Point. Periodically Rhoda reached over to give Orrin a hug of reassurance, but for the most part she let him remain silently in his own thoughts.

Although Orrin had visited the Blinn farmstead briefly before this day, he was looking at everything through different eyes, knowing that this was where he was going to live until he was 21. On either side of the road they passed areas of still pure forest. Orrin was struck by how much quieter it was than in the village, especially when he was surrounded by these deep woods. Periodically, they reached a clearing that had been created by one of the settlers who were coming into the area. Wisps of smoke drifted into the air above the rustic cabins that rested on these newly tamed pieces of land. It had been reassuring that he was still going to live in a cabin, since that was what he had always known. At least this would be familiar.

After a bit the horse and cart came to a wide curve in the road, and then a long decline. As the road flattened out and headed straight north Billy turned to Orrin, and brought him back from his reveries. He told him that they had just crossed the narrow neck of land that connected Willsborough to Willsborough Point. Through his tears Orrin glimpsed the vast body of water to the east that he had only seen when his father took him to the mouth of the Boquet to fish. The lake looked even bigger from here than it had previously. Seeing the water brought back a host of memories of the happy times that he and his father had had together when they went down to the mouth of the Boquet where the best fishing was. He treasured those moments, especially when they were alone and not surrounded by his many siblings. He would remember them always.

Suddenly the mare quickened her pace as they reached a clearing and passed a log house down by the water. Billy noted that this was the home of Rhoda's sister, Abalena, and her husband, Daniel Rowley had come to settle just a few months previously. Abalena's former husband, Daniel Barber, had died in 1802 and left her widowed with a daughter, Abilena. On February 19, 1807 she had married Daniel Rowley who born on April 6, 1752 in Kent, Connecticut, another town in the County of Litchfield that is located about 20 miles from Canaan.[37] After a disastrous first marriage in Amsterdam, New York, Daniel received a divorce and moved to Shelburne, Vermont where he met Abalena, who was born in Sheffield, Berkshire County, Massachusetts on June 22, 1775.[38] She was twenty-three years younger than Daniel. Needless to say, Rhoda was delighted that her older sister would be living so nearby. Abalena and Daniel followed in the footsteps of Billy and Rhoda and they laid claim to adjoining land on The Point.

Figure 3 The Blinn Log Cabin. Ashley Ahrent

This was where they had left their two-year-old son, Nelson, while they came to bring Orrin to his new home. Orrin was at full attention now because he knew that the Blinn homestead would be appearing very soon. Then, there it was—a simple, rough-hewn log cabin with a wisp of smoke rising gently out of the chimney that signaled its own kind of welcome to the family. Finally, it really struck Orrin that this was now his home, and the one that he had known for so long was part of a day gone by.

CHAPTER THREE

A HOME OF WARMTH AND LOVE

As the horse and cart came to a gentle halt Billy jumped down and grasped his steed's halter firmly while Rhoda and Orrin hopped down to the waiting earth—an earth that he would get to know very well during the months and years of indenture that lay ahead of him. The lad's eyes quickly roamed past the cabin and onto the woods, which formed a seemingly impenetrable barrier to all but the animals that called the forest home. The vastness of all that lay before him seemed quite overwhelming to this boy who had spent most of his young life in the village, or along the banks of the Boquet River. He remembered how sternly his parents had admonished him never, ever, to venture into the forest that surrounded the village, especially if he and his friends were alone. They warned that coyotes and wolves, inhabited it, and who knows what other vicious beasts might be roaming around in there that would love to have a child for dinner. This had been enough warning for the Clark children, and they did not go into the forest ever!

While Billy tended to the horse and cart, Rhoda opened the door to the cabin and, giving Orrin a big hug, she welcomed him to his new home. A cheerful fire greeted them and brought warmth and light to the room on this somewhat chilly fall day. Cooler weather was definitely taking over from the warm, sunny days of summer, and soon the door and small windows of the cabin would be closed to the outside world until the advent of spring. Orrin glanced around him, and quickly saw how neatly organized and tidy everything was. It was so different from his former home, which was always chaotic because of the presence of so many children. Here there was

27

only Billy, Rhoda, two-year-old Nelson, and, now himself—at least until Rhoda's next child was born, which would be soon. In his mind the small size of the family certainly accounted for the tidiness and order that lay before him.

Rhoda quickly donned an apron and said that she needed to get to the business of preparing the midday meal right away. Since he was not needed Billy seized the opportunity to invite Orrin to come on a brief tour of the farm, and the lad eagerly accepted the invitation. On their walk Billy gently took Orrin's hand in his, as a means of reassuring him that he and Rhoda would be good to their new "son". He could feel the child's pain at being wrenched away from the only place and family that he had ever known.

As they walked along together Billy pointed out various places and things that he said they would revisit later. He suddenly glanced up at the sky and noticed that the sun was almost directly overhead. This meant that soon Rhoda would be calling them in for the midday meal. He told Orrin that, for now, they would need to end their tour, but promised that they would continue right after their dinner. Billy had been instructed to walk over to the Rowley's cabin to gather up little Nelson and fetch him home, and he invited Orrin to come along. They walked quickly from whence they had come, and traversed the clearing that separated the two cabins, both of which were down near the lake. As they moved along what seemed to Orrin to be a wide-open space, the boy sensed that, here, he was going to be free from many of the constraints that had been placed upon him back in the village. Very soon he dropped his new "father's" hand and began skipping freely toward the Rowley cabin. The sight before him caused Billy to smile broadly. With feelings of relief, he could see that his "son" was taking the first tiny steps toward adjusting to his new surroundings, and the life that came with them.

When they reached the Rowley cabin, Abalena flung open the door to welcome them, with Daniel right next to her. Their children, four-year-old Abilena Barber and their year-old twins, Therza and Eliza, followed close behind. Two-year-old Nelson clung to Abalena's apron and was holding back a bit in uncertainty. He had been told that he was going to have a new big "brother", but this had meant little to him. After the usual greetings and then farewell hugs, Billy, sensing his toddler's unease, took Nelson's hand in his and led him out the door with his new "brother" right beside them. Orrin quickly resumed his former skipping gait and soon Nelson forgot his hesitancy, dropped his father's hand, and tried valiantly to imitate the older boy's actions. Much tripping and falling was the result for Nelson, but Billy simply picked him up, dusted him off, and set him back down on the ground to try again. He and Orrin could not help chuckling over Nelson's antics, and Billy was secretly relieved that the two boys seemed to be enjoying themselves despite the significant difference in their ages.

When they got to the house Rhoda explained that she was still behind schedule because of their trip into the village, so the midday meal was not quite ready. While they were waiting Billy thought that Orrin would enjoy meeting a few of the animals that lived on the farm. Nelson, who was already admiring his new big brother, begged to come with them as they made their rounds. He toddled along behind them quite contentedly. First, they passed a group of pigs that lay contentedly in a puddle they had created for themselves near the watering trough, while the rooster and his harem pecked away at the softened earth in their nearby enclosure. Suddenly, much honking and hissing greeted Orrin, and he turned to find himself face to face with a pair of geese who were letting him know that he was in their way. They flapped their wings noisily, and as Orrin stepped out of their path, they passed by somewhat imperiously. Orrin sensed that these birds were not to be tampered with. The mare was happily indulging in the hay that Billy had tossed down for her when he took her back to the barnyard, and a pair of cows stood nearby chewing their cuds contentedly. Around the corner Orrin caught sight of a pair of young, but sizeable, oxen. They eyed him curiously, and the young boy decided that it would be best to give them a wide berth, at least for now. As they turned to return to the cabin Billy told Orrin that he hoped to increase his livestock in the spring, but for the present he had all that he could care for during the winter that lay ahead.

Soon Rhoda called out to them and announced that their meal was ready. Billy took Orrin and Nelson over to the well that lay just outside the cabin door so that they could wash up before eating. He pumped some water into a nearby bucket, and then handed each of the boys a child-size bar of the coarse lye soap that Rhoda had made. They dipped their hands into the water and then lathered them with the soap. When they were finished, Billy began to pump some water over their outstretched hands, so that they could rinse off the lather that they had created. Finally, Billy repeated the process for himself. While they were doing this, he chatted amiably with the two boys, and seized the opportunity to reiterate to Orrin how happy he was that they could provide a home for him. Once again, he assured the ten-year-old that he would be loved and cared for as long as he lived with them. He also promised that, whenever possible, he would bring Orrin with him on his trips to the village so that he could see his mother and siblings.

When they entered the house Orrin could smell the delicious aroma of a savory stew in the big iron pot that hung from the crane over the fire. This reminded him so much of home, and his own family, who he was certain would be having the same experience about now, except without him. He had to fight hard to keep back the tears that threatened to come rushing down his cheeks. As his vision cleared, and he began to look around, he noticed strings of herbs hanging from the rafters. He recognized the aroma of some of them, especially the rosemary, which was one that he had always loved. Set back from the fire was a simple pine trestle table surrounded on two sides by rather crude benches that Billy had built as a temporary measure, and on one side of the fireplace was a settle, where one could sit and warm oneself when the weather was cold. Rhoda had woven several simple, but serviceable rugs that lay beneath the table and benches, and another in front of the settle. A pair of simple wood footstools was placed in front of the settle. These allowed one to lift one's feet off the bare, and often cold, wood floor.

As Rhoda took her long, tin, dipping spoon, and ladled the stew into the waiting earthenware bowls, Billy helped Nelson into a chair that was just the size for him to sit at the level of the rest of the family. In happy anticipation of the coming meal the toddler picked up his tin-ware spoon and banged it on the bowl before him, making quite a racket. Rhoda sighed and was grateful that the bowl was sturdy and took abuse without breaking. She admired the patience of the tinsmith in the village as he patiently repaired the eating utensils that had been twisted or bent, which was all too frequently. Billy and Rhoda, being pious people, offered a prayer of thanksgiving for

Figure 4 The Blinn Kitchen. Ashley Ahrent

the bounty that lay before them, and then began to eat. Orrin soon learned that prayer was the preamble to every meal.

Rhoda passed around a chunk of warm, freshly baked bread, and offered some to Orrin, who quickly used it to sop up the gravy in the stew. Then he used his spoon to bring the vegetables and meat to his lips. As he savored each bite he had to admit to himself that Rhoda's stew was almost as good as what his mother had prepared—well, maybe just as good, he conceded. They ate with gusto, and mostly in silence, and when they were done Rhoda whisked away their bowls, and came forward with an apple pie that she had made especially to welcome her new "son". With her triangular wood server she cut into the contents of the tin-ware pie plate, as Orrin admired the thick, tan liquid that oozed out as each slice was placed upon an earthenware plate. He could hardly contain himself. It smelled so good. Orrin, like most young children, loved anything sweet, and he had no problem consuming his share with dispatch. It was truly delicious and, as he sat back, replete and happy, he thought that this new home might be just fine.

When the meal was completed Billy suggested that Orrin stay behind to help Rhoda clean up from the repast, while he went out to finish harrowing the field that he had been preparing for a final fall seeding. Normally he would have invited Orrin to accompany him, but he thought that this would give Rhoda and her "son" a chance to converse, and get to know one another more. First, Rhoda needed to put Nelson on his small cot that was placed beside his parent's bed. He protested and begged not to have to rest just for this one time. He wanted to be with his big brother, but Rhoda prevailed and promised that, when she and Orrin had completed cleanup from the meal he could arise. In no time at all, the new mother and son heard gentle breathing emanating from the nearby cot.

Then Rhoda asked Orrin to join her as they began to clean up the dishes and other items from their meal. Orrin was a bit confused, since this was a new chore for him. At home Polly had always helped her mother, but he realized that here it was different because there was no big sister to offer this type of assistance. First, Rhoda picked up a large tin pail with a lid that lay just outside the cabin door and brought it over to the table where the dishes were still laid out. She picked up each item, and deftly scraped any remaining food scraps into the pail, while she explained that these slops would provide a delicious treat for the pigs.

With that done, Rhoda went over to the fireplace and swung the crane toward her so that she could reach the kettle of water that had been heating there. She poured some of its contents into a large tin-ware pan, which she placed on the table where they had just eaten, and then poured the remainder into an adjoining pan. Next she picked up a bar of homemade lye soap and rubbed it between her hands before swishing them around in the first pan of warm water. One by one she dumped the soiled items into the warm water, in order of their degree of food residue. She rubbed them vigorously with a cloth before transferring them to the other pan to rinse them off. Once this was accomplished Rhoda reached over to a rack beside the fire, handed Orrin a small towel of coarse linen, and showed him how to dry the various items she would be handing to him. While they worked together, with Rhoda chatting amiably beside him, Orrin began to relax a bit. As Billy had done, his new "mother" assured him that he was now a member of the family, and they were delighted to have him with them.

When these simple chores were completed, Rhoda urged Orrin to look around the house so that he would know where everything was. He noticed that Billy and Rhoda had a simple wood bedstead with a straw-filled mattress covered with tightly woven, striped ticking that she had woven. She said that the same was true for the pillows except that they were filled with goose feathers instead of straw, and the tight weave kept the quills from sticking through and piercing the sleeper. On top of it all she had placed one of her most prized family quilts. She had used the same rough linen to surround the bed, although it was not striped. That had made it simpler to weave since so much fabric was required for the curtains that did a fine job of keeping out drafts and providing some privacy. Beneath the bed was the inevitable chamber pot. He remembered that at home they used the nearby privy, but when the snow fell, and the winds howled the chamber pot was always welcomed. He thought that this would probably be true here also.

Rhoda explained that Orrin would be sleeping in the loft above so that he would have a space of his own, and the area beneath would be less crowded. This was just like home, except that he would be up there alone. He wondered how he would feel about that, but quickly cast that thought aside. Billy had constructed a wood ladder for access to the loft, and Orrin was eager to clamber up it to inspect his new sleeping quarters. When he reached the top, the light grew a bit dimmer, but he noted that there was a small window at one end of the area, and some light also came in from below. A simple cot, like Nelson's, but larger, had been placed near the ladder way. It, too, had a mattress that was filled with straw, and then covered with ticking, as was his goose feather pillow. Rhoda had laid another of her quilts across the cot invitingly. Above his head, Rhoda had hung herbs where they would remain dry, after being dried first by being hung from the rafters below. Here, also, were chains of sliced apples and pears. The aroma that they emitted was deliciously sweet smelling and very inviting. In one corner, there were several old trunks, and he briefly wondered what they might contain. Perhaps he would check one day.

After his tour of the small dwelling that was now home was completed Rhoda suggested that it might be good if he went out into the field to see what Billy was doing. In this way Orrin would be gone when Nelson awoke, and he would have some more one-on-one time with Billy. Orrin suddenly thought to himself that he would need to begin to think of Billy as his father. This would be hard, because the word itself conjured up so many memories that were still fresh with him, even though over a year had passed since he had seen his "real" father. He was glad that Billy had assured him that this was to be expected.

When he reached the field where Billy was working the land, he saw that the young oxen, that had intimidated him in the barnyard earlier, were hard at work. They were pulling a crude wood harrow, with spiked wood teeth, through the soil that Billy had already plowed. Billy walked beside the pair and encouraged Orrin to walk with him. The lad noticed that the oxen had to move in unison because they had a funny looking thing that Billy called a yoke joining them together. This seemed strange to him, and perhaps even a bit cruel. However, Billy pointed out that, if the oxen did not move together, they would be constantly jerking to and fro whatever they were pulling and wind up breaking it.

While they walked together, Billy explained to Orrin that he had recently acquired the team from a neighboring farmer, who had raised them until they were old enough to be trained to work the land. At a year-and-a-half he referred to them as yearling calves. Then they would become two-year-olds and, next, three-year-olds and, finally, they would earn the title of oxen until at age 4.[39] Since he had purchased them Billy had been working with them, using a small yoke that he had made for his oxen. He had progressively larger yokes for the animals as they grew larger. He pointed out that because they were young, they were still a bit willful and headstrong, and they often acted recalcitrant when he went to place the yoke over their heads and onto their shoulders. They seemed to delight in throwing their heads back, and high in the air, the minute they saw him approach with yoke in hand. Mercifully, man and beasts were getting to know and understand one another over time.

Billy told Orrin that he had taken many falls, and endured many bruises, while breaking them. However, in the end, he was winning, and they were becoming more submissive. His job was to teach them to respond, in unison, to a few simple commands, and he used his gad, a four-foot long elm sapling, as a whip. Some of the commands were the same as what he used with his mare, such as "giddy up", "whoa", and "back". They also had to learn "haw, haw" to turn left and "gee, gee" to turn right.[40]

As the sun began its downward course toward the western horizon and the harrowing was completed Billy turned his attention from his work in the new field and prepared to return his oxen to the barnyard. He asked Orrin if he would like to accompany him as he attended to the nighttime chores, to which the boy agreed instantly. First, they had to catch the chickens that had been loose in their enclosure. They could not be left out during the night because there were many foxes, and other animals that would gobble them up in an instant. Orrin volunteered to help with this task and quickly took to the job. In no time he had turned this into a game, as he found it was great fun to chase after the birds, and then get them in a corner. Once there he could pick up each one, as it squawked and flapped its wings in protestation. He shoved the hens into the coop, and then tackled capturing the rooster who had been crowing in a mocking manner. With all of them safely ensconced he shut the door firmly behind them, telling the hens that he expected to find eggs in their nesting boxes in the morning. Orrin was quite proud that he had been so successful with this endeavor on his first try.

With this accomplished, Billy asked the lad if he would like to try to do the same with the geese. Remembering his initial introduction, he was a bit hesitant at first. However, pride won out, and he said he would. The geese expressed their distaste for being distracted from what they were doing by hissing, honking, and flapping their wings. However, after Orrin had sized up the situation, he imitated their actions, flailed his arms in the air, and made loud noises that got their attention. Orrin moved quickly and soon he had them in their enclosure, and he firmly shut the gate behind him. Billy was truly amazed by the ingenuity of the boy and thought to himself that this lad had real promise.

While Orrin was tending to the fowl Billy was at work preparing the bigger animals for the night ahead. He never worried about the pigs being left outdoors, at least until it became very, very cold, and that would not be happening for a while. He knew that they could be extremely vicious if attacked, and predators hesitated to tackle them. He gave them fresh water from the barnyard well, filled their trough with the slops that Rhoda provided from the kitchen, and then turned toward the other livestock. His oxen were already in their shelter munching away on the fresh hay that Billy had given them when he brought them in from the field. He checked to make sure that they had sufficient water, and then walked over to where his mare stood waiting patiently for her evening repast. Billy always took a few extra moments to stroke his faithful companion's muzzle and run his hands through her mane lovingly. She had been such a wonderful friend to him in so many ways, and he had a special place in his heart for her. She then got a bit of hay and fresh water in preparation for bedtime. Rhoda had already been out to the barnyard to milk the cows and take care of their needs. That was her job twice a day, and she actually found it to be a pleasant interlude in her busy life. The bovines were happily eating the fresh hay they received as a reward for giving forth such delicious milk.

With their evening chores completed Billy and Orrin turned toward the cabin. They took off their outer clothes and boots, and seated themselves on the settle by the fire while Rhoda finished preparing the simple evening meal of tea, bread, jam and a piece of the cake that she had baked during the afternoon. Nelson was eager to have some time with his big brother and pulled up a little wood stool to sit beside him at the fireside. He was learning to talk coherently, and to express his thoughts more clearly these days. He bombarded Orrin with numerous questions, which his "brother" obligingly answered as best he could. With the preparations for supper completed the family gathered at the table once again and said their prayers as usual. Orrin simply bowed his head and listened curiously. He wondered why his own parents had never done this before meals but cast the thought aside as he dove into the food before him.

After supper Rhoda told Orrin that she would take care of the cleanup once she got Nelson settled in bed. While she was doing this Billy and Orrin returned to the settle, and Billy seized the opportunity to share with Orrin his plans for the days ahead. He explained the ways in which his son could begin to provide some assistance. Soon Rhoda came to join them. She settled into her rocker on the other side of the fireplace and began knitting as she and Billy talked about the day's events. Soon, they looked over to young Orrin and saw that he was yawning, and his eyes kept drifting shut, despite his best efforts to stay awake. He had had a long and stressful day, and his body was ready to bring it to an end, even if his mind was not.

Rhoda went over to him, and gently suggested that it was time for him to go to bed. She pointed out that they would be doing the same shortly, and said that, like all farm families, they arose early—earlier than those in the village. Billy stood up from the settle to give Orrin a goodnight hug, and then Rhoda climbed the ladder to the loft behind her new son. She stayed with him as he tried to get comfortable in his new bed, and before long he was fast asleep. When she returned to the fireside, she saw that her husband was snoring quietly on the settle. It had been a long day and he too was fatigued. Rhoda quickly undressed, donned her long cotton gown, and performed her nightly ablutions. Then, she gently tapped Billy and admonished him to do the same. Soon they were both on their knees beside their bed. Together they murmured a few prayers, and thanked God for their many blessings. They especially asked for His guidance and support with this child who would be spending a major portion of his young life with them. Finally, they, too, wearily climbed into their bed and snuggled under their covers. Soon the entire household, including the cat, was fast asleep.

CHAPTER FOUR

THE BRILLIANCE OF AUTUMN

Like most young children, especially those from large families, Orrin began to adapt to life with his new family over time. Except for increasingly brief moments when something would remind him of his former life, he plunged into his new one with enthusiasm, a cheerful demeanor, and a positive approach to life. Despite his young age, he accepted each new challenge eagerly and with great determination. The days fairly flew by as Orrin settled more and more into the rhythm of life in his new home. It was a significant period of observing, learning and adapting for this former village boy, and Rhoda and Billy were continually impressed by their child's powers of observation and the rapidity with which he learned new things.

True to his word, Billy invited Orrin to accompany him to the village from time to time. This was a special treat because it meant that he could visit with his old family while Billy went about his business. He loved his mother's reaction when he paid her a surprise visit. After he knocked on the door and entered the house, she would turn toward him as a wide smile crossed her face, while tears of delight rolled down his cheeks. She always greeted him the same way—first commenting, "How big and strong you are growing," as she pushed him forward to get a better view of her son. Then, she gave him a warm embrace as the rest of the children came scampering from every corner to do the same. These were moments that he would always cherish. Everyone clambered to hear about his life with the Blinn family, and Orrin delighted in reassuring them that he was just fine and very happy, while making certain that he also let them know that he missed them. As the eldest son, he was proud that he had been able to help his mother by giving her one less mouth to feed and child to care for.

Being a bright and observant young lad, it did not take Orrin long to master the chores that Rhoda and Billy considered appropriate for a child his age. Although still young, there were many tasks that he could perform, while he was growing taller and stronger. As it was becoming colder and winter was coming on, there was less that he could do to help Billy outdoors. His father was making the necessary preparations to ensure that he and his family would survive the months of snow, sleet, freezing rain, and bitter cold, that would come upon them inevitably. He was putting the final touches on his outbuildings and making certain that they were sturdy enough to bear the weight of heavy snow and withstand the rigors of the powerful north wind that tended to sweep down the lake with alarming force. Keeping warm was going to be a high priority, so he made sure that he had enough firewood stored under the lean-to that he had built close to the house. While Billy stacked the larger logs, Orrin was able to handle the smaller ones. Father and son were learning to work together quite remarkably.

As the days advanced, life for the newly forged family began to settle into a routine. Rhoda and Billy arose just as the sun began to poke its head over the horizon. Another day had begun. Nelson was still asleep on his cot beside their bed, and they could hear Orrin gently snoring up in the loft. While the boys were both still soundly sleeping, father and mother had a chance to slip out of the cabin just long enough to complete their morning chores. Billy looked forward to the time when their son would be able to help him with the rounds for all of the animals, not just the fowl.

The two "milch cows", as she referred to them, were Rhoda's responsibility. As she entered their enclosure, they turned their heads and eyed her longingly. Their udders were replete with milk, and drooping down heavily, which she thought must be very uncomfortable for them. They watched her carefully as she gave them each a handful of hay and then went about preparing to milk them. She had brought a small pail of water and a rag with her, and gently washed the first cow's teats. Then she reached for the milking stool that Billy had made for her, put a clean bucket under the cow's udders, and settled herself below the cow that simply kept chewing her cud contentedly. One by one Rhoda pulled down on each teat as warm, frothy, sweet-smelling milk came streaming forth. Rhoda loved this time of day. It was a special treat to be alone and free to enter her own private musings before she had to begin the routines of the day ahead of her. When she had milked both cows, she picked up her full buckets and headed back to the cabin. When he finished his other rounds Billy would give them a bit more hay.

All was quiet as Rhoda entered the cabin, set down her buckets and saw that Nelson was still sleeping soundly on his cot. She tiptoed to the bottom of the loft ladder, and gently called up to the sleeping lad above. Orrin responded, and snuggled more deeply into the warmth of his bed for just a moment. Then, with a yawn, he leaped off his cot and was immediately smacked by the cold air of the unheated loft where he slept. It made him think about how much colder it was going to be in the months ahead. He grabbed the clothes that he had put under his covers the night before, pulled them on as quickly as he could, and clambered down the ladder to the floor before, where light and warmth surrounded him immediately.

One of the first things that Rhoda taught Orrin was how to lay the fire for her. Before bedtime each night the lad went out to the woodpile by the door, gathered the necessary sticks and small logs, and brought them in to warm and dry overnight. Billy brought in the larger logs that would be used when the fire was going well. Then Orrin went back outside to bring in some buckets of water, which he placed by the fire so that they would not freeze. Billy had pointed out that this was a true safety feature, because if a fire erupted in the cabin during the night there would be a means of putting it out.

In the morning, Orrin's first job was to set up the fire upon which Rhoda would prepare the morning repast. If he were lucky there would still be a bed of coals in the fireplace. Then all he had to do was put the sticks directly on the coals and when they were burning brightly, he placed the small logs upon them. With this done he stood back and admired the flames before him. Sometimes he was not quite satisfied with his work and he would move close to the fire, puff up his cheeks, and gently blow until the wood burst into flames. Billy had already warned him that, in the dead of winter, it would not be as easy. Each morning he would have to lay the fire from scratch, light it from the tinderbox, and carefully nudge the pile of wood into action. Throughout the day keeping the fire going was to be his job, unless Billy needed him for something else.

When Billy came in from his morning chores he was tired and hungry, and the sight of a table laden with delicious food was very welcome. The morning meal was a hearty one, because Billy, like most farmers, believed that a full stomach made for a happier and more productive day. There was always an ample supply of bread that Rhoda had baked the day before, butter that she had churned, and jam that she had made during the summer months, when fruits were bountiful. As the days grew cooler Billy and the children were treated to a steaming bowl of oat porridge with fresh milk and maple sugar on top. As they approached the table Nelson was already in his chair, clapping his hands in delight at the sight before him. Much as he wanted to dig right into his bowl, he knew that he could not until the family had bowed their heads and taken a moment to thank the Lord for the bounty that lay before them. Orrin had gotten used to this now, but he still did not quite understand why this step was necessary. With the prayers completed spoons went to their lips, as each of them set about emptying their bowl with purpose and rapidity. In no time at all breakfast was consumed and Billy went back to his work while Orrin stayed behind to help Rhoda with the cleanup.

On Mondays Orrin usually found himself housebound. It was his job to help Rhoda with the family wash. Thanks to her previous preparation of a large supply of lye soap, Rhoda was prepared to go about the business of addressing the weekly pile of clothes and other household items, a process which some of her friends and neighbors referred to as the "weekly affliction". Orrin began to help his mother by fetching the two, big tin washtubs and a scrub board that lay in the cellar beneath the house. Then he began hauling what seemed to be an endless chain of pails of water from the well and pouring their contents into the iron pots that sat upon the fireplace coals. Once the water was hot enough Rhoda stepped in and poured it into the waiting washtubs. Orrin was happy to take a bit of a break and play with Nelson while Rhoda scrubbed the items that she had separated into piles, starting with the least dirty and ending with those that would take the most scrubbing. The latter were usually the things that Billy and Orrin wore as they went about their outdoor chores.

As she finished each item, she put it into the other washtub to rinse the soap out of the clothes. One by one she swished the clean items that she had washed around in the water. She pulled them out of the water, and she and Orrin wrapped them around a broomstick they held over the washtubs. Then, they wrung as much water out of the clothes as possible. Finally, Orrin held up each item so that Rhoda could hang it from the ceiling rafters. This turned the room into a bit of an obstacle course for Rhoda and Billy, who had to duck their heads each time that they went under a garment, or other item.

Although Orrin had to spend some time helping his mother on Tuesday, his task was far less arduous and time consuming. This was the day that Rhoda reserved for ironing the heaping baskets of sweet-smelling clothing and linens. The Sabbath Day clothing demanded very special attention. Once Orrin had gotten the fire to just the right level to heat the sad irons which were large and triangular in shape Rhoda put them near the coals while Orrin set up the old cloth covered ironing board between two chairs. Orrin was now done and what a relief this was! He was happy to leave Rhoda to sand, clean and wax the irons in preparation for the next ironing day.[41] The rest of the day was his, and he could hardly contain himself as he rushed out to find his father and join him in whatever he was doing.

One morning in early November some of the womenfolk in the area began to gather at the house, and Billy suggested that his son accompany him to the Village of Essex that lay to the south. Although Orrin had been there when he and his family crossed the lake from Charlotte on Charles McNeil's sail ferry in 1801, he was a mere lad of three years and had no memory of this occasion. After that there had been no real reason for his father to go to the tiny hamlet that lay ten miles to the south and had only been split away from Willsborough three years before in 1805. [42] After all, his needs, and those of his family, were easily met right in Willsborough, and he certainly had no reason to cross that wide expanse of water on the ferry as he had done many years before.

Billy did not reveal where they were going or why. He simply said that it would be an adventure. Orrin was filled with excitement as he prepared for what seemed to him to be a "journey". It would be even more special because only he was going with his father and he was going to ride behind him on the mare's back. This was an experience that he had never had, and he was a little nervous about it, despite the fact that he knew how gentle and calm the horse was. Soon Billy appeared, leading the mare by her halter. He instructed Orrin to retrieve the wooden mounting block that he had made to assist smaller people in getting onto the horse's back. Holding the reins firmly in his hands Billy mounted the horse, settled himself in the saddle, and told Orrin to step up onto the mounting block. He leaned over, hoisted the lad up and swung him into position behind him. Finally, Billy directed his son to put his arms around his waist and to hold on tight. The gentle mare never moved throughout the process. Billy assured Orrin that if the pace of the mare frightened him, he would slow her down. Then he gave his steed a gentle nudge with his heel and off they went.

Soon Orrin began to feel the steady rhythm of the mare's trot and, as he did so, he felt more comfortable looking at the sights he was passing by. First, they passed his Uncle Daniel and Aunt Abalena's farm and then they had crossed over the neck of land that separated The Point from the mainland, and proceeded along the well-worn track to the village. Before he knew it, the mare was taking them down the steep hill, over the bridge, and into the valley where Willsborough hugged the shores of the Boquet River.

When they passed by his former home, Orrin looked up the hill and felt a twinge of sadness as he remembered that his grandfather had finally listened to his mother's pleadings and invited her and her children to come to Stillwater to live with him. They were gone and now a different family lived where he had grown up in those happy days before his father's disappearance. He wondered if he would ever see his mother again. Then, he shook his head and refocused his eyes as he endeavored to dismiss this thought from his mind. With a small sigh he turned his thoughts back to today's adventure.

The mare climbed up the steep hill at the other end of the village, and for almost five miles the road flattened out remarkably. The landscape continued to be forested and, occasionally, punctuated by a small cabin set in a field with a few outbuildings. At one point they passed a little schoolhouse, which had been constructed for the children of the first settlers in that area. As they neared Essex Billy pointed out the log blockhouse that lay between them and the shore. He remarked that this had been built to protect early settlers in the area from the British. He also noted that Essex had been used as the seat of Essex County until a year ago. Then, in 1807, this distinction had been passed over to Elizabethtown, which was more central to the county. As they dropped down the hill and into the hamlet, Orrin looked out over the water to the east and the Green Mountains of Vermont beyond. The lake was so much narrower than it was where he lived, and he was struck by the appearance of a sandy beach upon which Charles McNeil's ferry was resting. It was not at all like the rocky beaches out on The Point.

The first substantial house that they encountered was a white clapboard structure that sat low to the ground and had a type of roof that Billy called gambrel. What a funny name that was! Billy explained that this was the first house to be erected in Essex, and for quite some time it had been the only house of substance. He gave Orrin a bit of history as they slowed to a gentle pace while passing it. Billy knew a lot about its builder, Daniel Ross, because he owned the land upon which the Anchor Shop stood as well as its business. He explained that Mr. Ross had married William Gilliland's daughter, Elizabeth, in Albany in June 1784 and Gilliland had given Daniel a parcel of land facing the lake as part of Elizabeth's dowry. Soon after their marriage the house had been constructed. As they rode along still further they came across a hostelry, which Billy said was called Wright's Tavern after General Daniel Wright who built it in 1796.[43] It was a perfect place to welcome travelers who were passing through on their way north or south, as well as those who had come across the lake on McNeil's ferry. Billy explained that this inn was very important for travelers. There were a few houses near the tavern, a ship's hull was on the ways at a shipyard, and a number of smaller boats were tied up on the shore.

Billy decided to take Orrin home by a different route, and soon the mare was climbing the hill that led westward out of the hamlet. The land flattened for a bit, and then there was yet another steep hill to climb. As they reached the crest Orrin gasped when he saw the massive set of hills that rose from the river below. They were gentler than the steep cliffs and abrupt mountains that lay on the western shore of Willsborough Bay, yet they were still majestic. His father pointed out that this was the same Boquet River that wended its way through Willsborough. He added that he had been told that it sprang from one of the many tall mountains that lay much further to the west. Billy turned the mare to the north toward home. As mile after mile clicked by Orrin found himself swaying with the mare and, several times, had to shake himself awake. He thought that this must be what it felt like to be rocked in a cradle.

They passed through the village, across the bridge and up the steep hill on the other side. As they crossed the neck of land onto The Point, Billy pulled his steed over to the side of the road. Billy dismounted and then reached up to help Orrin get down from the mare's back. Then he wrapped his arms around the boy and told his son that he had something very special to share with him. He said that when they got home Rhoda would be presenting a newborn baby to them, and there would probably still be some women at the house to care for his mother and her infant. He urged Orrin to enter the cabin quietly in case she was asleep. He assured him that one of the women would let them both see the newborn boy or girl. Billy secretly hoped for a girl who would become a companion to his wife in the future, but he knew that having a healthy babe was of primary importance. Orrin was very excited by this news and could hardly wait for them to get back on the mare and head for home.

As they opened the door, and father and son crept into the big room, they were greeted by a wail that was certainly not coming from Nelson, who was eagerly waiting to share the news with his father and brother. After all, he was the only one who was there when the baby was born, and he was feeling quite smug as a result. Suddenly, from behind the curtain that surrounded his parent's bedstead came Orrin's Aunt Abalena Rowley, with a wreath of smiles on her face, as she presented the newborn infant to his father and brother.

It was a boy! Orrin was in awe and wonderment. Even though he had seen and been part of the lives of his younger siblings when they came into the world, somehow this was different. Billy told him the baby's name was Mortimer. Orrin simply stood in awe as he gazed at the tiny infant before him.

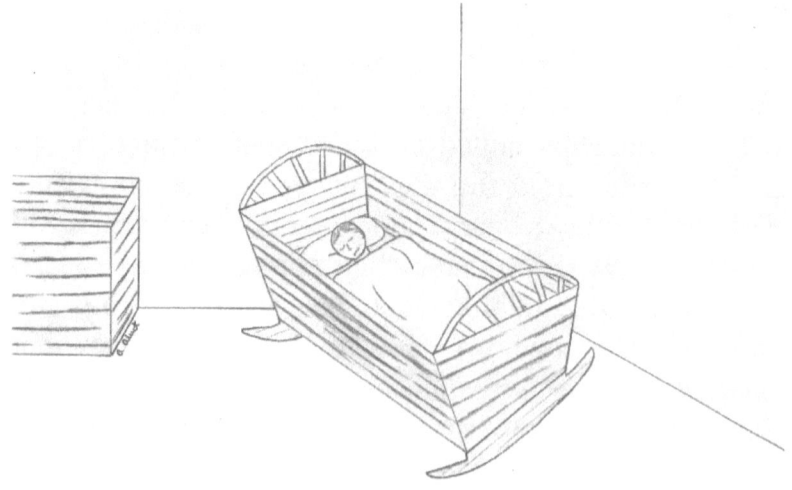

Figure 5 Baby in Cradle. Ashley Ahrent

CHAPTER FIVE

BITTER WINDS AND SNOW ARRIVE

In December Billy began the final preparations for the full brunt of the stormy blasts of winter that would be coming soon. He knew from experience how difficult it was to keep at bay the bitter cold that seeped in everywhere, forcing the fireplace to be kept filled and fully operational throughout the day and night. He was grateful that he had been so careful when he built the house and had paid special heed to chinking and caulking between the logs. First, he had inserted pieces of wood, and small stones, into every space that he could reach both inside and out. Now, with Orrin's help, Billy stuffed old rags into every aperture that he could find in the walls of the cabin. They were usually quite small, and Orrin's smaller hands did an excellent job of squeezing the rags into the crevices. Then he had taken clay, which was in great abundance on his property, and mixed in moss that grew freely on the edges of his woods and forced them into the spaces. As the final layer he took more clay and spread the daub out as evenly as he could.[44] Even so, he knew that the gales that swept across The Point would find cracks hither and thither. He had closed each small window's shutter firmly as another means of keeping the drafts somewhat in abeyance. They were as prepared for the full onslaught of winter as they could be. With no windows open the cabin became very dark, and the only light that broke the gloom came from the fireplace, and the candles that Rhoda had made.

As Billy introduced his son to new responsibilities, he was impressed by the speed and enthusiasm with which the lad continued to tackle each new task. He was teaching him how to help with the care and feeding of the animals—a task that

Orrin truly enjoyed, especially since he was no longer relegated to caring for the fowl. Each morning after his inside tasks were taken care of, it was time to attend to his outside chores. He pulled on his boots, wrapped himself in the warm wool coat that Rhoda had made for him, pulled his cap down as far as it would go, and wiggled his hands into the double wool mittens that she had knitted while rocking before the evening fire.

When he opened the cabin door, he sucked in the cold air that immediately attacked his face, and momentarily gasped. On days when the air was just right, he loved to watch the mist that curled forth from his nostrils, or his open mouth. He liked to pretend that this was what it must be like to smoke a pipe. If it had snowed the night before he loved the feel of the snow crunching under his feet. Billy had made a special wood shovel for him, with a short handle and a bowl that was just the right size for a lad his age, and had showed him how to help his father dig a path to the places where the various animals were housed. With his shovel in hand, Orrin dug into the snow mightily and then delighted in creating mounds of white all along the pathway that he was creating. When the snow was very heavy or icy Billy would come over to give him a hand. Otherwise, Orrin could do it all by himself while Billy attended to other chores. He felt so proud.

As he approached each animal's residence he was greeted by a cacophony of voices, signaling their urgent need for their morning meal and fresh water. It had not taken long for them to figure out who was responsible for responding to their demands and as Orrin grew closer their voices got more and more strident and demanding. The hens poked their heads out of their inside abode and, since they were by far the noisiest, he decided to tend to them immediately. First, he checked each of their nesting boxes. Often, there were precious few eggs and so when he found one it was a real prize. He had to remind himself that because hens instinctively respond to the hours of daylight that each season brings in winter their bodies simply did not produce at the same rate that they did when the days were longer. Orrin strew a special grain mixture on the ground and stepped back quickly so as not to be trampled by rush of well-clawed feet. Suddenly there was silence as they ate hungrily. Next, he tended to the two roosters, who were being incredibly patient for a change, even though they remained quite certain that they were the kings, or at least crowning princes, of their kingdom.

As he turned around a lineup of turkeys and ducks were following him and, finally, the geese came along, honking exceedingly noisily in hopes of attracting special attention to themselves. They always seemed to feel a bit slighted because, although they were bigger, they were consistently the last fowl to be fed. Orrin could not help thinking how impolite they were. Turn by turn, it did not take him long to satisfy the needs of each of the birds as he tossed more grain onto the hard-packed and often snow-covered soil. He knew that, after they ate, birds are anxious for some water to start their digestive systems flowing, so he picked up a sturdy hammer and smashed open the thick layer of ice that lay in their watering trays.

Next, Orrin walked over to the pen where the pigs were standing around their feeding trough and snorting loudly. He threw the slops from the kitchen into the trough and watched as they clambered over one another in a mad rush to attain what they perceived to be the very best place. Their antics were so comical that Orrin could not help laughing out loud. With that done, he turned to the pair of young oxen who were growing impatient, as most youngsters do. They had no interest in any special attention. It was all about food in their minds, and once they were served their ration of hay and oats they ate with gusto, ignoring their provider.

While Orrin had been attending to his chores, Billy was taking care of the many odds and ends that always seemed to crop up. Finally, it was time to be with his beloved mare. He always took care of her himself and, as he approached her stall, he could not help musing over his feelings of endearment toward her. To him she was a sweet and very special friend whose loyalty was unfailing. They had been through so much together. He wondered what he would have done without her. Before he fed her, and gave her fresh water, he ran his fingers over her mane, and along her backbone. She loved it when he did this and nuzzled him in appreciation. Then he poured some oats into a tiny bucket, just big enough for her nose to fit, and filled her crib with fresh hay and her tub with water. Giving her a final pat on the rump he turned toward the cabin.

Most days Orrin and Billy completed their chores almost simultaneously, which signified a good balance of duties. As they entered the cabin, and discarded their winter garb, they immediately inhaled the delightful aroma that emanated from the fireplace where Rhoda sat stirring the pots before her. As usual, their morning meal was a hearty one. As they sat at the table, waiting for their food, Nelson always chose the opportunity to bang his spoon upon the table in a demanding fashion that said, "Faster, faster." Soon Rhoda scooped luscious spoonfuls of thick gruel into the waiting bowls. She then covered it with rich cream and topped it with a bit of maple sugar. It smelled absolutely delicious! As always, the family bowed their heads in prayer as they thanked God for yet another bounteous meal. Then there was utter silence as each person dug into the food before him or her.

Rhoda was beginning to experience what was commonly referred to as "cabin fever" after being cooped up in a small space with the two children. As a farmer's wife her life was somewhat isolated during the winter. Her only break from children, and household chores, was during her twice daily milking of her cows. Occasionally she and her neighbors gathered at one another's dwellings to catch up on their doings, do a little handwork, or work on a joint quilt project. Rhoda always counted her blessings that her sister was nearby. They were devoted to each other and provided mutual love and support in countless ways.

With the repast completed, Rhoda was delighted that Orrin often lingered a bit in order to help her with the cleanup. She seldom asked for assistance, but with an infant to care for, she was grateful for his willing attention. Fortunately, Mortimer was proving to be a quiet and tranquil baby whose days and nights were focused on eating and sleeping. Rhoda was grateful for this since she still had many things to attend to. It pleased her that Orrin seemed to want to spend some special time with her, and this was an opportunity to do just that. He had really grown to love his new mother and when they were together, they chatted amiably about whatever came to mind. Rhoda had told him that the biggest help he could give was entertaining Nelson. After all, Orrin had some expertise in this regard because of his former interactions with his own younger siblings. He really enjoyed doing this and did not look upon it as a chore.

On cold, snowy days when the wind was howling, and the weather was not fit for man or beast, Billy retreated to his workshop. This was an opportunity for him to attend to all of the things that he had been too busy to worry about during the warmer months, when he was in the fields so much. Orrin loved to spend time with his father in the workshop. The best moments of all were when Billy had a moment to spare, for then he had the time to take a tool from its special place on the wall—or on a shelf, or even on the floor—and demonstrate its use. Some of the pieces were quite obvious and, occasionally, Orrin spotted one that he recognized from his own father's collection. However, he remembered that his father's work area was not nearly as neat and well organized as this one, but then again, he had seven children to care for in comparison to his new father's three.

In his workshop Billy had a small forge that met his daily needs. For bigger pieces he relied upon the blacksmith in the village. He particularly focused on making improvements to his farm equipment or repairing what he used, both outdoors and, in the house. Orrin especially loved watching Billy at the forge. It seemed almost like magic that he could take a chunk

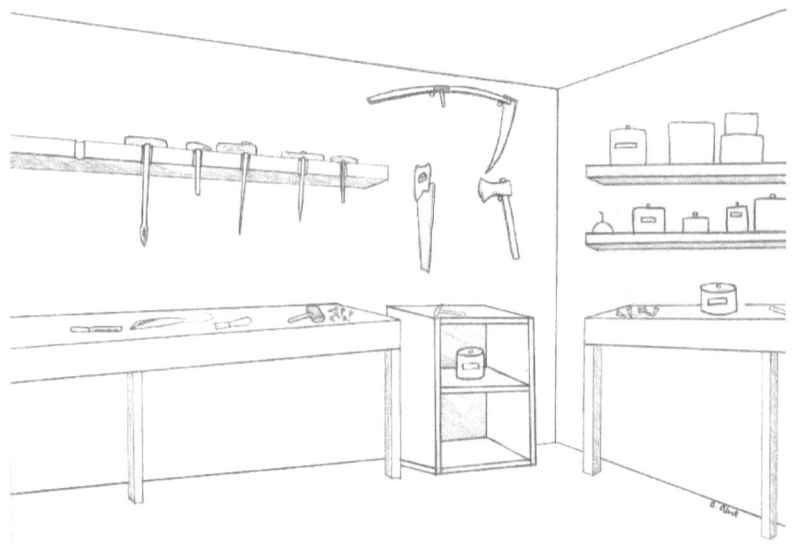

Figure 6 Billy's Workshop. Ashley Ahrent

of iron and turn it into a tool or use it to repair a piece. His skill and expertise were truly amazing. The boy was fascinated by his father's repetitive process of heating the metal until it was red hot, and laying it on the anvil to hammer it into the shape that he needed, then, with long tongs, dipping the piece into a barrel of water, where it bubbled and sizzled. Finally, he deftly lifted it out of the liquid and let it cool completely. Orrin wondered if he would ever be able to master that art and was certain that it would take a great deal of practice.

Orrin noted that his father handled his various tools and pieces of equipment with great respect for their importance in his life as a farmer, and he made a point of keeping them in excellent condition. Sometimes he was repairing or replacing the handle of an axe or saw. Upon other occasions, he was fitting an iron piece for his plow, or one of the other implements that he used in the warmer months. This was also a perfect time of year for Billy to build new pieces of equipment that he would need in the spring. In addition, he had begun to develop some very good woodworking and carpentry skills and was gradually making more permanent pieces of furniture for his house. He had learned a great deal from his brother-in-law, Daniel Rowley, who had been a cabinetmaker by trade. This winter Billy was creating a small cupboard in which Rhoda could store foodstuffs out of the reach of the ever-present mice.

When the days were cold, but fair and not too windy, Orrin was eager to don his warm winter garb as quickly as possible and proceed into the woods with his father. Because the ground was now hard, and solid, it was a perfect time to continue clearing the forest beyond the cabin. In the months before the bitter cold set in, Orrin had walked with Billy as he made a notch in each tree to be felled. Billy did not believe in wholesale clear cutting of his forest, and he made his decisions carefully and prudently. This winter he focused on an area where he planned to create pastureland, rather than a field in which to grow crops. Because of this usage he planned to leave a few trees to provide shelter from the sun and rain for the grazing animals. As he had in the past, he continued to seek out trees with fairly straight trunks. He knew that these provided the most useful wood for building more structures, erecting fences, cutting roof shingles, and even creating wood for building essential pieces of furniture.

When the two had reached the area of trees that Billy had previously notched for felling he brought forth a large felling axe which was among his most prized possessions.   He explained that there were many types of axes. Each had a specific purpose and had to be fabricated to the user's specific requirements. If the proportions were too large or small, if the axe head was not properly crafted, or if the handle was crudely formed, the axe would not perform to its full capacity. If it was made correctly a skillful axe man, like himself, could take a tree down without damaging the trees around it. Billy told Orrin that, although he had the blacksmith in the village fabricate his axe heads, he really enjoyed cutting and shaping the handles. He preferred to use ash because it was strong and durable. When the piece was finished to his satisfaction, he liked to carve his initials, or a symbol of his own design, into the handle. It was his mark of distinction.

Billy proudly lifted the felling axe that he would be using today. It had a long and graceful handle and a sturdy chisel head. He explained that this was the first tool that he used when felling a tree because, with every stroke, it cut deeper and deeper into the grain of the wood, resulting in a clean-cut stump.[45] With swift and precise swings he drove the axe through the tree's bark, and deep into its inner core. Then he turned to do the same on the directly opposite side of the tree, while making sure that his incisions would make the tree fall in just the place where he wanted it to land. With Orrin safely out of the way, he gave one final stroke. Suddenly, with a thunderous roar, the tree fell directly to the appointed spot on the ground. No matter how many times he saw his father repeat this action, Orrin never ceased to be amazed by the skill with which he handled the task.

After Billy took down each tree, he said that, first, he would cut the limbs away from the trunk. He handed Orrin a smaller version of the shorter handled axes that he would be using for the next step. He explained that some people liked to use a hatchet for this purpose, but he preferred a shorter handled axe. He emphasized how important it was for Orrin not to get too close to the trunk, and to keep his actions up and down in order to keep the axe from striking him. Orrin took his instructions very seriously and, although he worked far more slowly than Billy, he did so with great concentration and care. Laboring at opposite ends, the two of them went about the business of chopping away the branches until all that remained of each once stately tree was a long, round piece of wood with bark on it.[46] With that done, the two piled the remaining pieces of branches and leaves to burn at a later time.

Now Billy was ready to put his team of oxen back to work. It was time to place the yoke over their heads and attach a chain to the iron ring at the center of the yoke between the two animals. With that done, he stepped in and attached the chain to his large wood sledge. The team was pawing the earth in excited anticipation, expressing their eagerness to pull the sledge over the snow to the place where the fallen tree trunks were. As they lifted their hooves Orrin asked why there were spikes on their iron shoes. Billy explained that this gave them traction on the snow and allowed them to move more easily and safely. This morning the oxen were amazingly cooperative, much to Billy's pleasure, and soon they were where the tree trunks lay.

After several "gee-gees" and "haw-haws" they were in position. Billy and Orrin stepped forward and rolled the new logs onto the sledge with peaveys. When there was no more room Billy said giddy-up, and he and his oxen were off to where the logs would be piled for further use. Once again, to Billy's surprise his team obeyed instantly. For the rest of the day father and son repeated the process until what had once been proud trees in a dense forest were no more.

The day's objective was to remove the bark and cut the tree trunks into more manageable sections. This time Billy brought forth an axe that looked very much like the one that he had used to fell the tree, only its handle was a bit shorter and, therefore, better for horizontal work. At carefully selected intervals he cut deep notches into the tree trunk on one side. Then he drove an iron ring into that side of the trunk, so he could roll it over, and cut equally deeply into the other side. Billy disconnected the sledge, moved the team into position by the long trunk, and attached an iron chain to the ring in the trunk that he attached to the ring on their yoke. Once all was ready, he gave a lusty "giddy-up" and the team slowly moved forward. He shouted "whoa" as the trunk rolled forward, and over to the other side. It was time to notch the tree trunk just as he had done on the other side.

Then he reached for a broad axe. It was a strange looking device that had a handle with a flaring square blade at right angles to it. Billy deftly lifted it above the trunk, and with great precision inserted the newly sharpened blade into the wood at the notch and drew it back as it lifted the bark away from the trunk. [47] He repeated this all the way down the trunks that lay on the ground.

The next challenge was to turn the logs that had been stripped of their bark into useable pieces of wood. This involved making the basically round trunk into a square piece of wood. With some assistance from Orrin, they lifted each log onto short blocks that they had placed under either end. Then Billy instructed the boy to step aside as he picked up a broad axe with a chisel edge and grasped it firmly in his hands. As he walked along beside each log he swiftly drew the ax along the side of the log pulling out the round part of the log between each previously cut notch.[48] With Billy safely ahead of him the boy picked up the notched pieces that had fallen away and stacked them neatly on the sledge. He knew how perfect they would be for kindling to get the fire well started before placing firewood logs on top. When Bill reached the end of one side, he and Orrin rolled the log to expose another surface and he repeated the task before him. He and Orrin repeated this process over and over.[49]

As the rays of the sun lengthened to the west, and dipped further toward the horizon, Orrin and Billy realized that they had been in the forest all day, except for a brief respite. All too soon it was going to be dark and there were still evening chores to be done. They addressed these with dispatch. With their chores done father and son hastened across the snow-covered land and pushed the door to the cabin open, slamming it shut as quickly as possible behind them. Oh, how welcome was the warm air that greeted them, along with such a delectable aroma!

Suddenly Orrin remembered that he had forgotten to tend to the firewood and water. Before he took off his outer garments he rushed out to the woodpile and, in three trips, brought the wood inside for the morrow. Then back he went to the well, where he pumped several buckets full of water that he put beside the fireplace so that it would not freeze overnight. With that done, he drew off his outer garments and his hat and mittens, hung them on the peg to dry off the snow, and edged his way to the fireplace to warm himself, especially his hands and feet. Before he knew it Rhoda had put before them a pot of tea, some luscious homemade bread, a pat of butter, and a bit of jam. Mortimer was sleeping soundly, and Nelson was tired and very quiet, which was a joy. Together, except for the baby, everyone quickly said Grace, and then plunged into the last meal of the day.

As they ate, Orrin chimed in excitedly, sharing the adventures of his day. He really loved his hours in the forest with his father and was developing new skills with each passing day. Billy and Rhoda told him how very proud of him they were. After Rhoda had put Nelson to bed, Orrin went to her side to help her with the final cleanup. Just as it was in the morning this was a special time of day for them. He loved to tell his mother all about what he had done and what he had learned. He always seemed so happy with his work, his home and, most of all, his family. With cleanup behind them Rhoda settled into her rocking chair and picked up a sock that she was making for Billy. The candlelight and the light from the fireplace did not really provide a lot of illumination, but she knew the pattern by heart. Billy sat on the settle before the fire and put his feet up on the stool before him. He settled himself comfortably, enjoyed watching the coals in the fireplace that would suddenly leap into flames and, before he knew it, was snoring softly. All was at peace in the cabin.

Orrin had been sitting quietly on the other side of Billy and, as Rhoda looked over to the man and boy seated on the settle, she smiled to herself. In just a few minutes she noticed that Orrin had begun to rub his eyes and yawn. She went over to him, and gently suggested that it was time for him to climb the ladder and cuddle down under the covers for a good night's sleep. Who knew what the next day might bring! She took him gently by the hand and, with candle in hand, ascended the ladder behind the sleepy lad. She and Orrin said their evening prayers together. Then Rhoda gave him a kiss and adjusted his bedding and sat beside him until she knew that he was fast asleep. Then, she climbed back down the ladder.

Nelson was already asleep, and Mortimer was beginning to gurgle, which signaled the imminent approach of tears of hunger. She quickly scooped him up in her arms and went over to her rocker by the fire. In no time Mortimer had nestled into her breast and was sucking hungrily. Soon, Rhoda was dozing off a bit and she was relieved when the baby was satiated, and she could put him in his cradle. Next she turned to rouse Billy from his slumbers just long enough to get him into their bed. Then she pulled the curtains around them, and peace descended upon this little family of five—at least until sunrise heralded the arrival of another day!

CHAPTER SIX

SUGARING TIME

In the late fall, and before the ground began to freeze, Billy told Orrin that they would be sugaring for the first time in the very beginning of spring. There was an abundance of old sugar maple trees on his property, for which he was very grateful. He, like everyone else, depended upon maple sugar and syrup to provide a year-around source of sweetness. This would be the first time that Billy had actually sugared, although he had watched his neighbor, Samuel Adsit the year before.

In anticipation of actual sugaring season Billy said that they needed to make a few preparations before the ground froze. First, he chose the best place to set up a shallow fire pit over which the sap would be turned into syrup. Then he and Orrin dug out an area just the right size for the sugaring process and lined the sides with stone that would reflect the heat of the fire back into its center. With that taken care of, Billy hitched up the mare to the sledge that he would be using, and he and Orrin headed out into the woods in search of four strong ash tree limbs with sturdy crotches as well as two long straight ash limbs. He chose ash because it was very hard and durable. Since his was old growth wood that had never been touched, except by nature, it was fairly easy to find limbs that were close enough to the ground for Billy to reach. Once they found just what they wanted Billy took out his felling axe and cut the limbs neatly from the tree trunk while Orrin went to work with his hatchet and removed the peripheral small limbs. Billy knew that he had to remove the bark from the limbs because they would catch fire too easily when it was at the fire pit. He used his adze to make them bark free. As the final step, Billy cut the limbs into the correct lengths and Orrin whittled the ends of each to a thick, somewhat blunt point.

They loaded the prepared limbs onto the sledge and took them back to the fire pit. With Orrin's help Billy pushed the side-by-side crotched tree limbs deeply into the still frost-free earth on either side of the pit, where they would remain until needed. When ready for sugaring the pones that they had cut would be placed side by side and span the fire pit. They would support the weight of the sturdy iron sap pots that would be hung from them over the fire. For now, the poles would be stored up on the rafters of the hen house until they were needed. That was all that they needed to do for now.

One day during the winter Billy and Orrin went to the tinsmith in the village to ask him to make the pails that they would use to collect the sap as it poured out of the trees. He would need a pail for each tree. The tinsmith was already working industriously to meet the needs of the farmers who were asking for the same thing. They stopped to watch him for a few moments. He picked up a thin sheet of iron that was coated with molten tin, which provided a rust-resistant veneer. He carefully cut it to just the width and length that he needed and bent it around a rounded wooden form. Then he cut out the circular bottom for the pail. He explained that now came the trickiest part of making a pail. He had to hold the two edges together with the bottom and create a smooth, watertight seam. For this step he used an iron soldering rod with a copper head that was placed in a charcoal brazier. Once he had this just as he wanted, he took the molten tin and poured it along the seam. He had to work very quickly as he carefully applied the solder, or it would begin to harden before he had completed the process.[50] As the final step the tinsmith cut yet another rather thin piece of tin which he carefully folded over to make a double thickness. This would be the handle of the pail. His last step was to solder the two ends of the handle to the pail and, with this completed, he proudly held up the finished product for them to see. Orrin was amazed by the process and filled with admiration for this craftsman.

Their next stop was at the cooperage where Billy ordered the large barrels, he would need for collecting the sap from the pails. When they entered the shop, the cooper was sitting on a work stool with the makings of a barrel in front of him. Orrin noticed that there were two different kinds of barrels. The smaller ones were held together by wood while the larger ones, that would carry much heavier loads, had metal hoops. The cooper had already cut out the round wood bottom for the barrel he was making and had just finished taking his plane to the staves. Orrin stood by and marveled as he watched him reach into the pail of water beside him and draw forth a strip of wet wood that he deftly molded around the wood slats of the smaller barrel that was before him. He then overlapped the wet wood ends so that they would dry together and form a seal without needing to be nailed together.[51] Orrin could easily see that, as with the tinsmith, making these barrels demanded a great deal of skill and dexterity, especially the smaller one.

During the winter evenings Billy and Orrin sat before the fire and whittled the spiles that they would use to tap into the sapwood part of the trees and release the precious liquid to flow steadily into the tin sap buckets. Once Orrin had learned how to safely use a whittling knife he took over that process. First, he took a piece of sumac about 8 inches long and an inch around, and whittled it into a piece that was flat on one end and tapered on the other, so that it would fit into a hole in the tree. Billy then picked up each of the pieces that Orrin had whittled, reached into the bed of coals in the fireplace, and withdrew an iron-burning awl, which he carefully inserted through the spile in order to create the spout through which the sap could flow.[52] Although this was a laborious process, both father and son enjoyed having this time to work together, as they chatted about the day's events and plans for the future.

By the end of February, the lengthening of the days became visibly noticeable to Billy and Orrin. Even on a very cold day the sun was casting off a bit of warmth. On a clear, bright day they would occasionally take a break from what they were doing and turn their faces or backs to the sunlight for a few moments. It was delightful! Sugaring season would begin sometime between mid-March and mid-April, when the snow still lay on the ground, but the rays of the sun had gained more warmth. The sap would flow when the sun and warmth caused it to rise up into the tree trunk, and cold nights forced it back down in a rhythmic pattern day by day. This created a delicate balance in which the heat of the day exactly matched the frost of the night.[53] Samuel Adsit had instructed Billy that the optimal temperatures were between 32° and 40° during the day and down to anywhere between 31° and 24° at night. Both during the day and at night, Billy watched the outside temperatures as he carefully calculated the moment in which the sap would begin to flow.

One day in in the latter part of March the day-night temperature balance had reached its optimum. With great excitement Billy and Orrin set forth to the woods after completing their morning chores. As they came to each maple tree, Billy took a small auger, which the blacksmith had made for him, and slowly wound it slightly upward through the bark and into the sapwood, where the ultimate sweetness lay. He did this on the sunny side of each tree and about four feet from ground level. Orrin found it fascinating that each tree was different and seemed to have a personality of its own. Sometimes the auger barely pierced the bark before the sap flowed, and other times he had to go in several inches. Billy knew that he had reached the perfect place when tiny drops of sap began to ooze out of the hole. As soon as it came he quickly withdrew the auger, and Orrin handed him the spile, which Billy inserted into the hole.[54]Then they hung a tin sap pail from the spile on each tree.

Figure 7 Tapping the Maple Trees. Erwin H. Austin

Now came the time of waiting and watching. At last the sap began to really flow at a steady rate. Sugaring season had truly arrived. Each morning, after completing their chores, and indulging in their morning repast, father and son hitched their horse to a sled and placed on it the wood barrel for collecting sap that the cooper had made. They chose to use the mare instead of the oxen much to the consternation of the latter, which always wanted to be the center of attention. However, this was not heavy work that demanded the brute force of the team. The mare stamped her feet in happy anticipation for, in her mind, she had been spending far too much time idle. They quickly attached the chain that linked her to the sled, and all was ready.

Orrin and Billy picked up the shoulder yokes that Billy had carved for them, and extended a sap pail from the end of each. These yokes looked much like the ones they used to keep the oxen in line with one another. However, they had a very different purpose. They were made to rest on a person's shoulders and keep the weight evenly distributed across them as they carried pails of sap to the collection bucket on the sledge. Billy had made sure that the two yokes were of the appropriate size for each of them.

During the winter months after Billy had finished Orrin's yoke, he had the lad practice using it. He showed Orrin how to put it on. Now came the tricky part. It took considerable skill to lift the yoke with the sap pails hung from each end in a way that avoided spilling a drop. Orrin spent a considerable amount of time practicing with buckets of water rather than sap. At one point he became quite discouraged. He thought that he would never master this challenge and then suddenly one day everything fell into place. Orrin was so glad that he no longer had to worry about losing a precious drop of sap.

With everything prepared, Orrin, Billy and the mare set off for the woods. Once they reached a tree, they followed a measured routine. They took the sap pails down from the spiles on two trees and then donned their yokes, crouched down, and gently lifted the sap pails from the spiles and onto each end of the yoke. Rising was very challenging, but both father and son did this adroitly. With this accomplished, they walked over to where the mare was waiting patiently with the sled and emptied the liquid contents from their pails into the large sap barrel. It was time consuming, rewarding work that was never monotonous. At the end of each day the mare pulled the sled with the brim-full sap barrel over to a shed where Billy dumped the contents into a still larger barrel where they would remain until it was time to boil the sap. After many days the first sap barrel in the shed was full and Orrin brought forth the second one. He had three altogether, although he was not certain that he would need all three. It all depended upon the sap flow for a particular year.

When the flow of sap had come to an end it was time to start boiling the colorless liquid in the barrels. In preparation for this step Orrin had laid a fire of ironwood and shagbark hickory, which grew plentifully on the property and produced the hottest fire[55]. Meanwhile, Billy inserted the double pones into the holders. He had doubled both the pones and the holders for extra strength because the pots that would hang over the fire were very heavy. Then he got out the large iron pots that Rhoda used just for sugaring season because she could never get them completely free of sugar remains at the end of the season. He carried them to the fire pit and set them down. Once everything was in readiness, he would hang the pots.

The day for boiling the sap began with clear blue skies overhead. It was a perfect time to start the process. Billy hitched the mare to the sled and went over to the shed where the large sap barrels had been stored. Orrin helped him semi-roll the barrel out of the shed and onto the sled. With a tug on the reins, the mare pulled slowly forward as father and son walked on either side to keep the barrel steady. Once they reached the fire they set the barrel upright alongside the pit, and Orrin watched while Billy picked up Rhoda's sugar ladle. It had a very long handle that meant that he could dip out the sap right to the bottom of the barrel. It took quite a long time for him to fill each pot, so he asked Orrin if he would like to take over now that he had watched how it was done. Billy remarked that this was a good sugaring year and all three barrels were filled to the brim with the pale, sticky substance. Once Orrin had filled the pots in which he would boil the sap he hoisted them up onto the pone. Orrin lit the fire with the flint, and from then on, it was his job to continue to replenish the fire as long as it was needed.

Periodically Billy stopped to dip the ladle into the pot to determine whether enough of the water content in the sap had evaporated into the air, leaving only syrup behind. When Rhoda came out to watch what was going on, she had Nelson with her. She had admonished him to stay very close to her because this was a dangerous process and a child could be badly hurt by falling into the fire or being touched by the scalding hot syrup. Orrin helped Rhoda set up a sturdy, old table far enough from the fire to be safe from flying sparks. She placed her tin sugar molds on it so that they would be ready when the syrup had cooled sufficiently to pour it into them.

At last the first batch of syrup was ready and Billy told Orrin to let the fire die down naturally, so that the sap could begin to cool. Once it had cooled enough not to be dangerous Billy picked up the ladle and poured a small amount of hot syrup directly onto a clean area of snow away from the still hot fire. While Orrin and Nelson watched with great eagerness and delight the warm syrup immediately turned into a kind of snow cone. Orrin took Nelson's hand and, together, they rushed forward eagerly, scooped the frozen mass into their bare hands, and began licking eagerly so that they could go back for more. Billy and Rhoda followed suit, but in a much more genteel fashion.

As the sun began to fall lower in the sky, the syrup was cool enough to pour into the sugar molds, and the fire was almost out. Billy wound a number of rags around his hands, carefully pulled each pot from the pone, and put it on the table. It was time for Rhoda to dip the syrup into the tin molds, where she would let it cool completely overnight. Early the next morning she returned to the table to be sure that the syrup in each mold had hardened sufficiently to be dumped into the wood sugar tubs, with lids, that she had brought out with her.[56]

For several days Billy and Orrin repeated the previous process until all of the sap had been removed from the barrels and boiled down. They kept some of the syrup liquid and made the rest into maple sugar. Rhoda had special uses for this wonderful sweetener in both forms. When she made buckwheat pancakes, she preferred to pour the syrup on top of them. More often, she picked up her weird looking forked iron sugar devil and broke the amount of sugar that she needed.[57] No matter which form it was in, the sugar and syrup were wonderful additions to her cooking repertoire.

CHAPTER SEVEN

PLANTING SEASON IS UPON US

Just as sugaring season had come to an end in the latter part of April, spring finally showed some signs of coming. In early May, the last vestiges of the winter's snow slowly receded from the surface of the earth as it rose from its long winter repose. The days lengthened, the sun gained strength, and there was a slight softness in the air. The roosters were noisier than ever, the chickens went back to regularly producing eggs, the geese honked and flapped their wings with fierce determination, the cows gave forth copious quantities of sweet golden milk, the pigs lolled in the puddles that the spring rains continually replenished, the oxen stamped their feet in happy anticipation of being outside all of the time, and the mare's feet echoed the sound in return. Canada geese wheeled through the air, honking and shifting positions in a never-changing vee as they headed north for cooler climes, repeating a tradition that had lasted perhaps for millennia. Vernal pools emerged, and peepers began to regale those nearby with their constant chorus. Wisps of brilliant green peeked through the snow as it thinned and finally disappeared, giving way to lady's slippers, Dutchman's breeches and trillium. Tiny buds began to appear on the trees, producing fascinating patterns of colors, and fruit trees burst forth with wee pink and white blooms.

It was a time for rejoicing by man and beast. All had survived yet another harsh winter in the north. For Billy, these sights and sounds of spring signaled the commencement of the same backbreaking period of labor from dawn to dusk that his forebears had faced. With so much moisture in the earth from snowmelt, it would be late May before he could fully work his land. Frost heaves had forced stones to emerge from beneath the surface of the land, and tangles of roots and stumps were emerging from their winter place of hiding. They must all be removed before the land could be cultivated. If not, when he tilled the soil, his implements would be badly marred, if not destroyed, when they encountered them.

During the winter, Billy had put together a strong oak stone boat. Now it was time for the restless oxen to really go to work. Billy pulled down from the wall a yoke that was different from any that Orrin had seen before. With this one, the ends of the arched piece of wood that went under the oxen's heads came through the cross piece and made the yoke look like it had horns. Billy explained that this gave the yoke extra strength and was very useful when the team was doing heavy work because it helped to distribute the weight more evenly. Once they were securely hitched to the stone boat Billy led his team into the area that he wanted to work, with Orrin right beside him. There Billy, with as much help as a lad of 12 could give, shoved a strong iron peavey under a stone protruding from the damp soil and rolled it onto the boat. As they approached each stone, they repeated the process, until the stone boat was filled to capacity. Then Billy slapped the rumps of the oxen with his willow gad, and he and Orrin guided them to the place where he planned to build a wall. There he rolled the stone into position, and then returned to retrieve yet another load.[58] It was tedious and exhausting work, but it was work that had to be done.

Once Billy was satisfied that he had removed all of the stones that he could, he turned his attention to the stumps and roots that lay all around him. First, he and Orrin went to fetch the pigs. They were not the least bit interested in being forced out of their wallows. However, with much grunting and oinking, they hoisted themselves up and waddled along as Billy flicked his gad across their rears to keep them moving. When they reached the area that had just been cleared of stones, the pigs moved swiftly into the mess before them. There was still plenty of good eating there and, in true form, the swine exhibited their usual voracious appetites. After a few days, the pigs had done the best that they could, but some of these obstructions to progress remained, especially the roots that flared like the tentacles of an octopus. In many ways these were even more challenging than the prior removal of stones had been. Fortunately, the roots had a definite use. They would make an excellent border around the edge of a cultivated area or pastureland and were far less time and effort consuming than building an actual stone wall. Billy saw using these as a temporary measure that would serve him well until he had more time to build a real stone wall.

The procedure for removing the roots was a bit different from that used to dislodge the stones. Billy and Orrin began by prying just as they had with the stones. They did this simply to rock the root structure just enough to get in place a sturdy rope that they could use for pulling the root and stump out in one piece. After Billy secured the rope, he attached the other end to the iron ring on the oxen's yoke. Now, Orrin and Billy worked as a team. Billy walked along with the root to guide it as best he could with a huge peavey, while Orrin walked alongside the oxen, and gave them a sharp slap with his stick when he got the command to do so. Billy had discovered that yanking was not successful, as it dislodged or broke the rope all too often. Instead, his team needed to work, slowly, and steadily, until the deep under roots snapped loose, and the roots and stump lifted from the earth.[59]   Father and son repeated this process time after time until, toward the end of the day, they had accumulated quite a pile. It would take several more days to complete the process.

By mid-May the rains began to abate, and the frost started seeping out of the soil. What had been streams filled with rocks, tree stumps, whole trunks, and other detritus left behind by nature had receded to their normal course, or simply disappeared, leaving a lot of debris behind. When time permitted Billy and Orrin would tend to the mess, but not now. The land was beginning to dry out and become arable. By the end of the month it was plowing and planting season at long last. Billy looked upon this as the most challenging month in his life as a farmer. Every day from dawn to dusk was filled with immediate and pressing activities. So much had to be done—and so quickly. Just one rainy day or one mishap with his equipment could set him back irretrievably.

Billy turned his pigs out onto the land once again. Their job was to finish off the remaining small bits of roots and stumps. Then, he needed to take one more step before he actually began to turn the earth. During the winter, when his livestock had been enclosed most of the time, a large amount of manure had accumulated and been piled in a heap outside. A friend and neighbor had told Billy that even though he did not understand why this worked so well, it did. That was all he needed to know.[60] A morning came when there was no sign of rain in the skies. This was just what he needed to deal with spreading the manure. With Orrin's help, they dug into the rotting pile of animal waste with their wood manure forks and loaded the stinking, clinging mess onto their manure cart. Then the oxen pulled it to the place that they planned to plow.[61]

By day's end father and son reeked of manure. When they opened the door to the cabin, Rhoda protested loudly and demanded that they go out to the sap shed. There she had left a pile of somewhat cleaner clothes for them to don until they took their weekly Saturday bath the next day. Everyone was glad that this task was over, and Rhoda sighed deeply when she thought about the washing challenge that lay before her. She had to face this one more time when Billy and Orrin spread the manure out over the area they were about to plow.

A few months before, Samuel Adsit told Billy about a new, and better, type of plow. Samuel was always seeking new implements and methods that could help him to improve his land. A friend of his, from across the lake, had told Samuel about something called a mould board plow that had been in existence in England for fifty years. Samuel said he wondered why it took so long for this type of plow to come to the attention of farmers in America because it sounded so much better than the hand plow that he was using. He was convinced of its superiority and had acquired a mould board plow the previous summer. He urged Billy to purchase one for himself this year.

Samuel explained that the basic components of this new type of plow looked much the same as Billy's hand pushed plow except that the oxen provided the power, not the farmer. It was the farmer's job to steer the mechanism. This plow had two long bars between which the farmer stood to steer the plow that the oxen were pulling. A cross piece held the bars together. This part was reminiscent of the hand plow. However, the actual plowing mechanism was completely different. A triangle-shaped, wood board, called a mould board, hung beside the traditional iron plowshare. The board's purpose was to lift the slice of earth that had been cut by the share and then invert and pulverize it. A long, wood shaft extended from the steering mechanism and a chain went from there to an iron ring in the middle of the oxen's yoke. The farmer was able to control the oxen's yokes by this mechanism and could guide the team where he wanted it to go. [62] As Samuel demonstrated the plow, Billy quickly saw that it also did a much better job of turning the earth and it turned a two-step plowing process into one-step. He then tried it out for himself and was quickly convinced that purchasing a plow like this made very good sense, even though it was a costly investment.

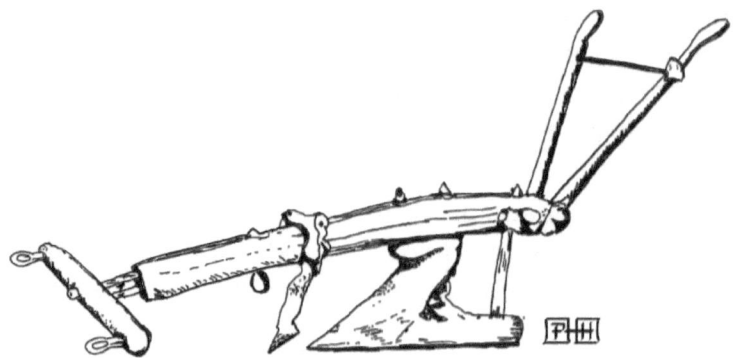

Figure 8 Mould board Plow. Philip Hall

Since he had come to Willsborough he had only used a plow that he pushed by hand. He had found that this presented several significant challenges. First of all, it took a huge expenditure of brute strength for him to force the plow blade into the previously uncultivated soil and bring up the clods of earth. Once this was accomplished, he had to turn the clods over and break them up by hand. Sometimes the ground was so packed that the plow would simply bounce over the surface of the land instead of digging into it. The thought of not having to endure these trials and tribulations was like music to Billy's ears. He was very excited, and yet a little nervous, about trying out his new acquisition. He could only hope that it would work as well as Samuel had claimed it would.

Finally, it had not rained for several days and the ground was dry but firm so Billy knew that there was no danger of him or his oxen getting mired in the mud. He went out to attend to his team. Orrin had fed them earlier, and he hoped that the beasts, with their bellies full, would be less restive, and more compliant, for this new operation. After breakfast and giving a quick hand to Rhoda, Orrin headed outside to see if he could assist his father. Billy seized the rope that hung from the ring at the center of the yoke and led the oxen forward. Periodically, they needed to be reminded to keep moving, rather than paying attention to the luscious tidbits of newly emerged grass that lay beneath their feet. When they were disobedient, Orrin gave them a good tap on their rumps with his long willow stick, and they moved forward grudgingly. It was almost as if they had a premonition that hard work lay ahead.

All was in readiness, and Orrin had a specific assignment. Billy instructed him to walk ahead of the team so that he could seek out any rocks, roots or other dangerous obstacles that lay ahead. He explained that he would not be able to see these because his visibility was greatly diminished by the oxen ahead of him and he indicated that Orrin should give him a signal to stop if he saw an obstacle ahead. Then Orrin would be able to try to clear the obstacle. If it was too difficult for him to do, the boy was to hold onto the plow handles while Billy worked at the obstruction. Fortunately, as hour after hour they worked together, they encountered very few obstacles that they had not removed previously. The team was surprisingly responsive to Billy's commands. It seemed like it was no time at all before man, boy and oxen were in sync and real progress was being made. Even with his new plow, the work was hard, but nothing like what it had been before. Seeing the results was immensely satisfying, and the humans were grateful for a moment of rest while they ate the noonday meal that Rhoda had prepared. Then back to the field they went until darkness descended and it was time for evening chores once again.

At last the plowing was completed and Billy and Orrin now needed to deal with the remaining clods of earth that had to be broken down further. Billy hitched the oxen to the wood tooth harrow, which he had built. Usually, by going over the ground with this he was able to eliminate the last few problems. However, when the harrow simply passed over the clods, Orrin's job was to jump forward with a hoe and knock the clods apart. Harrowing took a few more days, but then all was ready for planting this new 5-acre plot.

At last, it was planting time. The soil on The Point was somewhat thin, with a large clay component, and his neighbors, who had been there longer than he, urged him to plant Indian corn, oats and rye as the best staple crops for the soil. He also wanted to plant rows of barley and buckwheat that were such vitally important components of his working animals' diets. Next year, he planned to plant some turnips, carrots and pumpkins to supplement their usual fare, especially that of his pigs. However, there simply was not enough time this year. Of course, potatoes were the mainstay of everyone's diet, and so he was going to plant a goodly amount of these around the edges of his cornfield.[63]

When planting days came, Billy started with corn because it took a long time to germinate and bear fruit. During the previous summer, he and Orrin had kept an eye out for any corn whose silk had been successfully pollinated. They carefully gathered these ears and during the evenings sifted through them to separate the seeds from the silk in readiness for spring planting. The actual planting was something that Orrin could handle with ease. Billy marked straight rows with string for him to follow. Then on his hands and knees the lad moved along each row, pressing a pollinated seed into the ground to make sure that it had a covering of earth.

Next they planted the rye and oats. Rhoda had to use rye for making bread since there was no wheat. Unfortunately, the rye flour was difficult to work with, and produced hard, crusty bread, but they simply had to make do with it. Cultivating oats was very important for two reasons. The family loved the oat porridge, which was a very popular part of every morning meal throughout the winter. It was even more important as a staple of his livestock's menu. Both were planted and cultivated in a similar manner. For each, Billy ran his finger in a straight line, making a small declivity every few inches in each row. Then he gave Orrin a sack full of rye or oats seeds that he had collected the year before and instructed him on how to sow them. The boy walked along the rows gently dropping a small amount of the seeds into each declivity along the way. Once he had completed a row, he went back to turn a small amount of soil over the seeds. Orrin did so well at planting the corn, rye and oats that Billy determined that, after a few instructions, he could leave his son to continue the planting on his own.

Once the corn and rye were taken care of it was time to plant potatoes around the edge of the same field. While he had been harvesting the last of his potato crop the previous year Billy had saved some potatoes to use as seed potatoes for the next year's crop. He had kept them in the cellar throughout the winter, and in early May he had brought them out of their dark lair, and placed them in a tin tray on one of the cabin's deep window sills where he uncovered them to let light and air surround them. After that, he turned their care over to Rhoda who rotated them and kept them moist, but not wet. As the time for planting was drawing near, Billy showed Orrin how to prepare the potato planting area by creating a straight furrow that was several inches deep in which he would place the potato eyes. Orrin went to work right behind his father, and soon he had the soil ready for planting. With this accomplished, he and Billy returned to the cabin, and Billy showed the boy how to use his jackknife to pick up each seed potato, cut it into chunks that contained several eyes, and then carry them out to the field. Once there Orrin went to work quickly and deftly. At the intervals that Billy had marked out for him Orrin placed a chunk of potato eyes right side up.[64] With that done he went back and covered the furrow with soil. As he worked his way along, visions of luscious potatoes, with a pat of butter on top, made him slather with delight.

Once Billy had finished planting the crops for his animals, and some for human consumption, he was able to turn his attention to preparing an area for planting flax. Rhoda relied upon this for weaving her linens. Billy had prepared a perfect flax bed where the earth was a bit less porous, so it retained the moisture that flax liked best when the seeds were germinating. Every year he enriched the soil further by adding a healthy dose of manure that helped the flax grow prolifically. In preparation, during last year's growing season Rhoda had harvested the seeds and stored them for planting the next year. After broadcasting the seeds over the loam Billy discovered that the soil was so easy to work that he and Orrin could turn the seeds into the soil with just their wood tined forks.

With the main planting behind them Billy and Orrin had a bit of breathing time before they started new projects, including creating an herb and vegetable garden for Rhoda. This gave them the opportunity to build a small shed in which Rhoda could keep the tools that she would be using to tend her garden. In preparation, when the ground was finally really firm, they were able to hitch the team to their wagon and head out to the pile of prepared wood that they had stacked there over the winter. They loaded it onto the wagon and set forth to the sawmill in the village. When the sawyer had done his work, Orrin and Billy brought the newly made boards home and began to build the shed. It was a relatively simple project and only took them a few days to complete.

CHAPTER EIGHT

THE ONEROUS TASK OF MAKING SOAP

Early in the summer, when it was warm enough, but not too hot, it was time for Rhoda to make the lye soap that she would use in the coming year for washing clothes, washing people and for general wash up around the house. As she readied for this arduous and time-consuming task, she reminded herself of how wonderful it was to work outdoors in the sunshine and fresh breeze that usually came off the lake. Rhoda was grateful that Orrin had offered to help her because things would go so much better and faster with two people working together.

The previous year Billy had constructed a large, shallow fire pit that Rhoda could use for her soap making, as well as for doing her wash in the summer. It was similar to the one they used for sugaring, but this was divided into two sections. Half of it had two wood pones stretched between two crotched wood uprights. This section would be used for boiling various liquids. The other half was a simple, open pit that was used to turn wood into ashes. Orrin laid a fire of dry twigs in both sides of the fire pit while Rhoda hung her pots for heating liquids from the pones. Then he lit both sides with the tinder that Rhoda handed to him.

When the flames were burning brightly, Orrin topped the fire that would produce ashes with the hardwood logs that he had stacked beside the fire pit previously. Hardwoods produced the best ashes and there was plenty of hickory, maple and oak in the woods.[65]

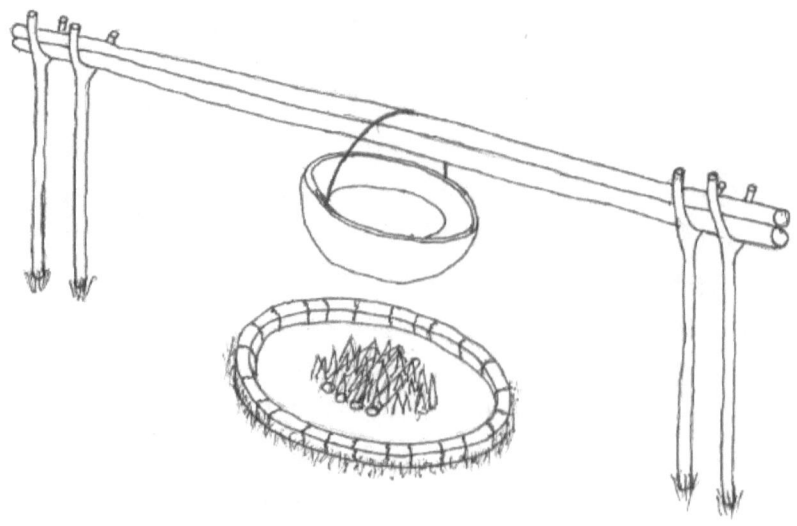

Figure 9 Boiling Lye for Soap. Bruce Hale

He watched the fire closely, turning the logs when necessary until all that was left was a nice pile of ashes. On the other side of the fire pit where the water was heating he used pine and spruce—softwoods that were readily available on the property.[66] Once the water was hot enough it was Orrin's job to lift down one of the pots down, and place it on the ground. Then Rhoda scooped up the hardwood ashes from the fire pit and put them in one of the pots of boiling water. They both stepped aside and watched the ashes settle to the bottom of the pot, leaving a layer of liquid lye on top.

At this point Rhoda needed to determine whether the lye was ready for the next step. She plopped a half potato into the pot and watched it closely. When the potato rose to the surface, she was satisfied that this step was completed. She removed the potato and discarded it. Then she skimmed the lye off the surface and put it into the other pot of hot water. Now came the tricky part. Orrin had to lift the heavy pot full of lye and water onto the pone without scalding himself. Rhoda worried about him doing this, but he managed just fine and soon the mixture began to boil down to a thick, syrupy liquid. Meanwhile, mother and son cut up cubes of fatty meat from the hogs that had been slaughtered during the winter. They carefully dropped these into the second pot of water, which Orrin then hung from the pone to boil. Rendering (heating animal remains to extract fat) was a very smelly process, and both Rhoda and Orrin stepped away from the fire while this was going on. Even ever-curious Nelson held his nose and fled from the scene as the odor became overwhelming. Rhoda kept dipping her very long handled spoon into the fatty water and when she thought that the mixture was successfully rendered Orrin took down the pot and set it aside to cool. This would take at least a day.[67]

As he looked up at the sky Orrin realized that, with the exception of a break for the midday dinner, they had been working together for most of the day. He heaved a sigh of relief when Rhoda told him that nothing else could be done until the morrow. She suggested that Orrin and Nelson, who had been standing by, might like to go down to the water to go wading before it was time for evening chores. The boys let out whoops of joy, and, hand in hand, ran down to the lake. It was somewhat comical to see twelve-year-old Orrin and four-year-old Nelson side by side. Their eight-year age difference made holding hands a bit lopsided. Rhoda smiled as she thought about how fortunate she was that Orrin really loved his much younger siblings.

The next day after morning chores, Orrin set about laying the fire as he had the day before.[68] Today they would only be using the side of the fire pit with the pone. Rhoda took the lid off of the pot of fat and water and sighed with satisfaction. The fat had risen to the top and congealed just as it should have. She skimmed this off carefully with a long-handled spoon and placed it in the pot of lye, stirring very carefully as she did so.

When she was satisfied that the ingredients were properly mixed, she asked Orrin to lift the pot onto the pone once again. It needed to be brought to a boil one last time. As the steam began to rise, Rhoda asked her son to remove the pot from the pone. She picked up her spoon, stirred the mixture again, and set it aside for the time being. Once it had cooled sufficiently, she would ladle the soap mixture into her tin molds where it would set and become soft soap cakes. [69] As Rhoda and Orrin turned to clean up the mess they had created, they wearily thanked God that this only happened once a year.

CHAPTER NINE

THE BOUNTY OF THE EARTH

Now it was time for father and son to create Rhoda's annual summer garden. The plot was relatively small, when compared to the areas in which he had been plowing and planting previously, and the land had been tilled and carefully managed for three years. His old, hand pushed plow was much less damaging to the soil than if he had used his team, or even his mare with the new plow. It was perfect for this work. Bright one morning Billy and Orrin set off to get the smaller plow from the shed. Because it had no wheels and would be heavy to carry any distance, they opted to hitch up the mare to the ever-useful sledge, roll the plow onto it and transport it to the garden by this means.

When they got to the edge of Rhoda's garden they pulled the plow off the sledge. Orrin was eager to plow his mother's garden and he watched carefully as Billy explained that he would make the first few runs just to see how easy it was to lift the soil and to demonstrate to Orrin how the plowing should be done. He quickly found that the fall additions of composted old leaves, as well as some of the winter slops that the pigs were not particularly fond of, had greatly enriched the soil. Also, careful weeding during the previous growing season had ensured that there was fertile, easy to manage loam in the spring. After the demonstration Orrin assured his father that he was confident that he could manage the plow, and Billy consented to let him try. After all, the boy was growing bigger and stronger with each day and he had quickly grasped other new challenges as they were presented.

Orrin assumed a position between the steering shafts So far, that looked pretty straightforward to the lad, and he said he was ready to try his hand at the task.[70] To his surprise, Orrin quickly discovered that this was more complicated than he had anticipated. He had to steer the plow to make sure that he moved forward in even lines and, at the same time, he had to watch to make certain that it actually dug into the soil and did not just skid along the surface. Turning the corners at the ends of each row was especially tricky until Billy showed him how to skid the plow around. For several hours Billy patiently walked beside his 12-year-old son and made suggestions as they moved along. Then, suddenly, it all came together for Orrin and he no longer needed guidance and assistance from his father.

For the rest of the day Orrin worked steadfastly at his task and by the time that the sun was lowering into the horizon he had completed plowing the garden. Billy praised his son profusely for his fine work. Over the supper table that night, Orrin spoke excitedly about his adventures. He was so proud of his day's achievements. Rhoda had taken Nelson out to the field to see what his big brother was doing, so every once in a while he interjected his own words of awe and praise. This made the little boy feel quite grown up, and not just four years old. On the other hand, two-year-old Mortimer, who had accompanied his mother and brother, was far more interested in picking up interesting stones and trying to stuff them into his mouth. After supper Rhoda could see that Orrin was very tired, and suggested that he sit by the fire and relax after his hard day. The lad barely settled himself when his eyes began to close with weariness. Rhoda roused him, and, without protest, convinced him to climb the ladder to his loft bed and get some sleep before the morrow's adventures.

The next day, as Orrin opened his eyes in response to Rhoda's cheerful "Good morning," he was reminded of yesterday's adventures by a few sore limbs, especially his arms, which had been in constant use. However, he eagerly jumped out of bed, donned his clothes, and headed down the ladder and out the door to do his morning chores. He had learned to handle these rounds quite quickly and soon was back in the cabin and settling down to breakfast with his family. This was going to be yet another very interesting day.

Rhoda had carefully planned her garden, giving much thought to the placement of each plant. She preferred to divide it into sections: one for herbs for cooking; one for herbs to use for medicinal purposes; one for above ground vegetables; and one for root vegetables. For culinary purposes she was especially fond of mint. She found that putting it in fruit drinks was a wonderful way to quench the thirst of her family during the warm summer months, and she always used it when she made candies for very special occasions. They all loved the very distinctive licorice flavor that anise, fennel, lovage and chervil put forth, and Rhoda had discovered that this did much to mask the taste of foods that were verging on becoming inedible. Summer savory and basil were excellent sources of imparting a peppery crispness and lightness to a wide variety of meat, vegetable and egg dishes. As she thought about it, she had to concede that she was particularly fond of sage, thyme, marjoram, tarragon and parsley because they enhanced both meat and vegetable dishes, and she knew just how much of each to use in which dishes. As a matter of fact, she knew exactly which herbs she wished to use with any vegetables, as well as with "flesh", fish, soup, and cheese, and egg-based dishes.[71]

She had learned to gauge when each herb was at its very peak of ripeness and she always did her picking on a sunny day when there was no dew or rain to rob them of their full aroma and strength. She harvested each type of herb individually, and then gathered them into small bundles and hung them in front of the fire to be certain that there was truly no moisture remaining. With that accomplished she carried them up the ladder to the loft that Orrin and Nelson now shared. There she attached each bundle to a line of thin rope that she had stretched across from roof eave to roof eave.[72] At first, Orrin and Nelson complained somewhat about the medley of scents and smells that bombarded them, but with time they had grown to rather like them, much to the relief of their mother.

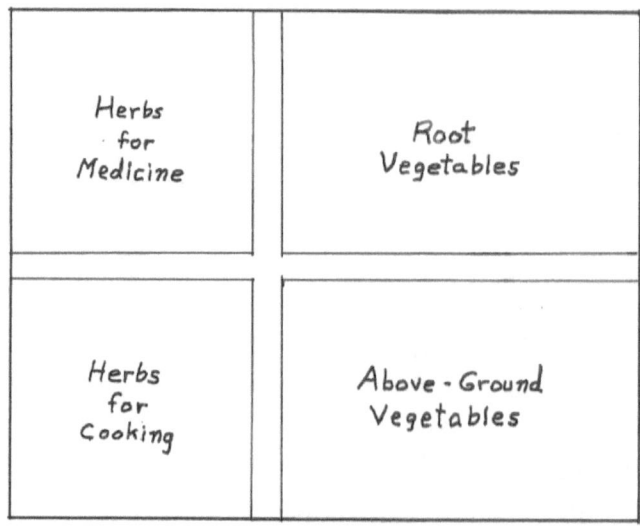

Figure 10 Rhoda's Garden Design. Bruce Hale

Each year Rhoda experimented with using different herbs to combat the variety of ailments and infections that bombarded her family, especially during the long, dark, and cold winters when so much time was spent indoors. She was well aware that death lurked just outside the door and she, like most women, had a wide variety of home remedies that she had developed over the years. Those who lived the somewhat isolated life of farming had had to be prepared to deal with any type of injury or illness that came their way. Injuries were very common and, thus far, Billy and his family had only suffered minor scrapes and bruises. Among other remedies, she had found that when she put dried yarrow flowers in her mortar and stirred them to a powder it did an amazing job of stanching blood. She had also discovered that if she squeezed the oil out of barberry berries and rubbed it onto sore muscles, it greatly eased the pain.[73]

From a medicinal standpoint mint was one of Rhoda's favorites. Once again, she had found that by putting it in tea it eased a sour stomach, stopped hiccups, kept eyes from watering, and, when family members had bad breath (usually from a rotten tooth), she rubbed their gums with it. She grew a bit of lemon balm, because Billy was particularly inclined to develop boils on his body for reasons she could not determine. If she gently rubbed a bit of the balm over them, it caused the boils to burst open, allowing the fluid beneath to seep out, and the pain to ease. Thyme was a favorite remedy for countless ailments. It made you sweat out a fever, helped with ague, decreased lethargy, dealt with diarrhea, calmed convulsions and controlled fits and madness. What more could one ask of a single herb. Rhoda almost always put marjoram, sage and basil in her stews, not only for their flavor, but because they seemed to control intestinal problems, which were an ever-recurring issue. She relied upon tarragon to help with insomnia and anxiety and was convinced that adding a bit of rosemary to her fire not only smelled lovely, but also purified the air. [74]

In her vegetable garden Rhoda grew an impressive number of plants that she found did well in The Point's soil and climate, including a variety of beans, lentils (which she dried), peas, asparagus, cabbage, peppers, and eggplant. She also grew onions, garlic, and leeks which she called her "stinky plants", so she planted them on the edge of the garden lest the odors that they put forth would invade the more pleasant aromas of the other vegetables and herbs. For ease of maintenance, and for making their harvesting simpler, she kept her root vegetables, including her carrots, radishes, parsnips, beets and turnips in their own area. For her "crawlers", including her squash, melons, and pumpkins, and floppy eggplants, she made a space where they would not reach out their ever-growing arms and suffocate what she called her "gentler" plants, especially her asparagus. Billy and Orrin never minded digging up the potatoes when they were ready, since they were the crowning glory of almost every meal. Billy grew two different kinds of corn—corn for animals and corn for people. There was a very big difference between the two.[75] The corn stalks looked so handsome as they lay behind the hillocks of potatoes.

Back in Shelburne, Rhoda's mother had shared one of the tricks that she had learned many years before. She had discovered that when she planted buckwheat between the rows of vegetables it kept the weeds down, thereby obviating much backbreaking hoeing. There was yet another benefit. The bees found it a fine medium for pollination, and the chickens delighted in the special treat that came their way when Rhoda clipped it back. More importantly, when she removed the chaff and ground the buckwheat, it produced a type of flour that she found more delicious than the usual rye, although she used both.[76] Just as she had done with other things, at the end of each season she carefully gathered the seeds and stored them for scatter planting the following year.

Except for occasional assistance with some of the more difficult work, the care of the garden was her responsibility. She delighted in every moment that she could spend there and never saw this as a burden. Usually, she rose early in the morning, when the younger children were still fast asleep, and, with basket in hand, and a bonnet covering her head, she crept out to the beckoning dew-covered plants that waved gently in the breeze as if to welcome her into their presence. This was a much-needed solitary time for her. As she walked along each row, plucking dead leaves, weeds, and overripe vegetables that had previously eluded her eye, she had time for reverie and prayer. She was continually reminded of God's blessings and the bounty of riches that she and her family enjoyed. So far life had been good for her and her family, but she was wise enough to know that death and tragedy could strike at any time.

When she was in need of agents for coloring fabrics Rhoda went out into the woods in search of the barks, leaves, ash, chips and other things that she would need. She enjoyed looking for these because both Nelson and Mortimer loved an excursion into the woods, over hills, through brambles, and anywhere that the things she sought could be found. At four Nelson was beginning to be a huge help to his mother and he really enjoyed his "special" times with her. Mortimer just liked to tag along behind his brother when any opportunity presented itself. As a toddler, he was still a bit unsteady on his feet and, as a result, falls were a common experience. Fortunately, he was a happy-go-lucky child and with a little reassurance, and a quick brushing off, he was up and running again—at least until the next obstacle just seemed to get in his way.

As Rhoda roamed the woods and hills, with the two boys close behind her, she looked for plants to her liking. When she found them, she snipped, peeled, or cut them out and then handed them to Nelson who was proudly carrying a basket to receive the bounty. She was always looking for plants that would provide color to her linens and articles of clothing. Her mother had taught her which of these would produce the best dyes, as well as which were most successful with certain fabrics. Alum served as a mordant, which was applied to certain fibers before they were dyed and helped the dye to adhere to the fibers. It was made from stale urine, wood ash, oak galls and chips of oak or alder wood, and had been readily available for many years.[77] Red came from pokeweed, yellow from goldenrod, and black from sumac tops.[78] There were an abundance of elderberries around the cabin. Their bark provided blue, and their berries, when mixed with salt, offered a good source of purple. She had also discovered that green and brown came from elderberry leaves, when she mixed them with alum.[79]

Throughout the summer the family feasted upon the bounty of Rhoda's garden. She had just begun to cultivate strawberries and rhubarb in a special corner of her garden. When fresh they provided the family with luscious fruit and, for the rest of the year, tasty sweetness on fresh-baked bread. This year Rhoda had asked Billy to put in some raspberry and blueberry bushes if he had time. She knew that it would be a few years before they would bear fruit and waited for that moment with happy anticipation. Making jam was one of her favorite summer tasks.

Rhoda was keenly aware that everything had to be preserved in any way possible, so that it would carry the family through the months ahead. The family devoured the more fragile vegetables, such as the peas, beans, peppers, lettuces and cabbage, as well as the creeping melons, as they came into season. It was almost impossible to preserve these. Her root vegetables did very nicely when she tucked them away in the cellar under the cabin where they would stay dry and cool until used. Potatoes, the staple of their diets, did beautifully in the darkness below as long as she kept an eye out for their showing signs of sprouting. When this occurred, she knew that it was time to use those particular items quickly. Other produce, such as the various types of lentils dried beautifully and were a tasty addition to stews and soups during the long winter days. She found that her pumpkins and squash did nicely when she packed them in barrels of straw to protect them.

CHAPTER TEN

SUMMER ANTICS

On warm summer days when neither Rhoda nor Billy needed Orrin's help, he was free to play with his friends. He and the other boys his age loved to go down to the banks of the lake. They wandered along the beach and over the rocks, looking for curiosities that had been brought in by the waves and winter ice. They were sometimes shocked by the amount of debris that came floating by and wondered where it had all come from. There were always old tree trunks, logs, and even boards that had fallen off a passing boat, and some of them were quite usable. They gathered these up as best they could before they disappeared once again and over the summer constructed some amazing "forts" which they used as the backdrop for war games. Even though they knew little about wars they had learned enough in school to fantasize.

Billy had an old skiff that he kept down on the beach and he had taught Orrin how to row it well. Once he was confident that his son knew how to handle the boat safely, he let him go out onto the lake, with a friend or two, so that they could fish. However, he admonished them that they must remain within eyesight. With their crude fishing rods and some worms for bait they were always amazed by the quantities of perch, smelt, whitefish, and even the occasional trout they caught. At the end of a day they would proudly present them to their mothers who delighted in preparing them for dinner the next day. The bounty of the lake never ceased to amaze the boys.

At other times the boys just enjoyed playing games together. Billy had helped Orrin make a pair of stilts in his workshop and Nelson was so excited about these that Orrin made him a smaller pair so that they could stomp around together. Orrin, being significantly older than his brother, thought that he would be the first to learn how to use them. However, much to his chagrin he had a hard time getting up and frequently fell right over. He was even more disconcerted when Nelson caught on more quickly and resorted to rationalizing this occurrence by saying that Nelson had less height to fall from.

When his older friends came to play, they usually brought their hoops with them. The boys would engage in mad races, rolling their hoops along as fast as they could and screaming with pleasure as they pushed each other's aside. When they tired of this activity, they simply took the sticks that they used to push the hoops along and pretended that they were swords. Orrin had been very strict with them and they knew that the sticks would be taken away permanently if their game became unduly rough. However, like most young boys he had to be reprimanded from time to time.

Many times, Orrin and his friends were quite happy to resort to their old favorites- tag, hide-and-seek or ball playing. It seemed that for hours they could run around aimlessly chasing one another just for the fun of it. They did not seem to care who tagged who. When Rhoda and Billy watched them, they were quite amazed by their display of the sheer energy of youth.

Often, they would go to the edge of the woods to play hide-and-seek. They all remembered that their parents had warned them never, ever to go deep into the forest. They never questioned this requirement. The blood curdling howls of the wolves and coyotes at night was enough to cause them considerable fear.

Ball playing was always a huge success. The boys kept their mothers very busy winding old yarns around and around until they formed a ball that would fit into the boy's hands. Once this was accomplished the women covered the ball of yarn with a leather cover to protect it. Despite their precautions it was inevitable that, over time, the leather would disintegrate, and the yarn would begin to unravel. Then the boys would turn to their mothers and plead for a new ball. The women complained from time to time that if their offspring were a little more careful this would not happen. However, their word usually fell on deaf ears, as it is apt to do when youngsters are involved.

One day when he was in the village with his father Orrin went over to pay a call on Capt. McCray who owned a lighter that carried pig iron to the anchor shop and anchors back to the waiting boats on the lake that would take the finished anchors to their ultimate destination in Troy. Orrin had heard that the captain had brought home a very young bear cub, whose mother appeared to have abandoned him. He wanted to make it a pet, so he kept it on a chain beneath the ladder to the loft in his log home. Needless to say, it scared a lot of family members and visitors who had an innate fear of these animals and many of them steadfastly refused to even enter his house as long as the bear was there.

The day of Orrin's visit there was much consternation because somehow the bear cub had gotten loose. Needless to say, the captain was delighted to have someone help him find the bear cub, and he had already recruited sixteen-year-old Norman Moore. He offered Norman and Orrin a reward of a bushel of corn in return for their services if they were successful. Eager to be rewarded, the boys set forth with gusto. They soon found the cub and started dragging it back to Capt. McCray's cabin.

Figure 11 Capt. McCray's Bear Cub. Philip Hall

However, the cub worked its way loose and, being a wild animal by nature, it began to attack the boys who clubbed it to death with heavy tree limbs. The captain was dismayed and saddened when they returned with the body of the cub but was true to his word and rewarded them for bringing home the cub as he had directed. Sadly, he had not said that he wanted an alive, and not dead, cub. Being young, impressionable and a bit wary of the bear cub to begin with the boys found nothing wrong with what they had done.[80]

All in all, the balance of work and play worked well for Orrin. On the one hand, he was acquiring many critically important skills that he hoped to be able to use when he reached his majority and had property of his own to maintain. More importantly, he truly loved and admired his father who had taught him so much with seemingly never-ending patience. Every moment that he could spend with him was very precious. From time to time he continued to wonder what his life would have been like had circumstances not led him down the path to become a member of the Blinn family. However, he gave this little thought because he was so happy and comfortable where he was.

CHAPTER ELEVEN

THE HARVEST

By early to mid-July Billy and Orrin turned their attention back to the fields, and the two of them set forth to bring in the first cutting of hay. This was always a very scary time for a farmer, because one was totally dependent upon the vicissitudes of the weather. He knew all too well that once the hay was cut, any rain, especially one that was hard, could deprive the hay of its nutritional value. At worst, it could completely destroy the harvest, leaving nothing but a sodden mass behind. During the winter Billy had asked the blacksmith in the village to make a scythe blade to fit into the snath that he had made for Orrin. He made it of willow, which he molded into the correct shape by dipping the wood into hot oil and then bending it. He was always a bit relieved when, upon occasion, he could find a piece of willow wood that was just the right shape, thereby eliminating the time-consuming task of shaping by hand.

One morning after viewing the clear blue sky above, Billy proclaimed that this was the day for haying. All was ready, and with scythes in hand, Billy and Orrin set off. They began by cutting the stems, which demanded a broad stroke of the arm, time after time. It was tiring work, and at the end of a day both father and son were happy to put their scythes away until the next morning. Each day, as his arms got stronger and stronger, Orrin was amazed by how much more he could do. After they had cut the hay, they picked up their rakes, which Billy had made for both of them. He had attached to a long wood handle a cross wood piece, set at right angles. Into this piece he had drilled holes and inserted short wood pegs for teeth. With these they tossed the stems high into the air for several days until they were quite certain that they had dried completely.

With this accomplished, they gathered the hay into sheaths. They loaded it into the small cart that had been scrubbed with lye after carrying manure to the fields in the spring. Fortunately, it was no longer odiferous. When the cart was filled to the brim Orrin led the horse to a small structure with a roof but no sides that would still give the hay some protection from the elements until it was used.[81] When it was a good year, Billy was able to get several cuttings of hay before the season ended, and he had been fortunate thus far.

Meanwhile, Billy was keeping an eagle eye on his field of corn for his family and his animals. For what seemed to be forever he waited for the first sign of tasseling, and then there it was. He knew that it would be almost another 3 weeks before the silky tassels would turn brown, while the husks stayed green for a bit longer. It was the season when the long-awaited harvest moon rose above the horizon. "The harvest moon is the full moon that falls nearest the autumnal equinox and is in that part of its orbit where it makes the smallest angle with the horizon."[82] The unique beauty of this time was that a few moonlit nights occurred when he and Orrin could work until long after what would become dark once the equinox had passed.

The long-awaited time for harvesting the corn had come, and Billy headed into the field with corn knife in hand, and Orrin followed close behind. Much of the time he only got one ear from each stalk, but when there was more it was cause for modest rejoicing. His corn knife was significantly different from his hay scythe, even though, at first glance, it looked amazingly similar. Where his scythe for haying had a long, curving handle ending in a slightly bent blade, the corn knife had a short handle and a blade shaped like a quarter moon.[83] With an adroit hand Billy separated the ears from their stalks, casting the stalks away until later when he would chop them up for rough bedding for his animals. Orrin was right beside him picking up the ears as they fell to the ground and hurling them into the two-wheeled cart.

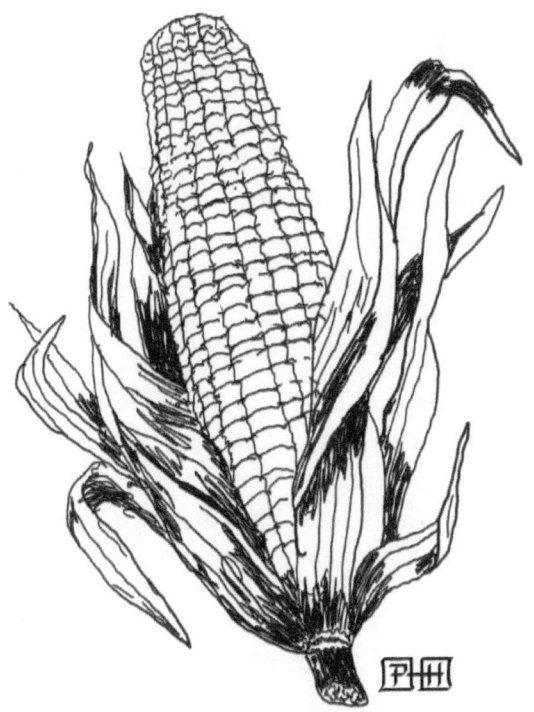

Figure 12 Harvested Ear of Corn. Philip Hall

When it was filled to the brim Orrin led the team to the small storage building that Billy had built specifically for this purpose. It was a strange looking structure that was narrower at the bottom and top than it was in the middle and it was raised well above ground level with stones.[84] Billy explained that this was to keep rats and other vermin from raiding the building and consuming all of its contents. Once the corn was safely put away, Billy and Orrin returned to the field to get the stalks. They brought them back to the barn where they laid them on a slab of wood and chopped them into small pieces for animal bedding.

Throughout the growing season Billy continued to keenly observe the flax field because the timing of harvesting the flax for future spinning was critical. He had to be sure to reap it after the plants flowered and before the seeds had formed. When the bottoms of the stems had turned yellow, and the soil was damp with morning dew, he and Orrin easily pulled each plant up from its home in the earth. This kept the fibers within the stalk as long as possible. Then they tied them into sheaves and stacked them in stooks to dry. After several weeks of drying Billy and Orrin were able to shake the plants vigorously, so that the seeds fell into the container they had placed beneath them. Later, they would pulverize the seed to release the linseed oil, which Billy used on the furniture that he was making for the house. Now came the most important task— retting. They took the stalks, which now had no seeds, and laid them out on the ground in an area where they would not be trampled. It was Orrin's job to periodically turn the stalks so that all sides got rain and sun. This went on for several more weeks until the stalks were ready for the next step.

Now it was time for Rhoda to take over. Just as she and her friends got together for quilting bees, they took the opportunity to work together to transform the retted flax stalks into useable fibers for linen. This was a three-step process. First the stems had to be broken by plunging a flat wood piece that looked like a chopper down on them. Rhoda found that this worked best if one woman held the sheaf of flax, while another actually hit it with the wood. With that done another woman "scutched" it. Then came the final step when another woman heckled it. What remained were the precious fibers that the women could spin for linen in their own homes.
85

CHAPTER TWELVE

FAITH OF THEIR FOREBEARS

Billy and Rhoda were god-fearing, devout people of faith, as were most members of their community. When death and life were ever-present and serious matters one tended to be afraid not to have faith or believe in God. Both of their families had been very strong Congregationalists for generations. Billy remembered his grandfather telling him that their religious roots harked back to the Puritans who strayed from the Anglican Church in the sixteenth century in England. This group wanted nothing to do with "the celebration of the Mass, ceremonial vestments for the clergy, or the hierarchy of archbishops and bishops".[86] There was to be no kneeling, making the sign of the cross, or any other "Papist" trappings. The Anglicans used the derogatory term "Puritans" as they mocked these dissenters who believed in "simplicity in worship and church organization".[87] However, these dissenters preferred to call themselves "the Reformed" people or "Independents", following the teaching and practice of the Protestant Reformer John Calvin.[88]

Unlike the Pilgrims, who wanted nothing to do with the Anglican Church, the Puritans hoped that they could find a way to create reform within it.[89] Billy's grandfather had gone on to tell him that many of these Puritans left England and came to settle in New England. They chose the name "Congregationalists" to reflect the fact that their "members had equal power and all of them were responsible to one another under the Covenant that formed the basis of their life together."[90] As such, they were free to create and follow Covenants and Statements of Belief that suited their particular group.

101

They also believed that the Bible only mentioned two sacraments: The Lord's Supper and Baptism. For them, these sacraments affirmed their "covenant" and were an outward sign of an inward spiritual reality.[91] The Lord's Supper was an act of renewal and a sign of redemption, and it could be taken at any time that an individual congregation chose. Baptism signified the washing away of sins, and rising to new life in Jesus Christ, not only for the infant being baptized, but also for the congregation in attendance. One can see the similarities to Anglicanism in both of these sacraments

Billy and Rhoda were very proud of their faith. Yes, it was all that they had ever known so they could not compare it to other faiths. However, they truly believed that, at its core, the basic Congregational premises, and the way of life that these underpinned addressed the needs of a group of recent settlers like themselves. They had pulled up their roots, left everything that was familiar behind, crossed a very large body of open water and, at risk and peril, were making their way in a place that was not what they had always known. They were still in transition, and seeking stability, hope and inspiration in their new lives. The young couple understood that they were "pioneers" in the true sense of the word and could see why Vermonters referred to the eastern shores of Lake Champlain as a "wilderness". Billy and Rhoda recognized that they were dependent upon their faith, as well as hard work and determination, if they were to build a new and better life for themselves and their offspring.

The Congregationalist's truly democratic approach to life and faith held great appeal to Rhoda and Billy, as well as to countless others in New England, and now in this part of New York. They prayed fervently that God would be patient with them as they sought their way in life as individuals and congregants, and they promised Him that they would make the fairest and best decisions they could for their families, their church, and their communities.[92] They were truly grateful that, even though they might err at times, reprimand and admonishment would not be coming down from on high, as it was in other faiths.

One cannot help asking what these basic theological principles were that rang so true to pioneers like Billy and Rhoda? Along with having been brought up in this faith they whole-heartedly embraced these tenets of Congregationalism. "The local church is complete and sufficient to determine its own matters of faith and practice. All members are spiritually equal... Christ alone is the head of the church, and the church is where Christ is active. Church members are bound together by covenant and therefore are responsible for the spiritual welfare of one another..."[93] This spirit of interdependency, and mutual respect and appreciation, was critically important to them. Each of these principles resounded strongly to people like themselves who had taken such risks in the hopes of a better life for themselves and their families. Billy loved and appreciated the fact that, while the Bible and belief in Jesus were indisputable, individual Congregationalists were given the freedom to interpret the Gospel as they understood it.[94] By this means, they were allowed to have a direct relationship with God.[95] They were not fettered by the dogma of the Anglicans and Papists.

Billy and Rhoda adhered to their parent's admonition to carry the mantle of Congregationalism into their lives. They fully embraced their faith and worked hard to see that it permeated every aspect of their lives. To them, being a Congregationalist was far more than just going to church on Sunday. It meant being true Christians in every way. As such they were committed to bringing up their children to respect and adhere to the basic tenets of Congregationalism, and they made every effort to see that their daily life experiences reflected this. Prayer was an essential ingredient in their lives. They faithfully welcomed each day with prayer, began each meal by thanking God for what they had, and ended each day with evening prayers. Sometimes, when life seemed particularly stressful, they would take a brief respite from their toils and troubles and look to the Lord for guidance and support.

The young couple remembered well the day that they took their infant son, Nelson, to be baptized in the Congregational Church in Charlotte. Although Billy was spending most of his days across the lake building the cabin that would be their future home, he returned to Rhoda's family home so that his son could be baptized among their family members in the Charlotte schoolhouse, which housed Congregationalists on Sundays. It was a truly beautiful and deeply meaningful experience. Nelson was now under the care of the Congregational Church and he had been accepted into a new life in Christ.[96] With the two-year-old's very own Bible in hand, they left the service with deep feelings of comfort and joy. The Holy Spirit had been with them all and had placed a mantle of love and wellbeing around their firstborn.

Although there were more Congregationalists than any other denomination in Willsborough, there was no church building. They felt that they did not need what they saw as the rigid reminders of the Papists and Anglicans, including their monumental structures that spoke eloquently of wealth and authority. Instead, they were happy to use the schoolhouse in the village for their Sabbath gatherings. By day it met the educational needs of the community's children, on Sundays it became a place of worship, and in the evenings, it was a center for community gatherings of all sorts.

Figure 13 Log Schoolhouse and Meetinghouse. Ashley Ahrent

For most families in Willsborough, the most important day of each week was the Sabbath, and they firmly believed that this day must be strictly observed. This was the day when Billy reduced his farm schedule to a minimum and his brother-in-law Daniel put aside his trade as a furniture maker. Saturday was taken up with the ritual of preparations necessary for the Lord's Day. Rhoda spent the day cleaning, cooking, baking, and seeing that proper clothes were laid out, ready for each family member to wear the next morning.

It was also the time for the Saturday evening bath. Out came the two big, old tin washtubs. In winter they were placed before the fireplace so that family members would not catch cold when they rose from the warm water. In summer they could bathe outdoors. This was much more for fun for the children since they could splash and play to their hearts content. Rhoda filled pots with water, and hung them from the fireplace crane to heat while she gathered up some rough, homespun towels in which the newly bathed family members could wrap themselves when they were finished. When all was in readiness, Orrin helped his mother fill both tubs. Then one by one, beginning with Mortimer, then Nelson, then Orrin, next Rhoda, and finally Billy, each hopped into the warm water, and lathered with the soft lye soap. With that completed, they moved to the other tub to rinse before stepping out to grab a towel and make room for the next occupant.

Sabbath Day arrived, and the family gathered for prayer and a small morning repast. Rhoda thought that this should be sufficient since none of them participated in any but the most necessary chores on the Lord's Day. Once these were completed, the family piled into Billy's small horse drawn cart that was reserved for such occasions, or onto the sleigh if snow had fallen. In the winter Billy filled tin boxes, with coals from the fireplace and took them out to the cart. He placed them where each person would sit and use them as foot warmers while traveling to the village, and while in church.[97] Rhoda sat on the short backward facing bench in the rear of the cart and held Mortimer firmly in her arms, while Nelson cuddled close to her. Orrin sat proudly upfront next to his father, taking full advantage of his senior position over his little brothers. Billy slapped the reins gently on the mare's back and off they went on the brief journey into the Village. They skirted along the edge of the lake until the track began to turn westward where it followed the Boquet River until they made the steep descent down into the river valley, across the bridge, and up the hill to the schoolhouse near Levi Higby's distillery that served as a place of worship on Sundays.

Since they had no regular clergy, except for an occasional itinerant, literate members of the congregation often led the prayers, readings and discourses. Billy wished that he could be one of those, but he accepted the fact that this might never be his lot. He was consoled by the fact that Orrin would be going to school and would be able to read and write well one day. Upon occasion there would be a baptism, and this was always an interesting and exciting time when everyone gathered around the infant as his head was covered in water by a congregant, or even a member of the clergy, if one was around. The first time Orrin saw a baptism he wondered whether the babe in arms would let out a lusty yell, and the infant usually did. He remembered that his mother had told him that he had been baptized in a similar way when he was an infant back in Canaan.

Upon other occasions, the congregation decided that it was the Lord's wish for them to share the breaking of the bread. For such occasions, an adult congregant had the honor of baking the bread, breaking it into small pieces, and passing it among the members of the congregation. Another congregant followed with a small carafe of grape juice, or whatever juice was handy. Billy tried to explain this to his son, saying something about these symbolizing the body and blood of Christ. To Orrin this made no sense. He could see nothing that looked like a body—even a small piece of it—and the juice did not taste like the blood he had tasted when he cut his hand and licked it to keep the blood from flowing forth. To him and the other children the bread simply tasted especially delicious, and the juice was a special treat. He just wished he could have more.

Orrin knew that being in church was a serious time, and much of what was said was far too complicated for him to understand, or just plain boring to the young lad. Occasionally, he found himself dozing off and was roused by a sharp tap from whichever parent was sitting next to him. The part of the service that he loved the most was singing hymns. He already had a very fine boy's voice and received much praise from parishioners when they heard it rise above those of the adults. He tried his best to maintain his focus, but it was hard not to keep thinking about what fun it would be when this was over, and he could go out and play with his friends. At other times he was a bit envious that Nelson was able to squirm and fidget without either parent giving it any thought. However, that was only a fleeting thought. Mortimer simply gave in and spent most of the time asleep in his mother's arms. Orrin understood that Billy and Rhoda would be ashamed if his actions did not show others that they were teaching him to be a god-fearing, respectful, and obedient young lad.

At long last the service was over and on fair days everyone would gather outside where the adults chatted and exchanged gossip with one another. When the weather was blustery and cold, or rainy, they would be forced to remain in the schoolhouse. This was not nearly as much fun. Because they were in their best Sunday clothes the children could only play games that would not sully their attire. This left out any activities of a boisterous nature and forced the boys to participate in nothing that might make them fall. Hide and seek was the game that they always fell back on and, upon occasion, they deigned to let the girls play with them, instead of standing by sedately with their dolls. Sometimes, he joined his friends from The Point, who were also coming into the village to worship. Upon other occasions, he took advantage of the opportunity to play with the friends that he knew when he lived in the village.

When it was time to go home, which always seemed to be much too soon, Orrin and his family climbed back into the cart for the journey to The Point. As they neared the cabin, Orrin's mouth began to water as he thought of the Sabbath repast that Rhoda had so lovingly prepared the day before. Sometimes, on special occasions, friends and relatives were invited to join them. He particularly loved it when his uncle and aunt, Daniel and Abalena Rowley, came over to join them for the midday repast, or when he and his family went to partake with them. Although Abalena's child was a girl she was halfway between Orrin and Nelson in age and preferred to play with Orrin. Because they lived so close to one another they frequently got together, especially on the Sabbath.

After the midday meal the family spent the afternoon in contemplation and prayer. Occasionally, one or both of his parents would nod off quietly. He was glad to see this since they got so little time to rest. Meanwhile, Orrin played quiet, imaginary games, either alone, or when asked to care for Nelson. Late in the afternoon Orrin and Billy went out to do their evening chores as quickly as possible and, as evening approached, neighbors congregated at Billy's house, or that of another neighbor, for an evening prayer meeting before the close of the Sabbath. Orrin always found it a special treat to visit someone else's home. Finally, everyone went back to his or her own home, and the family gathered by the fire to enjoy a bit of tea, and bread and jam. Often Mortimer was so tired that he just wanted to go to bed, even if he missed supper. It had been a strenuous day for a toddler. Nelson could hardly stay awake but was determined not to miss supper. However, he soon left the table and climbed up the ladder to his cot. Orrin was not far behind. Everyone knew that all too soon the cock would crow, signaling the beginning of yet another busy day.

CHAPTER THIRTEEN

SCHOOL DAYS FOR ORRIN

Billy knew that at least a basic education was essential for a man to be successful in any endeavor when he reached his adulthood. He was keenly aware of the paucity of his own education. Although he could read simple things, his reading was very slow because he often had to go over and over a piece to understand it. This was particularly frustrating when he wanted to read a passage from the Bible. Most farmers were just like him, and the itinerant preacher who came to the schoolhouse understood their plight and read things aloud for them. He was seldom called upon to write, other than occasionally having to sign his name, which he had learned to do. At least he did not use an X like so many farmers did. When Orrin came into his life, he vowed to give him the privilege of going to school for a portion of each year.

Fortunately, Samuel Adsit and William Crum, who were counted as the earliest settlers on The Point, had the foresight to build a small schoolhouse, which they indicated on their 1796 survey of the area.[98] Like most schoolhouses of its time, this simple one room log structure was set in a clearing of the surrounding woods just off the south-north track that led out to the end of The Point and quite near to Billy's tract of land. Knowing that the deepest cold came from the north, because the winds gathered momentum as they sped across the vast frozen, or almost frozen, waters of Lake Champlain, the builders of the schoolhouse took its location into consideration. They placed its entry on the south side, and next to it there was always a stack of firewood that had been delivered by one of the parents. This was one of the ways that they could pay for their child's schooling.[99] The fireplace behind the schoolmaster's desk was on the north wall. The schoolhouse windows were on the east and west sides, where they could catch the morning and afternoon sun, and an outhouse stood close to the building's facade.

Billy thought about sending Orrin to school in January of 1809, shortly after the boy had come to live with them. In the end, he and Rhoda decided to the contrary. Although the child was eleven, and definitely of sufficient age to attend school, his new parents felt that it was more important for him to spend his first winter adjusting to his new home as he dealt with his separation from his mother and siblings. Giving him this extra time made good sense in their minds.

When the fall of 1810 rolled in, and Orrin was twelve, his parents decided that it was time for him to be introduced to formal education. They explained that boys like him who were old enough to help their fathers with farm chores only attended school during the winter months. The animals still needed to be taken care of. However, father and son had developed an efficient plan for this twice a day endeavor. This meant that Orrin could attend school on weekdays from early January through much of April. The last day of school was very dependent upon the weather each spring, because it was keyed to plowing and planting season. Then it was back to work on the farm as spring, with all of its demands, was rapidly coming.

On opening day Orrin woke up very early and lay in bed peering at the bit of light coming from the fire below. He missed having his tiny window open, but understood that, because of the intense cold, its shutter had to be firmly closed until it got warmer outside. His thoughts were racing. On one hand, he was excited about going to school and yet a bit of fear and apprehension kept creeping into his musings.

He wondered if he would like the schoolmaster who came from a different community and would only be at the school during winter term. His father had told him that the teacher was a young farmer, whose family did not require his constant attention and assistance during this relatively slack period. When the last vestiges of snow and ice moved out, and planting season was not far away, the schoolmaster would be returning to his own home. In the meantime, this was a good way for him to gain some extra income that he could use to continue his own education, at an academy, or other institution. While he was at the school, he would find housing with the parents of his students, and he might even come to stay with them for a bit. That would be interesting, thought Orrin. Billy instructed his son to be respectful of his teacher, even though he was less than a decade older than Orrin, and he admonished him to listen well, work hard, and learn as much as he could during his short period of time in school.

After what seemed like an eternity, but was actually only a few minutes, Orrin was roused from his thoughts, as his mother called up to him softly. He jumped out of bed, grabbed the clothes that he had laid on the bench the night before, and made his way down the ladder as quickly possible. Even though he was going to be a schoolboy, he was still expected to take care of his morning round of chores. Because he, like most of the older students, had these obligations, the school day did not start until 9 o'clock. As he threw on his warm clothing and headed out to take care of his various duties, Rhoda promised him a special breakfast on this very important day.

An hour or so later, Orrin returned to the cabin along with his father and as he opened the door he was met with a delicious aroma. As a treat, his mother had made little potato patties and a chunk of bacon to go with them. Orrin ate with gusto, and his younger brothers and father also delighted in partaking of the feast. With his hunger assuaged, he soon forgot that he had had some ominous thoughts earlier in the morning. Soon there was a knock on the door, and in came two of his friends that had been his play pals during the summer.

Orrin was so glad that they were going to set forth on their adventure together. What a relief! He grabbed the lunch basket that his mother had prepared for him, got on his winter outdoor clothing, and set off with the others for the short walk to the schoolhouse that was very close by for him.

It was a crisp, clear, and sunny day. Only a thin mantle of snow covered the ground, and it was an easy walk. However, Billy assured Orrin that when there was an abundance of snow he and other fathers would take turns transporting their children to school by an ox drawn sled that could go through almost anything. As the boys departed Rhoda and Billy stood at the cabin door waving, with Nelson behind them looking very sad that his big brother would not be there during the day. As they turned to go back into the house both parents felt a few tears well up. It was a bittersweet moment for them. On the one hand, they were so proud to see him off to acquire the formal education that neither of them had had, but on the other hand it was hard to see him growing up so quickly. This young lad had truly become one of their own children.

It took very little time before Orrin and his friends arrived at the schoolhouse, and they were happy that they had a bit of time to play their favorite games before the schoolmaster would ring the bell loudly and their fun and merriment would have to come to an end. Sometimes they played hide and seek, or tag, or blind man's bluff. Today, with some snow on the ground, was a Fox and Geese day.[100] He and his friends stomped down the thin layer of snow in a circle, and then stomped once again from the outer edge to the center, thereby creating what looked like a wagon wheel. Then they created some trails that extended out from the wheel. Now it was time for play. Each of them selected a trail that he could not leave, except to go into the center, which was a safe zone where the Fox could not get him. When the fox tagged a goose it became the fox, and the fox became a goose.[101] The game continued, seemingly without end and Orrin, like all of his playmates, was tired and relieved when the school bell rang.

As he entered the schoolhouse, Orrin went through the big door that separated the outdoors from the entryway, where the walls were lined with rows of pegs for the boy's coats, mittens, hats and boots. These were at different heights so that short and tall boys could reach what they needed. After hanging up his coat and stuffing his mittens into his hat, and putting it on the shelf above, he sat on the bench below to take off his outside boots and replace them with the fleece lined wool booties that his mother had made for him to wear at school. They felt so cozy as he wiggled his toes around inside of them. As he walked over the cold wood floor, he was grateful that he had these to help keep his feet warm. While he was doffing his outdoor attire, he noticed that the girls slipped by into a small cloakroom with a window that lay opposite the boy's benches and pegs.

When all of the children had rid themselves of their outside attire, they opened the second door that led into the schoolroom itself. There, the schoolmaster doffed his hat, bowed, and greeted each with "Good morning." In return, the boys and girls said, "Good morning, Sir," and "made their manners" as the boys bowed respectfully and the girls curtsied.[102] As Orrin bowed, he remembered that he had been warned that if a boy failed to remember to do this he would get a swift boxing on the ears from the master. He certainly did not want that to happen to him.

When Orrin entered the classroom, he saw that each student had been assigned a seat, and the schoolmaster had a wide table with a candle, and a crude chair behind it. There was a small fireplace against the back wall and to the schoolmaster's right. The walls were devoid of any ornamentation—no pictures, no maps, nothing. This gave the room an aura of emptiness and foreboding, which was not abated by the children's clothing that, although serviceable, was drab, and brought no color to the scene. Today was sunny so a stream of daylight poured into the room, and that certainly helped. Orrin could not help wondering what it would be like when there was only a gray sky outside, and it was snowing or raining. It must be even drearier. He was grateful that on his first day of school there was light pouring through the east windows.

The older children, like Orrin and his friends, assumed their seats on long, backless wooden benches that faced into the center of the room. The boys sat on the east side of the room and the girls on the west. A center aisle on each side enabled the students to leave their places to stand before the schoolmaster for recitations. With their teacher watching them closely, the boys and girls assumed their appointed positions. Then the younger children took their seats in front. Their seats had a back, to which was attached a wide board. This served as a desk for the older students, who were sitting behind them.

The day began with the oldest boys, who were referred to as the "first class", reading two verses from the Testament. As Orrin and the other boys his age listened, he could not help but admire their ability to read so well. He hoped that he would be that accomplished in a few years. Writing followed this activity, and the boys were told to take their copybooks and pencils out and lay them on their desks. Orrin's parents, like all of the others, had helped their son to prepare a copybook for school. They had taken some loose sheets of very precious paper, sewed them together, and then covered them with rough brown paper for protection. Billy had made him a plummet, by taking a stick, cutting a groove in it, and then pouring molten waste lead into the groove. He was very glad that his father had even put a hole in it with a string through it, so that he could wear it around his neck, and not lose it.[103]

First, the schoolmaster gave Orrin a ferule to draw straight lines upon which to practice his writing. Because he was a new student with no former school education, Orrin needed to start at the beginning by simply drawing straight lines up and down. His teacher told him that once he had mastered this, he would be allowed to go on to drawing hooks and trammels that made him think of the fireplace crane and pots at home. The teacher told him that even though this was boring, learning to do this well would make it much easier for him when he was introduced to forming letters of the alphabet. Initially, he thought that this would be a very simple exercise, but he soon learned that it was much more difficult than he expected. All too often, his hand would wiggle out of control, resulting in work that looked like scribbles.

While he was struggling, he noticed that the oldest boys had graduated to using a quill that the schoolmaster had carefully cut with his jackknife, and ink that he had prepared for their use. They advanced their writing skills by copying from John Jenkins', "The Art of Writing", a 32-page pamphlet that presented an American approach to writing and replaced the English approach that had been used before he wrote this book in 1791.[104] "Jenkins instructed students to analyze the structure of letters carefully before executing them. This hand-and-mind combination, he boasted, would dramatically abbreviate the time needed to learn writing and bring handwriting mastery within the reach of all Americans."[105] A friend in Boston had sent the schoolmaster a copy, and he was eager to share this with his pupils. As he dealt with the earliest stages of learning to write properly, Orrin realized that doing well with his school work, as his parents expected, was going to be difficult, but he was determined to persevere and make them proud of him.

Spelling followed writing. The schoolmaster explained that there were no spelling books for his group. Instead, they would gather around him, as he pointed at the letters of the alphabet, and they responded in kind. Once the students had mastered the alphabet, the teacher said that he would point to combinations of letters and, as he did so, he would pronounce the sounds of the combined letters. While Orrin was engaged in this activity, he looked enviously at the oldest students who were using Webster's Spelling Book for both spelling and reading.[106] This all sounded so bewildering to Orrin and his friends, but their parents had made it very clear that they had no choice but to learn everything they could. The schoolmaster had already warned them that he would rap them sternly on their knuckles with his ferule if they did not do their lesson well.

Figure 14 Schoolmaster. Erwin H. Austin

At last it was time for lunch, and Orrin was eager to delve into the basket that his mother had prepared for him. There he found some nice bread, spread amply with butter, and topped with jam, and, in the bottom, he found a lovely piece of gingerbread—his very favorite. His mother was always so thoughtful! He thanked her, even if from a distance. Because the day was still fair, and no more snow had come, the children ate quickly so that they could go outside for the brief recess.

The boys really looked forward to the time to run around and do as they wished. They also knew that this was the only opportunity that they would have to make a visit to the outhouse. Orrin was very thirsty, and one of the older boys told him that when there was enough snow on the ground, they scooped it into their mittened hands, rolled it into a ball, and then carefully licked or bit the luscious moisture off, a little at a time. They warned him not to lick it when it was very cold, because his wet tongue would stick to the snow. Every once in a while, they said that some brave lad would try to show off by doing just this and wind up screaming in pain as a result. Sadly, there was not enough snow to make snowballs today. That experience would have to wait for another day.

Orrin felt sorry for the girls who seemed to be inclined to stay inside and play games or just talk. He thought that this was probably because their attire gave them little protection from the wind and weather. Their boots were quite low, and any snow could easily get into them, leaving the girls with an uncomfortable, squishy mess beneath their feet. Also, their skirts were so long that he was sure that they would get covered with clods of snow and ice that would freeze into little balls and make walking very difficult. Orrin could not imagine what it would be like not to be able to play freely outdoors.

All too soon the master rapped on the side of the outside door with his ferule, signaling that it was time to go back into the classroom for the afternoon's lessons. As they tumbled through the door they stopped just long enough to dip the scoop into the pail of water that lay at the classroom's entrance, and take a long drink before handing it to the person behind.[107] Then the students all filed into their seats for arithmetic. Because Orrin had learned to count at home, he was allowed to study Root's Arithmetic, and use a slate on which he did his sums. He was very proud that, for this subject, he could be with the older students who had been in school longer. He silently thanked his father for teaching him to count on his fingers and to recognize numbers. He worked diligently and usually his sum would be correct. Then he was allowed to put the problem and its sum into his ciphering book.[108] This gave him a great sense of accomplishment and pride.

Later, the schoolmaster brought out Webster's Spelling book once again. This time he used it to introduce the students in Orrin's group to the rudiments of learning to read. He began with the letters that he had asked the students to decipher in the morning. Once again, Orrin had an advantage over some of the other students because, even though his parents could not read well they did know the alphabet, and they had taught this to him. As a result, he was able to advance to the next level, in which the teacher put together two letters to form a word and asked him to say the words. He found this pretty easy and looked forward to having longer words in the days to come. He thought to himself that, if he worked hard, he would reach the level of the other more experienced scholars, and he might even be able to read the New England Primer that the schoolmaster kept on his desk. [109] He really looked forward to achieving this level since the book was filled with pictures, rhymes, stories and even proverbs.

Although there was no prayer in the school Orrin had been told that on Fridays, while the younger ones learned their ABCs and how to count by memorizing nursery rhymes, the older students would study the Catechism. It was a small book that had two parts: Historical and Assembly Catechism. The teacher explained to Orrin and his friends that they would begin with the historical portion since they were still new to school. Each week the master would require them to memorize the answers to a long list of questions after showing them a picture of a Bible scene. He told the students that, in the years to come, they would be taught the Assembly Catechism, which focused on questions of a doctrinal order. Then the children from that class would be required to go to the church where the minister would examine them on the Catechism, one by one. Orrin was not looking forward to this.[110]

As the children filed out of school, at the end of their day, the schoolmaster pulled Orrin and his friends aside. He told them that the older boys, including their group, were responsible for bringing in the firewood that was stacked outside the schoolhouse door and for laying the fire in the fireplace each morning. He explained that each evening, before school let out, he appointed an older boy to assume this responsibility. He told them that they would not have to assume this duty right away but, after a few weeks when they had adjusted to being in school, he would be requiring this of them. This would mean that they would have to arrive early in the morning in order to make all of the necessary preparations for laying and starting the fire before the schoolmaster arrived.

Orrin had noticed that the girls also had some duties, although in his mind theirs were far less difficult than what the boys had to do. It was their job to keep the schoolhouse as clean as possible. Their mothers had prepared these future young homemakers well. Just as with the boys, he found out that each evening a girl was assigned the job of coming to school early in order to dust and sweep the schoolroom before the schoolmaster arrived. Orrin had overheard a girl complaining that because the students were not always tidy when they were eating their noon meal, they frequently left lots of crumbs to be swept up. If they were not careful a mouse would be daring and venture out of its nest in the walls to partake of the feast that had been left behind. One of the girls told Orrin that she had reached down to sweep up some crumbs and had been badly frightened when a mouse scampered across her outstretched fingers. She said that from then on, she would be sure to look more carefully before extending her hands beneath the furniture.

At supper each evening Orrin delighted in telling his parents about what he had learned at school that day. Nelson, of course, listened intently, while Mortimer simply yawned, as evidence that he did not really care about this stuff. His parents listened to every word, with smiles on their faces and words of acclamation for their son. They were so proud of him for all that he was achieving and assured him that he would be returning the following winter to further his education. Both Billy and Rhoda were so pleased that Orrin was receiving the education they never got, and they vowed to do their best to see that Nelson and his younger brother Mortimer would be given the same opportunity that Orrin had.

Of course, his parents asked his son if he had behaved as he was taught. Billy had told his son that he, and other fathers, believed in being kind to their children when they were good, but when their behavior was bad both boys and girls should be punished in proportion to the offense. He had forewarned Orrin that his schoolmaster had their support in meting out punishments of miscreants. Orrin confessed that on his very first day he had seen one of his classmates being punished by the master because he had not presented a perfect copybook page to him. A rap on the knuckles was mild, but this poor boy had endured some very harsh punishment as the master had tied the boy's hands behind his back and, then, raised his ruler and hit the boy hard on his back and shoulders. Orrin told his parents that, after seeing this, he had vowed to never let that happen to him.

One day followed another in rapid succession. Then came Orrin's turn to take care of the fire at the school. He vigorously hoped that there would still be a few coals in the fireplace from the afternoon before, but he knew that this was probably wishful thinking. If there were no coals in the fireplace when he got to school, he would have to set forth to the nearest house to gather up some coals from their fireplace. In anticipation of such an event, he decided that it would be prudent to put his jackknife in his coat pocket. Along the way, he could cut off a wide strip of green hemlock bark to use as protection for his hands while he was carrying the hot coals back to the schoolhouse.[111] His caution paid off. He did have to get coals from a neighbor. When he got back to the schoolhouse, he laid these in the fireplace with some wood on top. Then, he squatted down in front of the wood and carefully blew until flames leapt forward. It took a bit of practice and he knew that, if he blew too hard, it would disturb the ashes from the day before and send them flying into the air. Sometimes, if the wood was still quite green, this process would take a while.

As the weeks unfolded, Orrin discovered that when it was bitterly cold and there was no way of preventing the strong winds from finding every little crack and crevice between the clapboards the wood supply that he had brought in before school would run short. This meant that when the schoolmaster directed him to feed the fire, he had to don his warm coat and boots, pick up the axe in the entryway, and head to the woodpile to get some more logs. It was cold and miserable to have to leave the semi-warmth of the schoolroom to fetch more wood and he tried very hard to avoid this extra task by bringing a bit of extra wood into the room when he laid the fire.

The days passed by quickly for Orrin. He had been a fast learner and a well-behaved lad, so he had had no significant negative exchanges with the schoolmaster. As a matter of fact, he quite liked him, and would be sad to finish school and to see him leave. As the end of the term approached in mid-April, the children began to prepare for closing exercises for "Last Day". There was much scrubbing and cleaning of the schoolhouse in preparation for this big event. Parents and siblings gathered in the middle of the schoolhouse floor, surrounded by the children's desks and that of the teacher. A Congregational minister attended these very important closing exercises, as did the committeeman for schools for his district.

First, the little ones recited their letters, spelled a few words and answered some questions from the Catechism. They also had to tell where they lived, the name of their minister, the governor of their state, and the president of their country. The students were very anxious, and a few even burst into tears but, overall, they did well, much to the relief of their parents. Then came Orrin's class. They demonstrated their reading and spelling ability as well as their understanding of abbreviations and Roman numerals. Then they read, spelled, and recited some simple addition and subtraction problems. They also named the books in the Bible and passed their writing and ciphering books among the audience. After each of the students completed their presentations they ended with a bow or a curtsy—something that they had learned exceedingly well after showing this respect to the schoolmaster every morning. As the ceremony ended, the minister admonished them to be good Christians, work hard, mind their parents, and keep up with everything that they had learned during the long period out of school. The events of the evening closed with prayer and a hymn, and each student received a small gift from the minister.[112]

As Orrin and his parents walked home with Nelson and Mortimer tagging along behind, Billy turned to his son to tell him how proud of him he was. Rhoda quickly expressed the same sentiment. It suddenly struck Orrin that he would not be back in school for almost a year. That seemed like a very long time to try to remember everything that he knew now. As excited as he was at the prospect of spending his days working with his father and helping his mother when she needed it, he knew that he would miss school and the sense of camaraderie that he had developed there. He was certain that he wanted to return to school to continue his education, at least as far as learning to read and write.

For the next few years Orrin continued to attend school during the winter months. Billy and Rhoda had decided that they did not want him to stop his education until he was 16, or a year or two earlier, if it was necessary. They recognized that this might mean that he would have to miss days when an emergency came up that Billy could not handle alone. They might also have to ask him to leave a little earlier in the year if, for some unusual reason, preparations for spring plowing could be done sooner. As much as Orrin enjoyed working with his father, he knew that he still had much to learn that would be helpful to him in his adult life.

CHAPTER FOURTEEN

PEACE AND PROSPERITY

Trading with Canada and England had met with some severe restrictions when Thomas Jefferson signed the Embargo Act of 1807 into law. His objective was to stop the raiding of American ships by the French and English, who were engaged in the Napoleonic Wars against one another. However, if the embargo had been successful, it would have stopped all shipping to and from Great Britain and France. Although responses to the embargo varied it had little, if any, effect upon smuggling enterprises in the United States.[113]

Fortunately, the embargo proved to be unenforceable. Otherwise, it would have brought a complete halt to the trade that Billy and others were seeing on the lake. As it was, the Act of 1807 was simply ignored for the most part, and those living on Lake Champlain saw no reason to comply with its restrictions. Furthermore, it is doubtful that Billy, or anyone else in Willsborough, knew anything of the Embargo Act. Even if they did, for young Americans their independent spirit prevailed, and they simply continued to send goods north. Smugglers, or not, there was financial gain to be had, and the lucrative trade continued.

Huge amounts of wood were being shipped to England. The tavern keeper told Billy that much of England's forestland had been stripped bare, and the country was hungry for this essential building material. Coincidently, settlers out on The Point, and other lakeside communities, found that after clearing the dense forest, taming the land that they had chosen, and creating a home and a homestead for themselves and their families, they had excess wood that potentially could have some value.

Wood was not the only thing being smuggled into Canada. George Throop used his excess wood to make potash and pearl ash to enter that thriving market, especially in England. Here again, that country's decimated forests left them with no production resources of their own. The first U.S. patent for the process of making potash was issued on July 31, 1790, to Samuel Hopkins, "for an improvement in making potash and pearl ash by a new Apparatus and Process." [114] By this time its usefulness had become significant. Potash had proved to be an excellent source of fertilizer, and an important ingredient of lye for making soap. Even more importantly, it was very useful in manufacturing glass, dying textiles, scouring freshly shorn fleeces, and cleaning flax among other uses.[115] In true entrepreneurial spirit, George took the process yet one step further by refining the potash into pearl ash, which he could trade with Canada and England at a considerably greater profit.[116]

In 1808 there was great excitement at Levi Higby's tavern when they heard news of the exploits of a 40-foot long boat called the Black Snake. Several people remembered her well in her earlier life when she had served Charles McNeil as a ferry that ran between Essex and Charlotte.[117] Now she had taken on an entirely different role. A traveler who came through town told them that for many months this boat had been the center of a bustling illegal trade in potash and pearl ash that England also needed badly. Somehow, month after month, the boat and its loads of contraband continued to elude efforts by Canada and the United States to capture her and her crew. The traveler said that the boat seemed to have taken on a life of its own. The Black Snake captain had set up a system whereby he and his crew would approach the border, offload their cargo onto smaller rafts, and then let them float into Canada with the prevailing winds.[118] From there they were picked up by Canadians and resumed their trip up the Richelieu River and into the St. Lawrence on their way to England. It appeared that both the Americans and the Canadians had found loophole after loophole by means of which they could continue this trade by water. The Black Snake took full advantage of this opportunity. Billy and his fellow townsmen were stunned by the sheer volume that they were being told about, and a bit relieved when they were told that the Black Snake had finally been captured.

1810 was a very exciting year for those who lived on the lake, and not just because on the smuggling of wood and potash into Canada. Early one morning, as Billy was working in his lower field, he looked up from his chores and saw a strange apparition coming south across the water. He had heard that there had been a steamboat on the lake called the Phoenix and that it had come to a dreadful end when it exploded, killing everyone on board. It was a queer looking boat with no mast or sails, which seemed very, very odd. He had no idea what type of watercraft this was, but it definitely was not a raft. As he regarded it he asked himself whether this was another steamboat, or just an apparition. Billy called to Orrin, who was working not far from him, and together they stared at the object while questioning, "How can something that big move with no sails, and why was it emitting big bursts of smoke from a pipe coming out of its roof." It was all very puzzling, and they could only hope that, if it were like that other ship, it would not explode right in front of them. This notion conjured up horrific images for both father and son.

Meanwhile, life in Willsborough continued much as it usually did. To Billy, although news of the Black Snake affair was interesting, he did not see that it had any relevance to him. He had always had an interest in local civic affairs and once he was somewhat settled in his new community, he became increasingly involved in Willsborough's affairs. Even though the population of the town was still relatively sparse, the usual responsibilities needed to be accepted if the town was to thrive. In addition to a town supervisor and clerk, there were three assessors, three commissioners of highways, one tax collector, three poor masters, three constables, nine fence viewers and damage appraisers, twelve path masters and ten-pound keepers.[119]

In 1809, Billy took on his first civic commitment when he was appointed as a fence viewer and damage appraiser.[120] This job had two prongs. Despite the fact that land surveys were very specific in their language of rods and chains, white oaks and large rocks, etc., there were still frequent boundary disputes between neighbors. When one arose, Billy was called in to review the survey and arbitrate the claims. He was also responsible for only approving well-constructed, sturdy fences, or stone walls, since those that were poorly built invited neighbor's livestock to wander astray. In addition, if a fence or stone wall was harmed Billy was responsible for assessing the damage and presenting a fair financial, or other type of settlement, for the damages that the landowner had encountered.

Figure 15 Steamboat. Ashley Ahrent

In 1810 Levi Higby continued as the village's postmaster, a position he had held since the first post office came into being ten years earlier.[121] George Throop remained as the Clerk to the Town Board, as he had been for the five previous years. The Town Government, for the first time, determined that barnyards could be used as legal pounds for the pound keepers,[122] and, but a year later, Billy was elected pound keeper for his district.[123] His experience as a fence viewer had really impressed upon him the importance of farmers keeping their livestock off of other people's property. He could not countenance irresponsible citizens who simply left their animals to wander about freely, causing particular havoc in the village.

Access to passable roads continued to be critically important, especially for the farmers who lived outside the village, and travelers who were passing through on their way to another destination. On The Point only one road stretched from the neck in the south to John Crum's farm at the end of The Point in the north. There were a few side roads off of it that led to a farmhouse, or to the other side of the Point, but the main North-South road was a lifeline. Like all adult Willsborough men, each season Billy was expected to spend a certain number of days working on "highway" maintenance in his particular district.[124] For a few years The Point only had one district. However, as the population continued to increase, it became necessary for highway districts to be adjusted, or for new ones to be created almost annually. In 1809 Billy was assigned 5 days of road maintenance per season that year.[125] (The number of days that one had to work was based upon the amount of acreage an individual had.) Although road maintenance could be a time-consuming and exhausting endeavor, the men accepted their responsibilities willingly. Their dependency left them with no choice.

Each season brought its own particular road challenges. When winter came, it was often a fight to simply keep the road to The Point passable. However, Billy, like his fellow Pointers, knew that it had to be done. If they did not try to stay ahead of the snow, even while it was falling, they could find themselves marooned for weeks on end. This was arduous work, especially when the winds drove high drifts across the road. Hour after hour the men had to shovel them aside. This was particularly discouraging when they thought that they had a section open and moved on to another only to find that the first section had filled back in while they were working on the second. If the winds were quiet, they could hitch their teams to their stone sledges and use these to flatten the surface. However, upon occasion, no matter how diligently they worked they simply had to give in to what nature had presented to them. Their work was bitterly cold when the wind came howling down the lake from frozen Canada and the snow was driven with such force that one could hardly stand. No matter how thick their clothes were, both snow and wind left men frozen, sometimes with frostbite. When dark descended and they were forced to stop their work, they would return to their firesides, shivering, exhausted and hungry. They had done their best!

When, at last, the winds had abated, and the land was no longer encased in snow, the roads presented different problems that were equally challenging. The rains came, often driven hard by the winds off the lake that continued to bring a chill to the air. The land became a sodden mass as the surface of the road turned into a quagmire that fairly sucked wagon wheels, and sometimes even a horse, down into it. Once they had heaved the horse and wagon out of the ooze, the job was not finished. The road crew had to rush to the scene to make the necessary repairs as quickly as possible, lest the next traveler meet with the same fate as he tried to get through the new ruts. Fortunately, the farmers had had the foresight to prepare themselves for this eventuality. In the fall, when the ground was still hard, they had stockpiled stone by the side of the road for use in the future. They used this to fill in the rut. Billy found their spring road maintenance almost as challenging and exhausting as shoveling the snow. However, at least they were not frozen stiff, as they had been previously.

Mercifully, the demands of road maintenance slackened during the summer months, except when a sudden, heavy shower passed through. This was an enormous blessing, since the harvest was very time-sensitive, and any loss of time could lead to disaster for the farmer. Nevertheless, they still had to be ready to attend to the aftereffects of a storm when the occasion arose. This was the time of year when farmers were hard at work on their own land, and they had little time for anything else. The growing season was so very short, and they had to spend every day, and often into dusk, in the seemingly endless cycle of plowing, harrowing, planting, weeding, and pruning. However, they continued to have to pay attention to the maintenance of their roads. Billy and his fellow farmers had to be able to travel safely and easily if they had any hope of transporting their saleable goods to a market. Fortunately, the roads tended to stay in good repair into the fall.

According to the 1810 Federal Census the population of Willsborough was 663 that year.[126] Residents of The Point were listed as Billy Blinn, Adam Patterson, Frederick Rueback, William Stroud, Daniel Bacon, Capt. Abraham Chase, Jacob Adsit, James Reynolds, Samuel Adsit, Caleb Smith, Asa Fisher, James Smith, Asa Frisby, Borhave Rueback and Daniel Rowley.[127] The 1810 census also indicated that Billy Blinn was listed as head of family, and his household consisted of two free white males under age ten (Nelson and Mortimer), one free white male between eleven and twenty-five (Orrin), one free white male between twenty-six and forty-four (Billy), one free white female under ten (new born Theresa), one free white female between sixteen and twenty-five (Rhoda). The

Blinns were listed as having a total of six household members.[128] (This is the first time that the term "free white" appears in the census records.)

Town records for 1810 show that there was a sawmill on the east shore of the river, along with Daniel Ross's gristmill. Across the river, on the west shore, there was Daniel Sheldon's blacksmith shop, and another sawmill a bit further down.[129] As yet, there was no shoemaker in the village so community members had to put together their own crudely constructed shoes and boots, which recognized no difference between the shapes of the right and left feet. Occasionally, an itinerant shoemaker came to Willsborough, but their skills were not much better. People just had to survive with ill-fitting footwear. Levi Higby and George Throop continued to be enterprising entrepreneurs in the village, just as they had been when they opened the anchor shop. In order to provide the villagers with some basic provisions they constructed a stone store just back from the river. This gave local farmers and craftspeople a local outlet for their excess produce and other goods and offered townspeople a source of items that were not available locally, unless a peddler came through and offered these.

Taverns continued to play an important role in the life of the town. Isaac Jones had a tavern near the east side of the bridge where he "distributed 'sperrits' to the thirsting palates at and about 'The Falls'."[130] True to his entrepreneurial spirit, Levi Higby established a distillery on the hillside above his store for the purpose of provisioning spirits for his own tavern; a tavern that lay not too far from that of Isaac Jones. Meanwhile, Levi Cooley had established a tavern on the west side of the river near the sawmill.[131] Billy was secretly relieved that, even though a person could purchase spirits on his own, there was no tavern out on The Point. His faith told him that the Devil lurked in such indulgences. However, when he was in the village, he did not hesitate to step into one of the taverns to gather the latest news, to converse with other men and, perhaps, to have a round or two of darts.

Much to Billy's consternation, his neighbor and good friend, Samuel Adsit, sold spirits at his store, as well as other things. He wondered why such an upright community member as Samuel would feel compelled to sell spirits, although he had to admit that it was undoubtedly a lucrative part of his business. Several entries in the 1811 records state that David Langdon purchased a quart of rum and two plugs of tobacco, Kenyon Adsit bought a gallon of gin and a pound of tobacco, and Jacob Adsit ran up a tab for pork, butter, wheat and, of course, a quart of rum.[132]

The year 1810 brought yet another Blinn child into the world. This time it was a girl whom they named Theresa.[133] Life in the Blinn family had definitely settled into a routine that, every two years, seemed to be punctuated by the birth of another baby. With each new addition family and household responsibilities for Rhoda increased. Being a kind, good-natured, and inherently patient woman, she accepted this with the same aplomb that most women did. The cycle of births and deaths was just a part of their normal lives. With regularity, during their reproductive years, women brought babies into the world and, hopefully, saw them grow into healthy and responsible adults. Far too often, families watched as death crept in, and their own progeny, or those of others, were lowered into the ground for their final rest. Rhoda and Billy counted their blessings that this fate had not befallen them, at least not yet.

As was to be expected, twelve-year-old Orrin, did what he could to relieve his mother of some of her daily duties. Now it was his job to milk, feed, and generally care for the "milch" cows, both morning and evening. As the first light of dawn crept over the lake Orrin threw off his covers, and hastily donned his clothes, which was never a pleasure during the colder months. If it was still dark, he grabbed one of the lanterns that were kept by the door and rushed across to the barnyard where he was greeted by baleful mooing as these sad-eyed bovines waited patiently to be relieved of their burdens. As he approached each of them, with bucket in hand, the heads of these gentle creatures turned to nuzzle Orrin, as they breathed their warm, grassy breath upon him. The lad had come to love these animals just as his mother did. Although not very smart, there was something special about their sweet manner. What he could have seen as a boring job was not that way at all for him. Instead, he, like his mother, found it an undemanding and quite peaceful prelude to the day that lay ahead.

Four-year-old Nelson had grown into a young lad now and left his toddler days behind. Like his big brother he was very observant and a quick learner. He worshipped his older brother and tried to emulate him in every way that he could. As a result, he became a sort of apprentice to 12-year-old Orrin and this, of course, made the older boy feel very grown-up, and even important. Orrin realized that it would not be long before two-year-old Mortimer followed the path of his older brother, but, for now, he was content to cling to his mother's apron strings. That way he could be sure that she gave him as much attention as the newborn baby was getting.

As he had since he became a member of the Blinn family, Orrin continued to ensure that there was always a fire going in the fireplace, both for cooking year-around and for warmth and cooking in the colder months. Nelson loved participating in this activity with his brother. Each morning this lively four-year-old would run back and forth from the door to the fireplace, carrying the twigs and scraps of wood that Orrin used to start the fire. Then, while Orrin laid them in place, Nelson trudged across the floor, huffing and puffing, as he carried one log at a time to the hearth. Sometimes, the burden was simply too heavy, and he condescended to accepting some assistance. When all was ready and Orrin pulled out the tinderbox and lit the fire Nelson clapped his hands with glee as he saw the tongues of fire shooting high toward the mouth of the chimney. In the evening, if he was still awake, the youngster helped with preparations for banking the coals in the fireplace until morning. When this was done the brothers loved to sit on the settle, where Orrin would share his vivid imagination by telling Nelson stories. Often, they were about his own antics and his friend's.

After the morning meal Nelson and Orrin set forth to tend to the chickens and other fowl. Just as Orrin had done when he was younger, Nelson picked up the basket that lay just inside the chicken coop door and set off to fetch the eggs that the hens had left behind. They were usually well nestled into the straw, where the hens had deposited them, and Nelson loved reaching in to see if anything was there. It was like a game of hide and seek. While he was doing this the hens clucked around as if to say, "Look what I left for you. Aren't you pleased with me?" With a well-laden basket in hand, Nelson triumphantly returned to the house, carefully bearing his trophies. His mother always greeted him with a hug and a wreath of smiles.

With that job dispatched the child would quickly run back to the coop, reach into the pail of mash that Orrin had left for him and carefully place the hen's morning libation in their feeder. Under Orrin's ever-watchful eye he would feed the roosters who, as usual, were noisily protesting that they had had to wait too long. Meanwhile, Orrin did some general cleaning, then fetched a big bucket of water from the barnyard well and poured its contents into the troughs. With the chickens taken care of, the boys set forth to take care of the turkeys and geese. Because they were bigger and, often, quite testy, Orrin took over this chore while Nelson eagerly watched his every move and dreamed of the time when he would be able to do this, also.

CHAPTER FIFTEEN

STILL SAFE ON THE HOMEFRONT

As the year 1812 rolled in life in Willsborough continued pretty much as it always had. Billy was appointed as a Commissioner of Highways for District #9 for the second year. A new regulation stated that rams could not be allowed to run loose from September 1 to November 11 lest they disturb the carefully planned breeding cycle of the town's sheep owners. Crows had become a terrible nuisance in the village, as had wolves a few years before, and a bounty of 12$^{1/2}$ cents was offered for each of the birds that was destroyed.[134] The surveying of roads, both old and new, was a constant and ongoing process. In addition to new roads being built, those that had been built previously, and were no longer useful, were taken off the official list and ceased to be maintained.[135] Because traffic over Willsborough Mountain had increased, a new survey of the road between the bridge and the north boundary of Willsborough that was a vital link to the inland towns was also undertaken.[136]

Each day, as soon as the ice was gone from the lake Billy saw the heavily laden, huge rafts floating by with some regularity. He asked himself, why he should not participate in this lucrative endeavor. Yes, he was an honest man and an upright citizen. However, the temptation was there. After all, who was to know? There appeared to be no legal oversight on the lake and, in his mind, what he wanted to do, and others were already doing, was actually a benefit of the area. After all, it was generating revenue. Following considerable thought, he determined that he would become a part of the smuggling enterprise and set about finding a way to do this.

It did not take Billy long to learn that there were individuals in the area who actually executed the smuggling trade. When they first started out they needed to make a major investment of time and capital because they had to build huge rafts of wood to carry their contraband—a process that demanded a considerable amount of hard work from the time that they first cut the wood until the raft was completed. When the lake was at its lowest level in late fall, they began to build their rafts on land that would be swamped when the ice on the lake thawed and spring rains came. Then they could easily float the rafts into the lake.[137] Once the structure of the raft was completed, the builder erected a parapet, loaded it with staves and saw lumber, on top of which he placed tents, or even a log cabin for the crew. Cooking was a necessity, so he built a clay foundation for the hearth that sat on top of the staves.[138] This process could take most of a year. However, once completed the crewmembers began to load their completed raft with potash, pearl ash, lumber, pork, fish, cheese, butter, tobacco, grain and other tradable goods.[139] Then, they were ready to set forth on their journey north with dreams of good fortune for their futures.

On a visit to the tavern a crewman on one of the smuggler's rafts, who was waiting for it to be loaded, described the voyage that they took going north with their booty. Usually they proceeded northward and down the Richelieu, sailed past Isle aux-Noix, a Revolutionary War relic with a few sunken ships, and on to St. Jean in Quebec.[140]

Figure 16 Smuggler's Raft. Ashley Ahrent

Soon after they left St. Jean, they encountered the rapids at Chambly. Except for a brief period when a spring freshet allowed small vessels and rafts to pass over the rapids, the raft would have to be winched or carried overland to the St. Lawrence.[141] The other possibility was to off-load the crewmen and goods onto land and proceed overland to the markets of Montreal and Quebec—a journey that could be filled with peril. Some American smugglers, particularly in Vermont, were even taking large numbers of cattle, sheep, horses and oxen through dense woods along the shore until they reached the border where the same type of transfer occurred.[142] Whatever route they chose, it was heavy and miserable work. In addition, "Other than the elements, ... they were at the mercy of Quebec middlemen, the relentless laws of supply and demand, inflation, and the scarcity of hard cash."[143]

The crewman went on to explain that the Canadian smugglers who were going south had to do almost the same thing. As was the case for those going north into Canada, border protection was thinly spread across northern New York and Vermont, so once the Canadian goods got past the challenges on the Richelieu, they could proceed without having to be especially cautious. They were bringing in salt and a variety of manufactured European goods.[144]   "The most persistent smuggler, a non-resident but frequent visitor [to Canada], was John Jacob Astor, whose traffic in furs became the foundation of his fortune. His Burlington agent, "Admiral" Gideon King, fitted his 30-ton sloop, *Lady Washington*, with a false bulkhead, behind which an invaluable amount of illegal or semi-legal contraband escaped the eyes of the authorities."

Strong winds helped the smugglers heading north with a heavy load, especially since the prevailing wind on the lake at that time of year was from the south and the lake and river flowed to the north. Unless foul weather prevailed the trip to the border and on into the Richelieu was eased considerably when the south wind filled the sail on the raft and pushed it forward. In addition, wharves had been constructed at the border so that the wood could be off-loaded and taken overland as far as St. Jean if necessary.[145] From there it would be an overland trip no matter what. Unfortunately, the opposite occurred when they had to slog home, tacking back and forth, against the south wind and the northward flow of the river and the lake until reaching their destination. Of course, this was also true for smugglers bringing goods from Canada into the United States.[146]

As the crewman was describing all of this, he laid out a rather crude map, which helped Billy to understand what he was describing. When he pondered the map of these places that seemed so very far away to him he began to understand why both the United States and Great Britain saw the Richelieu River and its Chambly Rapids that lay just to the north of St. Jean as a formidable barrier between Lake Champlain and Canada's St. Lawrence River. The lake was huge and wide, the river was narrow, and the rapids were forbidding. Billy went away from the discussion with great respect for the men who plied these waters, often at great peril. He was glad that he only had to trade his excess wood for things that he needed and did not have to make their journey.

Smuggling into and out of Canada continued unabated until it came to a halt, usually by the latter part of June. Until then, the number of heavily laden rafts that continued to float by his field each day amazed Billy. After he had decided to enter the smuggling trade, he began to take any excess wood that he had to one of the smugglers who assured him that it would be sold at a profit. He knew that this was a long chance but also figured that he had nothing to lose. Even if the raft sank, or the smuggler never paid him, he had only lost wood for which he had no use—at least at this time.

On April 30, 1812 the first reference to a freed person of color appears in the Town records. On that date Joseph Sheldon, a freeholder and inhabitant of the Town, appeared before Thomas Stower, a judge in the County Court of Common Pleas. There Mr. Sheldon swore that he was acquainted with Philip Barber, a man of color, aged twenty-eight, who was born in the State of Connecticut, and "was reputed to be manumitted" at the age of 25. Joseph Sheldon swore that he believed this to be true.[147] Like most of the men in the community, Billy had heard enough about slave holding to express his strong disapproval of the system. He even knew of a few persons who had slaves in their households, including Daniel Ross,[148] who seemed to be an honorable person otherwise. He wondered how a person of his stature in the community could countenance such a position, but let it go at that. Billy simply thought that as long as the slaves in his area were being fairly treated, and presented no problems to anyone, they should be an accepted fact of life in the community.

On June 18, 1812 the United States of America was forced, yet again, to face a daunting challenge. It was one that brought back memories of the Revolutionary War—memories of a bloody confrontation that were still too fresh in the minds of many; memories that left wounds and scars that would never completely heal. Nevertheless, the gauntlet had been thrown to the ground. The Congress of the United States, with the full support of President James Madison, had declared war on Britain! Once again, the country was forced to lock horns with its former enemy, just as it had been a little over thirty years earlier.

By this time over 100,000 people lived in areas of New York and Vermont that abutted Lake Champlain. Economic growth there was stimulated by trade with Canada (both legal and illegal), and with major population centers as far south as New York City and east as Boston. Because of this, towns like Burlington, Plattsburgh, Whitehall and Vergennes were becoming dominant centers for commerce.[149] According to the 1810 Federal Census the population of Clinton County was 8,002 and Essex County was 9,477, and those numbers were continuing to climb.[150] The position of Lake Champlain, as a strategic commercial conduit, was soon to play a significant economic role far beyond its shores.

Events that would have a bearing on the future of Lake Champlain, and Willsborough, were soon to come closer to home than Billy and his fellow community members realized. Once Congress had declared war with Great Britain, it left the United States border with British-controlled Canada vulnerable for both the Canadians and the Americans. Conflict along this border was not only possible but also highly probable. Quebec City, the center of Lower Canada's governance, as well as the metropolis of Montreal, had the potential to become major targets for invasion by the Americans, or vice versa.

In the months following the President's Declaration of War on June 18, 1812, serious rumblings began to reach south from Plattsburgh. During his tavern visits Billy heard that local militias had already begun to be formed in the border towns of Clinton County. These were particularly vulnerable because there were no fortifications there. Any that had existed during the War of Independence had decayed, fallen down, or been taken over for another purpose. A few attempts at defense had been made earlier on. In 1809 a brick arsenal had been built in Plattsburgh, then a town of 3,112 inhabitants and 28 slaves.[151] A year later another arsenal was built in Elizabethtown, the Essex County seat of government, but this was a significant distance south of the border and, seemingly, could be of little help.[152]

Billy continued to hear disquieting news from time to time. However, as far as he was concerned, in general, the news seemed to have little, if any, bearing on his life. When he had heard about the Royal Navy's impressment of sailors, he simply shook his head with complete lack of understanding of what this was all about. Neither could he relate to things that were occurring at "Detroit, on the Niagara peninsula and along Lake Ontario".[153] These types of events meant nothing, because they were taking place elsewhere and elsewhere meant any place beyond the shores of Lake Champlain. Billy only knew the names of the large population centers such as Boston, New York, or Philadelphia. Even Washington, the seat of the Federal Government, was something he had only vaguely heard about. He still had a problem fathoming` why Congress would have felt forced to take such an aggressive and terrifying step as declaring war on Great Britain. This meant that the Americans would be pitted against their neighbors across the border in Canada, and that could have dire consequences for the Champlain Valley. That much he understood quite clearly.

During the late summer of 1812 Rhoda gave birth to another baby boy that they named Edgar. Now they had three boys and only one girl.   Fortunately, he was yet another relatively easy baby who was quite content to spend his early days sleeping and eating. Rhoda was grateful for this and hoped that she would have a bit of a respite from childbearing. However, she was wise enough to realize that this might not be the case. Only time would tell.

When the days began to grow shorter Billy and Orrin started to make preparations for the cooler weather that would come before they knew it. Fortunately, they had planned ahead and had built a few additional structures for their livestock and for storage. Now, they had a corn crib set up on stone posts, so that rats and other vermin could not get in and have a feast. They also built a small shed in which they could store their plow, harrow, various sleds and sledges, and all of the odds and ends of farming under cover. Billy was confident that this would ensure the longevity of these pieces.

For some time, Rhoda had longed for a quiet space away from the hustle and bustle of the big room where all of the family activities took place. Billy realized how crowded they had become, and he decided to put a small addition onto the cabin. He built it against the west wall of the house where there was usually less wind. It was a simple one-story structure with a doorway into the main room, a window facing south where it would be warmest, and one facing west to bring in more light. This provided he and Rhoda with a bedroom, and the removal of their big bed and the cradle offered the children more space in which to play in the big room. When they had completed this endeavor Billy and Orrin looked back on their accomplishments with pride.

Later in the fall of 1812 Billy heard that militias and regular troops were gathering in Burlington and Plattsburg and there was a rumor that they were preparing to invade Canada.[154] In a somewhat derogatory vein, one man described the group as

"400 militiamen, not in uniform, and distinguished only by a military badge worn as a cockade in their hats".[155] Meanwhile, with no memories of the previous conflagration, some young Willsborough townsmen who were filled with patriotism, and without families, joined the militia that had been forming in Essex County, with its headquarters in Elizabethtown.

In October, citizens on both sides of the lake were told that a young and daring sailor named Thomas Macdonough who, at age 28, had already distinguished himself had been brought to Lake Champlain from Maine to take command of the "fleet" on Lake Champlain. It consisted of two gunboats, one of which lay below the water's surface at Basin Harbor, Vermont, as well as six sloops, one of which had been built in Essex, New York by John Boynton. This hardly made it a "fleet" in the true sense of the word.

Rumblings continued to become even more intense, bringing a sense of foreboding and unease to those in the Champlain Valley. By the end of November news reached Willsborough that an invasion of Canada by the Americans had taken place and it was a disaster. The militia and regulars from Burlington had joined those in Plattsburg in two groups and they had headed due north, one behind the other. Shortly after they crossed the border into Canada the first group laid siege to a blockhouse but did not take any prisoners because the Canadian and Indian occupants had fled. The other group advanced, and mistakenly engaged in warfare with another group that they mistook as British, when they were really Americans. When they discovered their egregious error, they retreated in shame.[156] Billy and the others at the tavern were horrified that such a thing could happen to their own countrymen. They simply could not imagine how this could have occurred. After assisting with the disastrous foray into Canada in November, the young lieutenant took his boats to winter quarters in Shelburne Bay.[157] There he planned to upgrade them and make them into a true "fleet".

From time to time news continued to travel south to Willsborough. Billy was deeply concerned by reports of the conditions under which the shamed militia from Clinton and Essex Counties were living during the winter months of 1813. At least those who had gone back to Burlington had a dormitory. Crude as it might be it provided some degree of shelter from the horrors of winter.[158] He was told that a ragged, demoralized, cold and hungry group dragged themselves back to Plattsburgh where they would have to spend the winter— unless, of course, they defected and headed home. Those who remained had to survive in tents with nothing to cover them from the ravages of winter but a thin 3 by 4-foot blanket. Food was always in short supply since private contractors, whose sole goal was financial gain, provided this.[159] The result was to be expected—disease and death.   Most prevalent were measles, fevers of all types, typhus, dysentery, rheumatism, diarrhea, jaundice and pneumonia. Dr. Beaumont, a physician who was left to minister to the bedraggled and sick group, stated that the men's ailments "made the very woods ring with coughing and groaning."[160] His only tools to help them were bleeding, opium and emetics. When alcohol was smuggled in, as happened frequently, it simply made things worse.

Spring 1813 finally arrived, and with it the usual round of plowing the earth came again. By this time, 15-year-old Orrin had grown into a lean, strong, and energetic young man who was Billy's right hand. The two of them worked side by side in almost everything that they did. Orrin had continued to be the observant, quick learner that he had been since he first came to live with the Blinns. Even more important, he had developed into a kind and thoughtful young man who seemed to always be there, when and where he was needed most. Orrin now knew how to operate every piece of the modest equipment they had. He had developed a fine relationship with the horses and oxen, and was skilled at making them do exactly what he wanted. The fact that he could now handle so much of the hard labor left Billy with more time to do the things that he loved the most—working in his shop, and in the woods, and teaching Nelson skills that were appropriate for a 7 year old.

As Billy and Orrin went about the business of turning the earth for yet another crop, planting seeds, and watching anxiously to see the fruits of their labors begin to emerge from the loam they had created more disquieting news of impending war came their way. Despite this, Billy and Orrin had no choice but to focus upon their lives as farmers. They prayed fervently that those rolls of thunder that they heard coming to their quiet and peaceful community would pass them by. They had worked hard for the life that they had achieved for themselves, and their families and, more than anything, they did not want to lose sight of this. The days of fear, skepticism, worry, endurance, pain, and endless hard work seemed to be coming to an end for the pioneers on The Point. All that Billy, his family and his friends, wished for was a time of peace in which they could rejoice in God's love and the bounty he had bestowed upon them.

Out on The Point Billy Blinn, his brother-in-law Daniel Rowley, neighbors Asa Frisby and Job Boynton, along with Asa Fisher, Truman Nash, Jacob Adsit and Samuel Adsit, Caleb Smith, James Reynolds, Adam Patterson and Frederick Ruback were part of highway district #8.[161] They formed an important core of settlement on The Point at that time. In the same year a new dam was built to provide waterpower to the sawmills and the gristmill in the village.[162] Daniel Sheldon had recently set up shop as a blacksmith on the west bank of the river, an area that was developing as rapidly as the east bank.[163] Also, the Lake Champlain Steamboat Co. had been established in an attempt to provide boats that would outrun the sail ferries. Its future remained to be seen.

In the late spring a raft hauled into the small bay in front of Billy's property. It was there to pick up the goods that residents on the Point had ready for trade. The crew brought disquieting news. They related that, earlier on, as they had sneaked up the Richelieu River, and past Isle-aux-Noix, they had noticed that large numbers of workers were engaged in improving the old fortification. The island was in a perfect location because of its defensible position with the Chambly Rapids to its North and several new outposts to its south. The men could see that it was being transformed into an important British military and naval base. It even had a dry dock for shipbuilding and repairs.[164] Because of its location, and the many improvements, it had been transformed into an ideal place to assemble troops, as well as the ships needed to transport them south to conduct raids along the north shore of Lake Champlain, and perhaps even further south.[165] There was an even greater shipyard at St. Jean where the larger British ships such as the *Confiance* were being built.[166]   Billy and his neighbors found this very disquieting news since they knew that they would be very vulnerable if the British made their way south as far as The Point.

Increasingly disquieting news was coming to Willsborough at a rapid rate. In June 1813, against Major Commandant Macdonough's advice, his headstrong deputy took three gunboats north down the Richelieu where they encountered the large military presence at Ile-aux-Noix and fled, but to no avail. All 112 men were captured and imprisoned in Montreal and Halifax, and the British took their ships.[167] This frightening occurrence proved how defenseless Lake Champlain really was.

In late July 1813 more unsettling news travelled to Willsborough. This time it was that a large body of British troops had assembled at Isle-aux-Noix. The bearer of these bad tidings was a man who said that they had been warned not to take their raft north as far as the island because of all of the activity there. Thus, they had been forced to offload their goods and carry them overland all the way. As the smugglers trudged through the woods to the west of the island, they could see the massive number of military men busily preparing for an assault on the Americans.

Just a few weeks later, Billy and others at Levi's tavern heard another report from the north. They were told that on July 29th the British troops and ships had entered American waters and were sighted off the coast at Chazy. Word of this alarmed the citizens of Plattsburgh greatly. They were certain that their town would be the primary target. Gen. Mooers, who was in Plattsburg, immediately mobilized the militia in Essex and Clinton Counties. However, it took several days for the Essex militia to assemble and march north to provide assistance. In the meantime, a group of prominent Plattsburg citizens begged Mooers not to fight back, since they were certain that the much larger British forces would overwhelm the American militia in short order.

Two days later the British bateaux entered the Saranac River and disgorged their troops onto the streets of the hapless town of Plattsburg. There they pilfered the arsenal, one of the blockhouses, and several storehouses. Not content with that, they looted furniture, books, clothing, cooking utensils, groceries and dry goods, leaving Plattsburg in shambles.[168] There was no opposition to their attack. Following the directives that he had received from the citizens, Mooers had taken his men to the west. The bearer of the news continued his report. He said that, as the British headed back north, they wreaked havoc in Pointe au Roche and at Chazy landing. They ended their northward march in Champlain, where they destroyed two blockhouses, the barracks, and a warehouse full of hay before heading across the lake to Swanton in Vermont, where they proceeded to burn the American barracks, the hospital and the other government properties.[169]

Billy and his fellow citizens at the tavern were stunned by this news. They asked themselves how this could be. All too soon word got to Willsborough and Essex that the British were coming their way again, and the towns mustered together their militia as best they could. Meanwhile, the British continued south to Shelburne Bay and onto Charlotte where they captured several American ships before turning northward to return to Canada. In all, they captured 8 ships.[170] There was nothing that those on the western shore could do but stand by helplessly. Billy prayed fervently that they would find no reason to warrant a landing at The Point. Their prayers were heard, and the fleet passed them by.

With this behind him, Macdonough turned his thoughts to the 1814 winter ahead. He desperately needed to be given a chance to make necessary repairs to his damaged vessels and, more importantly, to set about building new boats. In order to do this, he had to have a safe place to do his work. He chose to build a shipyard up Otter Creek as far as the falls at Vergennes, Vermont. There he spent the winter constructing six 70-ton row galleys, a 27-gun ship, and converted a steamboat hull.[171]

Meanwhile, as 1813 was drawing to a close Rhoda produced another son just eleven months after she had given birth to Edgar. She had fifteen-year-old Orrin, seven-year-old Nelson, five-year-old Mortimer, three-year-old Theresa, one-year-old Edgar, and now another tiny infant to care for. They named him Washington. Needless to say, her days and nights were filled with her duties as a wife and mother. Although she was concerned by the news that Billy shared with her, she had little time or opportunity to think about anything but her duties. Carrying and bearing five children in a period of seven years had sapped her of some strength. However, like most women her age, she had no recourse but to endure what life brought to her and to thank God that each of her children was healthy and filled with life.

CHAPTER SIXTEEN

A CLOUD OF WAR HANGS OVER US

Prior to Orrin's 16th birthday on January 3rd, 1814, Rhoda and Billy had decided that Orrin's assistance with the many aspects of his father's growing farming enterprise was so badly needed that Billy could no longer spare him. That was the end of Orrin's formal schooling. Coincidentally, and much to the advantage of future children in Willsborough, in that same year, the Town established a formal Commission of Common Schools, and appointed its first Inspectors of Common Schools. The town was divided into various districts, each of which was to be overseen by these inspectors.[172] The Point became one of these districts. Billy was delighted that his town had made this decision and looked upon it as insurance that his younger children would be guaranteed an appropriate education. In the meantime, the schoolhouse near his property continued to function as well as it had in the past.

Things on the lake appeared to be relatively quiet during the early winter months of 1814, yet citizens of the towns along Lake Champlain continued to become increasingly wary. News of ongoing mounting tensions, and the potential for escalating aggressions on the parts of both the British and Americans, told Billy, and his friends and neighbors, that they needed to brace for more military and naval activity in the months to come. When Billy gathered with his neighbors, or he visited the village, there was talk of little else. Everyone began to sense that the winter quiet was merely the lull before the storm and that formidable challenges lay ahead.

News reached Willsborough that to the north the British were engaging in massive shipbuilding activities at Isle-aux-Noix. This was a clear indicator that they had plans to launch another major attack on the lake in the warmer months that lay ahead. From the south they received reports that Macdonough and his men were heavily engaged in building a viable fleet in their winter headquarters at Vergennes where the river became non-navigable because of the falls. They were making good progress there. It seemed to Billy and others that the British and Americans were totally locked in competition to see who could build the biggest and fastest fleet first. Inevitably that would identify which side would be the aggressor. It was clear that both sides were fighting against time to mount a major campaign.

Billy was an enthusiastic and patriotic man and by this time he had willingly joined the growing Essex County militia. Brigadier General Daniel Wright, who was also the owner of Wright's Tavern in Essex, commanded the 40th Brigade of the New York State Militia. Lieutenant Colonel Ransom Noble, also of Essex, led the 37th Regiment of Infantry under the 40th Brigade. The Regiment was made up of ten companies from Chesterfield, Willsborough, Essex, Elizabethtown, Westport and Lewis. Within each Regiment there were several Companies. Billy served as a Private in Captain Abraham Aiken's Company Three.[173]

Sensing their tremendous vulnerability and exposure, especially along the shores of The Point, the men of Willsborough began to devise plans for the safety of their families, their livestock, and their land. Billy and Orrin were earnestly planning for what lay ahead. Through his training as a militiaman, Billy knew that he might be called up on a moment's notice, so he carefully reviewed with Orrin every aspect of the farming operation that he might have to manage in the months to come. He was confident that he would be leaving his property in good hands, should the need arise. He was also heartened by the knowledge that Rhoda, and their eldest son had formed a very tight bond over the years, and he was certain that Orrin would look out for her and four children.

As portents of war became stronger and stronger Rhoda, like most wives, became increasingly terrified for her husband, her 16-year-old son and the rest of her family. She briefly contemplated gathering up her brood and heading across the lake to her family in Vermont but thought better of it. After all, word had it that Vermont and Shelburne were probably just as vulnerable as her side of the lake. In any event, she could not bear to leave her home—the home that they had created together. Billy tried to reassure his wife that he would always do his best to care for and protect her and the children.

Upon receiving increasingly upsetting news about the probability of an invasion from the north, General Wright put the Essex County Militia on alert while he tracked the ongoing movements of the British. Billy's Captain, Abraham Aiken, brought his men together, informed them of the impending danger and told them to make ready to leave their homes and families on a moment's notice.

The lake had thawed by the end of April 1814 and the British fleet, under the command of Captain Daniel Pring, was confident that they could safely head south from Isle-aux-Noix, and then on to their destination, Otter Creek. Once there they planned to go up the creek to Vergennes, where they would capture the fleet that Macdonough was building. Captain Pring saw this as a relatively easy way to cripple the Americans and regain control of Lake Champlain. However, fate intervened, and things did not go as he had planned.

On the 10th of May, as Pring's ships passed to the east of Plattsburg, they were detected and word that the British were moving south spread like wildfire along both shores of the lake. General Wright responded to this word in all due haste and ordered his Essex County militia officers and men to assemble and prepare for action. Billy brought his family together and told them the news. Orrin assured his father that he could manage the springtime farming activities on his own, and that he would take good care of Rhoda and the children. Rhoda wept and trembled with fear as her husband gathered his things together. This was the moment that she had come to dread, and now it was here. The little family group, like all the others on The Point, gathered by the roadside and waved as friends and neighbors headed into the village to join the militia. There they would convene, receive their firearms, and await further communications from General Wright.

Meanwhile, Macdonough was keenly aware of his shipyard's vulnerability. He realized that if his fleet could maneuver down the creek to the lake, the British could certainly bring their own ships up the same waterway to his shipyard. The latter could lead to the destruction of his ships and shipyard. With all due haste, he ordered the erection of a fortified earthen battery at the mouth of the creek. He named it Fort Cassin for one of his trusted officers.[174] He equipped it with seven twelve-pounder cannons on ship's carriages that the rapidly assembling militia would aim at the British ships as they approached.[175] It might be a long shot, but Macdonough was determined that the British were not going to destroy or impound the ships that he and his men had worked so hard to construct, over a very short period of time.

Figure 17 Cannon. Philip Hall

As it turned out, instead of heading straight south to Otter Creek after passing Plattsburg, Pring decided to spend three days anchored off Providence Island, which lies a bit south of Valcour Island. He spent the time there scouring the shores for any boats that he could steal and load with stone. The amassing of these was an important part of his plan for the assault on Otter Creek.

If for some reason he was prevented from actually entering and sailing up the creek, he planned to jettison the boats and stone at the mouth of the creek, thereby blocking Macdonough from getting his newly constructed fleet out into Lake Champlain. After he had gathered what he deemed to be a suitable number of boats and stone, he sailed south with his fleet.[176]

As they passed by the home of Charles McNeil, the owner of the Essex to Charlotte ferry, the captain of one of Pring's boats, who was very drunk, broke away from the other ships in his own vessel. As he approached land, the inebriated captain shouted to McNeil that he was going to open fire on them without giving any further explanation. The terrified McNeil family had no place to hide on such short notice, so all that they could do was drop to the ground as the captain fired round after round. Fortunately, since he was so inebriated, his aim was poor, and the shots went above the cowering McNeil's and plunged into the embankment behind them. The family survived unscathed and only the horse barn had been harmed. Needless to say, when the captain rejoined his group of ships, Pring, noting the man's drunken state, inquired as to why he had left the fleet. In order to excuse his murderous behavior, the man claimed that he had seen soldiers in uniform up on the embankment behind the house, and felt it was his duty to fire on them. Pring was not taken in by this fantasy since the man had no evidence to prove his story.[177]

While the British fleet continued southward, Billy and his comrades were following orders to move rapidly along the western shore of the lake and assume a firing position on the cliffs directly opposite Fort Cassin. At the same time the British fleet converged near Split Rock Mountain for the night of the 13th, dropped anchor and prepared for the invasion of Otter Creek the next morning. This delay gave the militia sufficient time to get into position for the inevitable events that lay ahead. In the early hours of May 14th Pring moved his ships across the narrows between Split Rock and Thompson's Point in order to get into position to head south to Fort Cassin. Much to their surprise local farmers, who had responded to the militia alert, fired on them. Many of them were Revolutionary War veterans, and they took aim at the British with their old muskets. However, once the British fired a salvo the old guys decided it was time to withdraw and were not seen again.[178]

Continuing on their way south, the British approached the mouth of Otter Creek and began firing rounds. Much to their consternation, rounds from the cannons that Macdonough had placed there fired back at them. Meanwhile, Billy and his Company were lined up along the shores in position on the western flank near Westport. While watching the drama unfold before them, they were at the ready to fire on the British upon command. They and the Americans at Fort Cassin were determined not to give the British the opportunity to be successful in this campaign. Pring found himself receiving fire from the west and from the south. The British were never even able to get close enough to the creek's mouth to sink their rock-filled boats. They were caught in a virtual logjam. After nearly two hours the engagement had done little damage to either Pring's ships or the earthen battery at the mouth of Otter Creek. Pring wisely decided this was a futile engagement, withdrew his ships and headed back north.

As Billy and the other men in Abraham Aiken's company, as well as others in Colonel Ransom Noble's 37th Regiment of Infantry, turned to make their way back north, they could not help chuckling in disbelief over what they had witnessed at the debacle at Fort Cassin. As they marched along the lakeshore, Aiken had seen that Pring was sending part of his fleet up each side of the lake. He was certain that Commander Pring was among the ships that were taking the western route, and that he was planning to stop in Essex to pick off the sloop hulls that he had been informed were being built there. Billy's captain, Abraham Aiken, brought his men back to reality when he informed them that there was still business to be dealt with in Essex.

Essex was prepared for this possibility. A few days earlier, when news of Pring's activities reached the shipbuilders in Essex, they decided that it would be prudent to remove the hulls that they had on the ways. They floated them south to the bay at Barn Rock Point Mountain where they covered them with boughs to disguise their presence.[179] It is curious that Pring had not seen that there were no boats in the shipyard, as they sailed toward Split Rock. Perhaps they were just too focused on the mission that lay ahead.

As the British stood off the Village of Essex, they aimed their guns directly west to protect their commander as he came into the harbor in a galley. When Pring got close to land he noted that General Henry H. Ross was on the shore waiting to receive him. Pring asked him if he would like a truce to which Ross simply signaled him to come ashore. When the British commander saw that there were no boats in the shipyard, he asked about their whereabouts. Ross cleverly responded that they were in Whitehall which, of course, was far from the truth. At first the frustrated and angry commander told his crew to destroy the spars for the boats that were still lying by the water's edge but, for some reason, then decided it was not worth the time and effort. On that note, his ships continued on their northward progression.[180]

In hopes that he could claim that he had accomplished at least something of note when he returned to Canada, Pring saw Willsborough as an easy target. He had been informed that the American government had stored flour at the gristmill there with the intention of having it available to the militia and navy, when needed.[181] Since his own flour and other stores were running low, Pring thought that this would be an excellent source of replenishment. Once this mission was accomplished, he reasoned that they would simply set sail and head back north to Isle-aux-Noix. But not so!

As they approached their target, he ordered his ships to stand off the mouth of the Boquet River. There he launched three row galleys. He was so confident that his mission would be successful that he chose to remain with his ships while several of his galleys went up the river. He had been informed that William D. Ross had a small sloop at the mouth of the river, which he fully intended to capture and add to his own fleet. However, just as in Essex, the sloop was nowhere to be seen. It, too, had been moved, and temporarily harbored with the others at Barn Rock Point Mountain. Having failed at this, the disgusted captain sent some of his men ashore to plunder the property of Aaron Fairchild who lived at the mouth of the river.[182]

What Pring did not know was that Colonel Ransom Noble had already anticipated that the next foray for the British might well be to steal the flour, and other stores, that were in the gristmill at the falls. He had ordered Abraham Aiken's Company to proceed directly to Willsborough and sent militiaman Jonathan Lynde to alert the citizens of the town to the impending attack.[183] This was a shock to Billy and his comrades who had believed that they were mustered out until called up again. This change happened so rapidly that, technically, the militia was not even mustered back into the

United States Service. In this case the men in the militia might never receive compensation for their efforts. However, none of the men in Billy's group stopped to think about that. Their loyalty to their young country was fierce and, no matter what, they were eager to defend her, when called upon.

Brigadier General Daniel Wright wrote a letter to Governor Daniel D. Tompkins on May 15, 1814, stating that"...at about three o'clock three of the enemy's row galleys passed up the river Boquet and landed at the falls, where they demanded the public property (which had timely been conveyed to a distance) and when they learned that the Militia were in force a few miles distant and were on the march to intercept their retreat, they precipitously embarked in their boats and made for the lake."[184] By the time the galleys approached the mouth of the river Lieutenant Noble's militia was assembled on the banks of the river and waiting for their prey. The skirmish was quick and decisive. The overwhelmed galley crews rowed fast and furiously as they desperately retreated toward Pring's awaiting ships.

Pring and his men were completely taken aback by what was happening before their eyes. It seemed that out of nowhere swarms of armed men appeared at the river's mouth and began to fire. It all happened so quickly that Pring and his men in the ships had little time to aim and return fire. In his letter to Governor Tompkins, General Wright went on to say that due to the militia's fire from the banks of the Boquet one of the galleys was "so disabled as to oblige them to hoist a flag of distress when a sloop came to their assistance and towed her off".[185] As soon as they could hoist their sails, a further humiliated Pring and his crew headed north, following yet another failed mission.

Although Billy came through the skirmish unscathed, his good friend and fellow militiaman, Job Stafford, was less fortunate. He was hit by one of the few three-pound cannon balls that the British fired. As it struck the sand ahead of him, he jumped aside to get of out of the line of fire. Unfortunately, the cannon ball hit a stump, glanced off it, and struck him before he could jump aside again. As a result, he lost the calf of one leg.[186] Billy and the other nearby militiamen, rushed to his aid, and lifted him out of the line of fire. Once they had him where he was out of harm's way, several of them stripped off their shirts and hastily wrapped them around the wound in order to stanch the blood. Job was screaming in agony and begging for mercy, as they placed him on a litter and carried him off to a place where they could safely and properly tend to his wound. Thanks to their excellent and immediate care, he made a slow, but successful, recovery. However, he was never able to serve in the militia again, which caused him great distress.

With the skirmish at an end, the militia was disbanded, and Billy and his comrades were eager to return to their homes to pick up the threads of their lives. As he trudged along the road toward home, exhausted by the activities of the past four days, his thoughts swiftly turned to his home and family. It felt like he had been gone for weeks on end and not days. Just as he crossed the neck of land that led him onto The Point, Orrin came rushing toward him on horseback. He was the bearer of bad tidings and wanted Billy to know what had happened before he got to his home. The boy assured his father that no one had been physically harmed, but that they were badly frightened and had been forced by the British to give up some of their carefully put up stores. Orrin was proud that he had been able to handle the situation as well as he did, and rightly so, as Billy reassured him.

Orrin recounted the episode that had just occurred several hours before. As the British moved up the western shoreline, and away from the disastrous scene at the mouth of the Boquet River, Pring ordered his ships to stand off at the small bay that lay just before the beginning of The Point. He had several wounded men that needed to be attended to, as well as needing time to regroup before heading back toward Isle-aux-Noix—a trip that he dreaded. He was certain that a reprimand from his seniors would await him and certainly was not looking forward to this eventuality. As he came into the bay Pring noted two log houses in clearings not far from water's edge, and the well-cared-for farmland that lay behind them. He figured that these properties would be excellent to raid for some much-needed stores, in place of the flour that they had not secured in Willsborough. Pring offloaded two galleys—one to go to each homestead—and gave the crewmen strict orders to take what was useable, but not to lay a hand on people or livestock.

As Rhoda looked up from her work in her garden she was terrified by what she saw. The galleys were bearing redcoats to her shore and would soon be landing. She scooped up baby Edgar, who had been playing in the fresh earth beside her, and rushed to gather up the other children and drag them into the house, where she bolted the door tightly shut. The children had no idea of what was happening and thought it all quite exciting. Orrin had been working in the upper field and, upon sighting the boats, dropped his rake and ran down to the cabin as fast as he could. When he came to the rear of the cabin, which faced away from the lake, he peeked in a window and saw that his family was huddled together as tightly as possible. As he rounded the cabin, he saw several Redcoats pacing outside the firmly secured door. Orrin went over to greet the intruders and inquire of their business. The sailors were a rough and tumble, motley lot, but protested that they were not there to harm the family or their livestock. Instead, they were looking for flour and other stores that they were certain the Blinns would have. Orrin sensed that the best thing to do was to oblige them and, when they had taken what they wanted, the men got back into their galleys and rowed out to the waiting ships with their loot safely in hand. Pring sighed with relief as he thought to himself that, at least, something had gone in his favor!

As Billy flung open the door to his cabin, an ashen, fear-ridden wife, who was still clutching the children to her and sobbing loudly, greeted him. The children, as children are wont to do, broke loose from her grasp and rushed over to their father, clambering for him to pick them up. Orrin intervened and gathered them to him, promising that a fun game lay ahead. Meanwhile, Billy went over to his shaking wife, and gently brought her into his arms as he tried to soothe her as best he could. Then he gathered his family around him and led them in a prayer of thanksgiving that the visit of the Redcoats had not ended in tragedy, and that he had returned from his militia duty unscathed. After what seemed like hours, Rhoda pulled herself together but the scars of the event would remain with her for a very long time.

CHAPTER SEVENTEEN

WAR

The summer months following the abortive British confrontation at Fort Cassin and the other stops Capt. Pring made along the lake were uneasy times for Billy and his family as well as for everyone who lived on the western shore of Lake Champlain. In flagrant violation of the law, Billy and his fellow countrymen were continuing to smuggle goods into Canada without regard for the fact that their enemy—Great Britain—controlled Canada. Frequently, Billy would see some portion of Macdonough's fleet sail by as they patrolled the lake in an ongoing effort to suppress the rampant smuggling. On July 31, General George Izard reported to the Secretary of War that the few revenue officers there were at the border simply could not make a dent in the trafficking. He wrote, "...on the eastern side of Lake Champlain...supplies of cattle are pouring into Canada. Like herds of buffaloes they press through the forest, making paths for themselves." It is likely that the same was happening on the western side of the lake. Some smugglers had even resorted to selling naval supplies to the shipyards at Isle-aux-Noix, and there was active trade in selling ship spars to the British.[187]

The British were unrelenting in their determination to seize control of Lake Champlain and Macdonough was equally determined not to lose his. Throughout the summer of 1814, the race to build the biggest ships continued both in Vergennes and at Isle-aux-Noix.

Everyone needed time to emerge fully prepared for the battle that was now viewed as inevitable. By July, Macdonough was actively training his crews.

These were times in which Billy and Orrin tried to go about their business as if this was just another summer, but deep down they knew better. As the weeks and months wore on Macdonough's ships, as well as laden smugglers' rafts, began to pass by his cabin almost every day. Sometimes he wondered why they did not collide when they came very close to the shore. All of this activity simply intensified Billy's awareness of their somewhat perilous condition.   Rumors were flying everywhere, and it was difficult to determine fact from fiction.

Rhoda had not fully recovered from her fright in May and always seemed a bit edgy. She kept the children close beside her so that she could protect them, if the need arose. She was very dependent upon Billy and Orrin for constant reassurance and it made her loving spouse very sad to see her this way. However, the Blinns, like everyone else, bravely continued to go about their daily routines as best they could, always alert and always at the ready.

Knowing how well Orrin had kept things together in May gave Billy great confidence and a sense of security. His son was a very mature lad whose judgment and actions had proved to be sound over and over again. Orrin swelled with pride that his father had such high regard for him. Rhoda, of course, was much relieved that Orrin had not joined the militia like so many of his friends, and would be remaining at home with her. At sixteen he could have joined the other youths who had signed up for militia duty. Billy knew some who, imbued with a sense of patriotism and a thirst for action had forged their birth dates, but no one had time to worry about that.

By the end of August, in addition to their own militia and army, the British had amassed 13,000 troops, many of whom had fought in Europe and were highly experienced.[188] Plattsburg was the ultimate target of the British troops. On August 31st the first group of British soldiers crossed into New York.[189] Upon receiving news of this Gen. Benjamin Mooers and Governor Chittenden of the Vermont called out the volunteers in Clinton, Essex and Franklin Counties and about 700 militia from the three counties began the march to Plattsburg. On September 1st British Captain George Downie arrived at Ile-aux-Noix to take command from the disgraced Captain Pring.[190]

As they made the final preparations for Billy's departure, he called his family to him, and together they prayed for his safety and wellbeing. Then they gathered by the side of the road, exchanged final hugs, and waved as Orrin took Billy to Willsborough where Captain Aiken would assemble his militia once again. With heavy hearts the little Blinn family turned back toward their home. Rhoda understood that life would not be the same without Billy, but she knew that she must be strong and the family must live their lives just as he wanted them to while he was away. When Orrin reached the village with Billy, his father quickly gathered with the other militiamen as they received their orders to move north, where the fighting was sure to begin. Aiken's Company, like other Essex County units, was given a rousing sendoff of speeches, music and tears.[191] They assembled in the village and quickly began their march north.

Meanwhile, Macdonough brought his fleet into Plattsburg Bay on September 1. The latter, being an excellent strategist, had reason for choosing this site. He banked on the British sailing south, taking advantage of the north wind that prevailed this time of year. Then they would have to tack to get into the Bay and this would put the British at a distinct disadvantage. Meanwhile, Macdonough would have the advantage of engaging in close quarters—the tactic that worked best for his fleet.[192]

Figure 18 War of 1812 Ship. Philip Hall

By September 4th, Captain Aiken, his lieutenant, Azariah Flagg, and their volunteer company of independent riflemen, including Billy, were assembled north of Plattsburg on the Beekmantown Road near West

Chazy. They were quite certain that at least some of the advancing British would come their way. As they had passed various villages and hamlets along the way there, Billy was shocked by the numbers of people who were fleeing their homes and seeking shelter anywhere they could, even in the woods, cellars or beside stream embankments. They left their homes with only the clothes on their backs and a few meager treasured possessions.[193] The looks of terror on their faces were terrible to behold, and all Billy could think about was his own family back on Willsborough Point. As he witnessed these happenings, time after time he prayed that this would never happen there.

On September 5th Aiken's Company moved slightly south to Beekmantown Corners. The British did, indeed, decide to move in the direction that Aiken had foreseen but, much to the enemy's distress, Aiken's company, among others, had effectively blocked their route from Beekmantown Corners south. At midnight the Americans engaged in a brief clash with the British. Mercifully no one was harmed. On Sept. 6th, Eleazer Williams, an Indian half-breed who played an important role in various capacities at this time, wrote, "There is no corps more useful and watchful than the one under the command of Captain Aiken and Lieutenant Flagg."[194]

That same day another group of British forces continued pushing forward toward Plattsburg. They marched south steadily, with Aiken's Company moving before them to Halsey's Corners in East Beekmantown. One of Aiken's men, Saint John B. L. Skinner, recounted that Captain Leonard had finally arrived with his small cannon and "...that Leonard's first shot cut a swath through the middle of the perfectly marching column..." of the British. However, the enemy was unrelenting and Billy and his comrades began being pushed back inexorably. The British headed toward the shores of the Saranac River as they kept marching forward toward Plattsburg. Meanwhile, Aiken's Company had no choice but to keep moving south toward the same river, with the hope of at least being able to keep the British from crossing it.[195]

Once at the river the Americans were split into two groups. One group crossed the upper bridge on the west side of the Saranac River and removed all of its planks after everyone had crossed, thereby preventing the British from having an easy way to cross the river at that point. Aiken's Company headed for the sawmill on the east side of bridge over the river where they assumed sniper positions in order to protect the group who were removing the planks on that bridge under heavy fire. Both groups were successful and with the two bridges over the Saranac River out of commission the militia hoped that they could keep the British at bay. That night Gen. Mooers praised the men who had performed so valiantly during the day. However, he did note that, sadly, some militiamen had fled the scene "...thereby disgracing themselves and furnishing to their fellow-soldiers an example of all that brave men detest and abhor".[196]

While Gen. Macomb was desperately trying to complete building the American forts at Plattsburg the British kept up a steady stream of attack and took the town by storm. Once there they proceeded to destroy the courthouse, as well as a number of other structures.[197] The town was in chaos as people fled in every direction, many without any idea where they were even going. It was a tragic scene. Word of the attack spread quickly to Vermont, whereupon hundreds of men sprang into action, many of whom crossed the lake in such haste that they came with nothing more than their knapsacks. Since Plattsburg was in British hands, they had to land to the south at the mouth of the Salmon River, where General Macomb saw that they were provided with arms and ammunition.[198]

On Sept. 9th, several of Billy's comrades were nearly captured when they sneaked behind enemy lines in an attempt to get supplies from a nearby barn.[199] He was grateful that he had not been a part of this attempt and felt great relief that no lives were lost. Minor skirmishes continued each day until Sept. 11th when Billy and his group made their way back to the Saranac River. At about 9 that morning they heard the first shots from Plattsburg Bay, where Macdonough had lined up his ships to the south of the town. He had them in a position to take on the British ships as they rounded Cumberland Head. At the same time, the British who were still in control of the town began a huge bombardment, which was met with an immediate response by the militia who were lined up and ready to fight.[200]

By 10 o'clock the noise from the battle in the Bay of Plattsburg was deafening. Billy and the other militiamen were ready to move forward into the battle scene but were halted until all of the militia had gathered. When all was in readiness, they received a message that the British fleet had surrendered to Macdonough's Navy and the militia was ordered to retreat. However, the British troops, who were on land did not stop pressing forward, and so fighting continued despite the earlier, initial retreat order. Perhaps they had not yet received word of the surrender or, perhaps, they wanted to win their own battle on land. In any event, at 3 o'clock in the afternoon the American troops received definitive news of a cease-fire.[201]

Not surprisingly, the militiamen's reactions to the cease-fire were varied. In the first blush of reality some, like Billy, were greatly relieved that the conflagration was over. They were eager to leave behind the scene of carnage, devastation and destruction that had lain before them. Everywhere they looked they saw those whose lives had come to an end, many of whom had such promise for the future. Worse still were the pitiful wails of the dying, and those who were sobbing quietly as they waited for some angel of mercy to come to their rescue. As they looked down from the height of land and onto the waters of the Bay they saw two broken vessels which, for now, could not sail anywhere in amongst the pools of blood.[202] Much to the shock of Billy, and others, some of the younger members of the militia who had been eagerly awaiting another opportunity to see some action, were sorely disappointed. One of these described the scene, as "Never was anything like the disappointment expressed in every countenance. The advance was within shot, and full view of the Redoubts, and in one hour they must have been ours."[203]

After the cease-fire General Macomb gathered his militia and the Vermont volunteers, around him. He praised them for their acts of courage and bravery before saying his farewells. As he brought together Captain Aiken's men he thanked each of them and handed each man and boy a rifle as a demonstration of his appreciation. " His quartermaster probably reminded him that he would be personally accountable, and so he asked Aiken to get them back, promising at the same time to refer his commitment to Congress. [After twelve years Congress provided that each (now a man) receive a rifle inscribed with his name.]" The militia, except for Captain Abraham Aiken, was mustered out and sent home. He stayed behind to see that the various accouterments of war were disposed of. The weary men and boys began to gather together what was left of their few possessions and prepared to make the long trek home. Only the Vermonters remained for the night while they awaited transportation.[204]

Having no knowledge of the cease-fire, Rhoda sent Orrin north with clothing and provisions for her husband, as many of the wives of the militiamen had been doing. Orrin saddled up his horse, and made the trip over Willsborough Mountain to Plattsburgh, some 30 miles away. When he reached his father's encampment he was met by a mass of tired, dirty, and somewhat bedraggled men who were scurrying around—some of them quite aimlessly in their confusion. Orrin was, however, much surprised by the air of jubilation that greeted him. He asked himself what this was all about. The moment Billy saw Orrin, he rushed over to him, gave him a handshake, and then wrapped him in his arms in a big bear hug. After catching his breath, he shared the news that a truce had been signed. He quickly instructed Orrin to make the trip back to Willsborough with all due speed so he could tell the folks there what had happened. With this incredible information, Orrin leapt back on his horse, slapped the reins, and headed south.

Within what seemed like no time, Orrin rode down off the mountain and into Willsborough, sharing the remarkable news as he went along. The word spread like wildfire as house after house emptied out onto the main street. Citizens quickly mounted their horses and went forth to tell the news to those on outlying farms and in neighboring communities. The people of Willsborough now knew that it was only a matter of time until their loved ones, no matter in what condition, would be back with them. This was cause for celebration and plans began to unfold with lightning speed. Capt. Aiken and his Company had truly served their country to the utmost.

CHAPTER EIGHTEEN

LET THERE BE PEACE

Sadly, although the September 11, 1814 truce at Plattsburgh Bay had been reassuring and provided relief to those who lived in the Champlain Valley, its residents were wise enough to know that this was temporary, and they could be facing continued actions between the British and Americans. The nerves of the militiamen, including Billy, were put on edge when news got to them that the British were engaged in large-scale building at Isle-au-Noix once again. It was apparent that they had not given up and the truce had merely given them time prepare to invade Lake Champlain once again. Billy and his fellow militiamen knew that they could, and probably would, be called into action at some time in the future. However, for now they just needed time to regroup at home, if at all possible.[205]

Tavern talk was abuzz when they heard that Macdonough had gone up to Chazy Landing to retrieve a large amount of ammunition that he had been informed the British had sunk in their hasty retreat back to Canada. After success there he had crossed the lake to Isle La Motte where he raised a British sloop that was loaded with naval stores. Billy and his friends felt certain that the enemy had no thoughts of giving up so easily and was planning to return to the lake to retrieve these sunken "treasures" in the near future. They would be very disappointed when they found nothing at either place. Billy had also heard that once Macdonough had raised and repaired his ships enough so that he could move them safely. He planned to send them to Whitehall to be more permanently repaired in a safe place.[206]

Meanwhile, smuggling continued without a break, and the rafts laden with wood and potash, as well as other tradable goods, continued to pass in front of The Point on a regular basis. Revenue men were scarce and received little support from the general populous. This certainly became very evident in November, when news that a confrontation between the smugglers and revenue men had taken place. Apparently, some revenue men spied a heavily laden rowboat off Rouses Point that was heading toward the nearby Canadian border. The men suspected that it was carrying smuggled goods and gave chase, at which point the smugglers turned south and fled over 110 miles to Whitehall where they hid their booty. When the revenue men got there the boat owners and a band of local citizens gave them a severe beating. Needless to say, the revenue officers hastily withdrew, leaving the booty still in the hands of the boat owners. News of this event quickly spread to every tavern and meeting place along the lake. There was a general sense that the revenue men got what they deserved. After all, most of them, including Billy, were benefiting from the smuggling trade in some way.[207]

Upon occasion, Billy would hear a bit about affairs in Europe, but that was a place so far away that it had no meaning to him. However, all too soon, word reached the tavern that the British were still at it, but in other areas of the United States. They had invaded Maine, and, worse still, had burned the nation's capital at Washington. Some tavern patrons had heard of this man named Napoleon. They had been told that the British had defeated him. They shrugged it off saying that the struggles between the British and French in Europe were of no consequence to them. All that mattered to Billy and his fellow citizens was that they would not have to defend themselves from the British again.

Everyone basked in the aura of success and pleasure, except those who were in the regular army. Their joy was a bit more restrained since they had received no pay since the truce at the

Battle of Plattsburgh on September 11, 1814 and had been discharged without this affirmation of their service to their country. This had caused considerable bitterness among this loyal group of men who were returning to their lives feeling very unappreciated.[208]

Now that the British had been defeated once and for all—at least the citizens of Willsborough and all-around Lake Champlain hoped so—talk of their country became a prime topic. Because of America's success in trouncing the British the men were imbued with a new sense of pride and patriotic fervor. As they lifted their glasses, they proudly boasted of the greatness of their country. By God, they had defeated those dastardly British, who thought that they were so powerful that they could take over "our country". Best of all, they had forced them to turn tail, and sent them packing back to Canada to lick their wounds. With the war now officially over, when Billy and his friends gathered at the tavern they found themselves slipping back into their normal conversation about their crops, their fishing and hunting exploits, and their daily lives in general.

The reunited Blinn family rejoiced that they were together. Orrin was particularly glad that his father had returned and could help him with the very busy harvest season. Although he was proud that he had been able to manage the various farm activities in his father's absence, and to help his mother with her chores and with the little ones, it had not been easy. However, he had gotten a taste of what life would be like for him when he married, had children, and became a farmer on his own. Fortunately, he still had almost four more years before he would reach his majority and would no longer be bound out. He knew that he still had a great deal to learn and was eager to do so.

Life was very busy for Billy and Orrin, as well as for Rhoda. The days were getting shorter and shorter, and night descended earlier and earlier, yet there were still crops to be harvested and stored away for the long winter that inevitably lay ahead. Orrin and Billy were out of bed as soon as the first rays of the sun poked their heads over Vermont's Green Mountains and laid a path across the waters of the lake. On a clear day, how beautiful it was!

It seemed like a perpetual race against nature when it was time to reap the fruits of their labors. Storms of all sorts came up quickly and seemingly out of nowhere. When Orrin asked why this was the case Billy explained that it was partly because they were surrounded by mountain ranges on both sides of a large expanse of water. Just to make things more complicated, The Point was surrounded by water both to the west and east and its tip pointed directly north, where the worst storms often arose. As a result, storm systems could be brewing to the west of the Adirondack Mountains, or the east of the Green Mountains, and not be seen until they suddenly popped up. As much as Billy studied his Farmer's Almanac, he still found himself tricked by the weather all too often.

It was time to harvest the grain crops and with forethought during the previous winter Billy had made a scythe for the lad. He made a cradle that was perfectly proportioned to fit his son's hands and arms. He selected ash for the handle and the sned that held together the handle and the fingers. When the weather was a bit better, he had taken Orrin outside and showed him just how to hold his right hand on the nib and his left on the snath. Then he told his son to practice using this awkward looking implement correctly. Before long he had gotten the knack of it. He had learned to swing the cradle back on his right side and then bring it down swiftly at right angles to the stalk of grain that he imagined stood next to him. It took a bit longer before he got every aspect of the process in a proper sequence and rhythm, but then one day it all came together.

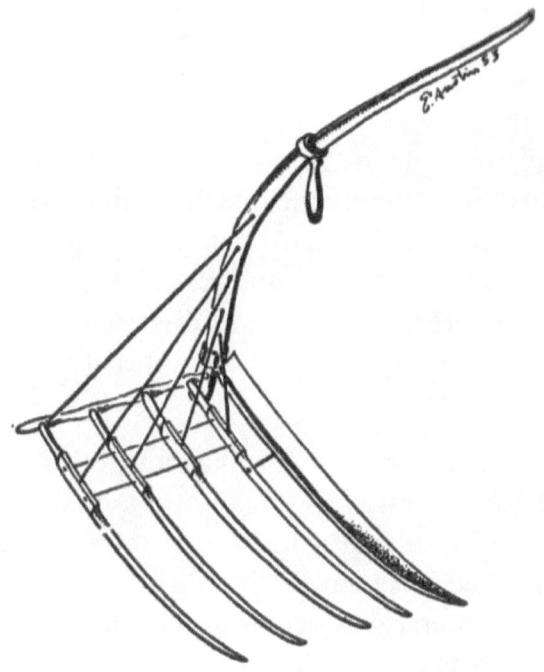

Figure 19 Grain Cradle. Erwin H. Austin

When the ripe grain began bending in the wind in the field behind the house harvest day was upon them and together Billy and Orrin set forth to cut the grain. They carried their scythes to the field and began the rhythmic process that Orrin had perfected previously. As they moved forward the grain dropped to the ground in swaths. Every so often they would cease cradling and turn to binding the swaths into sheaves that they dropped to the ground until they had time to pick them up later. At the end of each day they hitched up the mare and the cart, loaded the sheaves onto it and took them to a shed where they would be under cover.[209] During the winter they would begin the process of pulling the grain away from its stalks, but this was enough for now. There were still other things they had to take care of right away.

During the summer Rhoda's garden had done exceptionally well, and she was very busy drying her herbs, as well as preserving her fruits and vegetables. She found all of this work immensely satisfying, but her favorite of all was working with her herbs. Most of them sent forth a unique aroma and she often thought that even if she were blind, she would be able to tell them apart. Over the years she had experimented with the best way to preserve them since each seemed to have some unique characteristics. She had also tried various uses for them. Some were medicinal, and some simply made the bedding smell sweeter, or the clean clothes seem even fresher. Many of them were hung up in Orrin's loft that he now shared with Nelson and Mortimer.

Throughout 1814 all of the responsibilities of town government had continued to function in a business as usual manner and Billy, like all of the men in the town, had done their parts to ensure the safety and wellbeing of its citizens. Wolves remained a major menace to people and livestock so there was still a bounty. During the war Levi Higby's distillery continued to flourish. One of its best and steadiest customers was the government. It was customary to provide whiskey as a part of the soldier's rations since common belief was that this would keep the men satisfied and willing to accept authority from their superiors. Little regard was paid to the negative consequences of this action.[210] Likewise Willsborough Town Justice and tavern keeper, Jonathan Lynde, had a fine business selling whiskey, rum, and gin to his "guests". He also ran a distillery and regularly bought corn, hops, rye, potatoes, and apples to use for this purpose.[211] Gin was by far the most popular of his alcoholic offerings. As part of his other business he had set a regular charge of $1.25 for weddings, including supplies, lodging and a place for the horses. The schoolhouse behind the stone store had burned and been rebuilt.[212] Although initially distraught over the destruction, the Congregationalists were very happy about the outcome since the new school was a much nicer place for them to hold their worship services.[213] For all intents and purposes, things were gradually assuming their normal rhythm of life.

In the early months of 1815, news traveled across the Atlantic that on December 24, 1814 the British and Americans had signed a treaty that ended the war. The Treaty of Ghent was formally ratified by the United States on February 17, 1815.[214] The citizens of Willsborough had no interest in the terms of the treaty. What mattered was that the war was over! Needless to say, there was much general celebration!

Out on The Point Samuel Adsit's store continued to flourish. It was a vital link for those like Billy who lived removed from the village. The finances of the store were handled by barter, as was very much the custom in that day. Asa Frisby's Adsit Store account for April and May of 1815 was typical of the times. On the credit side, Asa worked with Samuel's cattle for 2 days, and his oxen for 1. Then he spent 3 days preparing to build a stone wall, and 2 days laying the stone. In return he received cash upon 3 occasions, and purchased flax seed, salt, wheat, and pork, as well as 5 gallons of gin and 1 qt. of rum in return.[215] We can see where his tastes lay when it came to spirits. Frequently one of his customers would work for Samuel and use his credit there to purchase from another store, such as those owned by Noble or Throop.

The Adsit store provided access to goods, and a means of paying for these, availability of cash upon demand, and a variety of opportunities to purchase goods Billy and others needed. It sold tobacco, sugar, flour, boots, leather, paper, tapes for shoes and boots, cotton, brandy, teapots, socks, mutton, bolts, knives, aprons, beans, wool, turnips, mittens, and plaster. The list goes on and on. Billy was grateful that it lay just up the road and was easily accessible. This greatly reduced the number of trips to the village he had to make.

Nelson was now nine and was growing into a fine young boy. He was bright and alert like his older brother and loved being out with "the men" as he called them. Billy was proud of him, and appreciated the time that Orrin spent teaching his younger brother the same skills that he had learned at that age. Mortimer, at seven, was torn between being with his mother or with his father. He loved to emulate his two other brothers and to pretend that he was as old as they. At times he attempted to perform tasks for which he was not really ready, and these often resulted in tears of frustration. Theresa, who was now five, was deeply attached to her mother and loved donning a little apron and pretending to be a mother herself. The two of them spent endless hours together chatting aimlessly about the activities of the day. Three-year-old Washington was an inquisitive toddler who liked to get into mischief if not watched carefully and his two-year-old brother, Edgar, toddled around the cabin and constantly got underfoot. Upon occasion, "Little Mother" Theresa would become exasperated with the youngsters' antics and led them to the settle where she would try to distract and amuse them by telling them stories, many of which were quite fanciful. Life in the Blinn household was very busy indeed.

CHAPTER NINETEEN

1816—A YEAR OF PAIN AND ANGUISH

As 1816 rolled in the mild winter weather seemed a bit odd but, living where he did, Billy thought it was just another no uncommon anomaly. He had seen this before and was certain that it would not last for long. In the village it was so warm that people only used their fireplaces for cooking in January. It was a bit chillier out on The Point because the temperature of the lake water was continuing to decrease, albeit slowly. The children particularly enjoyed the opportunity to play outside. The warmer weather prevailed through March, which came in like a lion with high winds and continued with occasional coldish days and some light snows. But all in all, it took on aspects of the lamb. It seemed so strange not to have any snow on the ground and no ice out on the lake. Billy and Orrin continued to ask themselves why this was happening. This was not following the usual pattern at all. The smugglers, of course, took full advantage of the situation and the seemingly endless parade of loaded rafts kept passing along the shoreline. Billy took all of this as a sign that he was going to have an early growing season. He delighted at this prospect.

In April, when the days were getting longer and temperatures should have been moving upward, they did just the opposite. This too seemed odd to Billy. He asked himself, "Why isn't it getting warmer now? I thought that I would be planting by this time. What does this mean?" However, once again he shrugged it off and chalked it up to the peculiarities of the weather along the lake. May came and Billy, like his fellow farmers, decided that he would proceed as usual. It was a bit chilly for the season, but not enough so to make him hesitate to move forward. He and Orrin did their early plowing and seeding as well as shearing their new sheep, just as they always did. Billy continued to consult his almanac frequently, as he had always done, and although it was not as accurate as usual, he shrugged it off once again.

The first few days of June were lovely and warm. They lulled everyone into a sense of complacency. Billy welcomed the new month with enthusiasm as he saw the temperature rise up to 80° on the 5th. He watched the miracle of new growth with the wonder and delight that he usually felt at this time of year, and he was humbled by the fact that the forces of nature seemed to be turning in a more positive direction. Alas, his hopes were to be dashed dramatically. He and Orrin awakened the next day to be greeted by temperatures that had plummeted overnight. They were horrified to see skim ice on the top of the animal's water buckets. After such a beautiful few days how could this be?

Worse was yet to come. The next day sleet was followed by snow and high winds. The snow drifted up to 18 to 20 inches in places. The newly shorn sheep huddled together in utter misery as they looked at Billy and Orrin with plaintive eyes.[216] One person reported that on the 6th of June, while on his way to work wearing thick woolen clothes and an overcoat, he had to lay down his tools and put on mittens. He continued on to say that on the 10th of June his wife brought in some clothes that she had spread on the ground the night before. They were frozen stiff, as in winter.[217]

Billy, Rhoda, Orrin, and the children huddled together by the fire hour after hour when they should, by all rights, have been outside working or playing. When the men had to go outside to tend to the animals they were greeted by a dismal world. The leaves on the trees had withered and turned brown. The ground had heaved up with the frost and brought with it shriveled masses of once promising vegetation. Rhoda shivered, as she looked at the garden that had looked so promising just a few days ago.

When Billy and Orrin reached their animals' shelters they were met with looks of such sadness that they found it hard not to weep in sympathy. The cows and horses huddled together in an effort to keep warm and mist came forth from their nostrils just as it did in the middle of winter, not in summer. Even the pigs looked depressed and were a bit off their feed. The fowl, which were usually so active and demanding, lay in silence and as close together as possible in the same nest area. Billy could not help thinking about how dependent these animals were upon him. It made him feel so very helpless.

Then, as quickly as the calamity had struck, it came to an end. The sun came out and cast a spell of warmth over the freezing land. With hope and renewed energy, Orrin and Billy turned back to the fields that had shown so much promise. They were certain that this time they would be successful. Their first chore was to use their plow to turn the masses of dead and dying plant life under where they could provide some nutrient to the soil. They reseeded and replanted with determination and courage as they turned to God for reassurance that the worst had passed. By the last ten days of June the tiny sprouts had emerged once again. What a blessing this was to behold!

July began just as June had, and then the cold descended once again. Orrin and Billy faced yet another disaster, as the wind swept past them bringing unwanted snowflakes with it. Billy kept thinking about his family and his livestock. How would they all be able to survive if they lost everything that sustained life for them? Meanwhile, Rhoda stood in the cold, with her shawl wrapped tightly around her, and wept as she saw those sprouts that would become beans, squash, cucumbers, and her other vegetables, succumb once again. Why was this happening? She questioned whether she had done something to offend God, but reason told her this could not be true because her friends and neighbors were suffering just as she was. The same man who had spoken of the cold on the 6th of June sadly declared, "On the fourth of July, I saw several men pitching quoits ... with thick overcoats on, and the sun shining bright at the same time. A body could not feel very patriotic in such weather."[218]

As if this were not enough, before they knew it, they had been plunged into a drought, yet it remained unseasonably cold. The grass that he and Orrin had counted on for grazing for their livestock, as well as for hay for the winter ahead, turned brown before their eyes. The corn that was so vital to the health of their animals suddenly stopped growing, and the awkward, gnarled stalks never tasseled this year. They could be chopped up and used for bedding at best. Just when all seemed lost the sun emerged from its cocoon and brought with it light and warmth. Once again, Billy and his family gathered in the village schoolhouse for prayer with their fellow community members. With fear in their hearts, and tears in their eyes, they beseeched God for mercy.

August came, and all was well until the later part of the month when cold and frost descended upon the land. For the foreseeable months ahead, every farmer would have to scratch for life. Billy heard that some families already had nothing to eat themselves or to feed to their animals. Fortunately, Billy, being a frugal man, had planned ahead and made certain that the bounty of the year before was conserved, and not used frivolously. What little remained in the cellar and the loft would have to suffice for the winter that lay ahead. He had also exercised caution when doling out the hay and grains to his livestock. He prayed the he would have enough to keep them alive, but on very short rations. He knew that his formerly healthy, well-fed horses, oxen, sheep and swine would not look corpulent when spring and new sources of food came their way. He prayed that they would survive at least. The chickens complained bitterly about their meager rations, and they let

Billy and Orrin know how dissatisfied they were by continuing to bring forth very few eggs.

Orrin and Billy were fortunate that they could turn to the nearby lake as a source of food. Although this was certainly not what they expected, at a time when they usually would have been harvesting their crops and storing them away for the winter, the abundance of fish in the lake would help to sustain life. With fishing poles in hand, they found themselves spending significant amounts of time in their little scow and they were almost always rewarded. They salted some of the fish they caught and packed them away in barrels where they would be safe from vermin, and they smoked some of the other fish and stored it in the same manner. In addition to turning to the lake for fish they looked to it for waterfowl as another source of food. With a rifle in his hand, Billy would walk down to the shore in search of the ducks and geese that were usually walking along the beach, swimming, or soaring about their heads. He had become quite a marksman as a result of his militia experience and had been teaching Orrin how to use a gun safely and responsibly. When they were successful Rhoda rewarded the family with a sumptuous feast.

On land father and son would set forth in search of deer which were in abundance in the forest. When they were successful, they had quite a feast for a few days. They also hunted small game such as hares, muskrats and squirrels. He had heard that some people were so hungry that they had resorted to eating woodchucks, opossums and raccoons. One person even shot a bear, and although greasy and strong tasting, he said that he and his family had eaten it because they had nothing else. Billy and Orrin had learned how to flush pheasant, grouse, partridge, and even wild turkeys out of the forests and bring them to earth adroitly.

Figure 20 Deer Hunt. Erwin H. Austin

Rhoda had met the challenges presented by the hunter's bounty with great skill as she sought various means of turning something unpalatable into a feast for a hungry family. She was constantly amazed by the way that the various herbs and spices that she had grown magically changed something totally unappetizing into something that was modestly edible, even if barely so. They simply made the best of it and survived on a high protein diet, since the usual stores of fruits and vegetables were very, very limited.

When the men gathered in the taverns, they puzzled over what had befallen them. Some of their friends and neighbors had had enough and simply packed up their goods and chattels and headed west to the new lands being opened up in western New York.[219] Those who held fast to their community gathered together as never before. They wanted to rail out at God, but were afraid to, so they simply attended church services more faithfully than ever. The womenfolk came together, with their children in tow, and shared recipes that would allow them to offer things that they never would have dreamed of serving in the past. This was truly frightening! They were worried beyond belief and felt utterly helpless—many of them for the first time in their lives.

At last the weather gods had expended their wrath. Winter came with weather that was much as it always was. In years past Billy and his friends and neighbors would have seen this as business as usual. Now they were only guardedly optimistic. During the winter of 1817 those who were more fortunate shared what little they had with those in need, but everyone's stores were depleting rapidly. Orrin and Billy continued to brave the elements and risk life and limb as they went out for their last days of fishing before ice formed a barrier to what lay below the surface. When they were not fishing, they were hunting in the woods, aiming their rifles toward to sky or scouring the beach for waterfowl. Normally, in December, Billy would have slaughtered a few of his hogs, but they were so thin and malnourished that the meat he would get would be meager. Anyway, he could not bear to do this when the animals were looking at him so balefully, as if pleading for help. He felt that this would be truly heartless and cruel.

As the winter continued, life for many became more and more a desperate and futile struggle. When they went into the village Billy and Rhoda dreaded hearing news of the dead and dying. Death was always around the corner, but usually it was from disease, an accident or neglect, not from starvation. The only way that many weakened men could obtain any of the provisions that they needed so badly was to go into the woods, cut down trees, and leech the wood for potash. Once it was made, they put it into barrels and transported it to William D. Ross's store where they traded it in exchange for supplies. Ross was the largest provider of potash and lumber for the Canadian market, so he was happy to have what they brought to him. However, when he ran out of provisions to offer in exchange for potash he could only give them cash in return for their goods.[220] The receipt of cash would have been helpful at another time, but it was not when what one desperately needed was goods, not funds.[221] "So close and pressing was the destitution, that the indigent, gathering from many miles about a mill, would crave the privilege of collecting its sweepings, to preserve the lives of their families."[222]

Spring came at last, and 1817 brought new hope to those on The Point and elsewhere. The weather continued to be what one normally expected. Billy and Orrin set about their usual chores with guarded optimism. Because they had no idea what had caused this massive and devastating weather change in 1816, it left them with a sense of unease. Could history repeat itself? How would even the most prudent individuals survive if this happened? [They had no idea that their disaster had been precipitated by the eruption of Mount Tambora, a volcano in Indonesia, which spewed forth huge amounts of ash. Unusual cold and lack of sunlight covered much of the northern hemisphere in 1816.][223]

At least there was warmth in the sun this spring and, as thin as his animals were, they seemed more cheerful. However, he knew that he had to make accommodations for their conditions. This was especially true with his oxen and his mare, which he relied upon completely at this time of year. Until they could get proper nourishment and begin to gain back the weight that they had lost throughout the ordeal he was aware that they would tire easily. As Billy and Orrin set about plowing, harrowing, and preparing the ground for planting they shortened the periods of work for them, giving them more periodic rests than they would have done normally. Spring planting went well, and warmer weather came a bit earlier than usual. Days were sunny, with just the right amount of rain at appropriate intervals. As in the years before 1816, the fruits of their labors began bursting through the earth. As he watched this beautiful explosion of nature, he prayed fervently that all that was before him would not suddenly wither and die, as it had the previous year. With each passing day of good weather, Billy and Orrin began to be more confident that all was well.

Even though Billy had been very prudent in his use of their meager resources throughout the fall and winter, he worried that they might not last until he could harvest his earliest plantings several months later. As spring continued the very meager stores of food continued to plague the residents of Willsborough, and beyond, until their own crops would be ready for harvesting. Wheat was in such short supply that, if it were procurable, it cost $3 a bushel and rye flour sold for $11 a barrel.[224] In past years this would have been unheard of. Billy was one of the fortunate ones who, by sheer chance, had cut out the corn kernels in 1815 and set them aside for future planting. Had God told him not to plant all of his seeds in 1816? He did not know but was grateful that he had been prudent. While many traveled as much as fifty miles to procure corn seed, he had enough for his planting, and a bit more that he could share generously with his neighbors.[225]

The clouds of doom finally lifted when summer brought with it the kind of weather that one usually expected. Yes, there could be the occasional cold snap, but it quickly lost its strength and warmth returned. Once in a while a high wind, especially from the south, was accompanied by a hard rain, but this too disappeared before it had done any serious or lasting damage. As the weeks went on the children and their parents began to lose their former gaunt features and their cheeks became rosy again. Rhoda worked in her garden while the little ones played beside her. Billy and Orrin did their daily chores and relished the warmth and sunshine that prevailed as they went about their work. The old routines were established once again. After what they had been through it seemed almost too good to be true.

Grass grew, oats sprouted, and corn stalks poked their heads through the warm soil. Haying season produced a plentiful supply of future nourishment for the livestock. The mare and team of oxen stepped forth with new energy as they happily savored the sweet, green grass that lay before them. Mother hogs lay contentedly in their wallows, surrounded by piglets that eagerly tugged at their mother's teats and cows' udders poured forth streams of rich, creamy milk.   What had often seemed like endless days of grinding work for Orrin and Billy in previous years now filled them with joy and wonder as nature's bounty surrounded them. God was surely showering his blessings upon them all!

Throughout the summer of 1817 shipping on the lake increased rapidly as boats of every kind plied the waters, both south and north and east to west. Although steam was gaining in importance, sail still prevailed as the most reliable means of shipping. Business relationships between communities across Lake Champlain flourished once again and legal commerce with Canada resumed, although at a lesser pace than before the war. In Willsborough, as in other communities, roads had fallen into serious disappear from the years of neglect. This meant that, without a safe and reliable means of travel by land, commerce and communication were difficult. As a result, those who had been assigned to highway duty took time from their farming and other responsibilities to make the necessary repairs and improvements whenever they could. In the village they constructed a true public highway that linked the bridge in Willsborough, over the mountain and onto the road to Plattsburg.[226] Out on The Point they built a better road that replaced the one that was hardly more than a mere track. It intercepted Asa Frisbie's road that came in from The Bay on the west and extended all the way out to John Crum's property at the end of The Point.[227] Communities that had been isolated were linked to one another yet again.

On August 22nd, Rhoda's women friends gathered around her and prepared her for the birth of yet another child. Even though painful, bringing a child into the world was a joyous time. One never ceased to be amazed by the beauty and holiness of birth. In due course, Rhoda delivered a baby boy and then, much to everyone's surprise, she gave birth to yet another baby. This time it was a girl. Once they had recovered from the surprise, they named the new babies Oscar and Amanda. As always, Rhoda's friends took turns lending a helping hand. One of them even provided a second cradle that she did not need, at least at the moment. All was well!

Nelson, who was eleven, and Mortimer who was now nine, were now able to help their father and Billy with some of the lighter chores. They especially delighted in following their big brother, Orrin, everywhere that he went. As soon as each meal was completed, they were out the door to see what activity was on the list for the day. Theresa, who was seven and up to then was the only girl, spent her days at her mother's side and was actually quite a big help, even though she was still quite young. Then there was five-year-old Edgar, who could never quite figure out who he wanted to be with the most—his older brothers or his sister. Since he was much smaller, keeping up with his brothers presented some special challenges. Sometimes they taunted him mercilessly, and brought him to tears, until Billy or Orrin came to the rescue and severely reprimanded them for their poor judgments and rude actions. Four-year-old Washington followed his next brother constantly and always wanted his attention. Then there were the newborn babies. It was quite a family!

Theresa, who had been surrounded by three brothers, was overjoyed to have another girl in the family but was puzzled that, in addition, there was yet another boy. She clung close to

Rhoda's side and, like so many little girls her age, she now saw herself as a little mother to the babies, especially to Amanda. She would happily watch over her, when she awakened from her slumbers, and she loved to rock her in her cradle. Theresa had even learned how to sit in just the right position to hold the babe in her arms, just as her mother did. Her help, even though mainly with Amanda, gave Rhoda the relief she needed to take care of Oscar who had proven to be a bit more fretful than his baby sister.

September rolled in, and all was well in the Blinn household. The children were happy and healthy, the harvest was going well for Billy and Orrin, and the two babies were thriving. Then one day, in the early hours of the morning before dawn, Rhoda arose from her slumbers to feed her babes. She reached into the first cradle beside her and drew Oscar gently to her breast. Without even seeming to awaken, the baby nestled up to his mother and began to savor the delicious, warm milk that was entering his mouth. When he was sated, she put him on her shoulder, patted him gently until he let forth a loud belch. Then she placed him back in his cradle to return to the Land of Nod. Next, she turned to her baby daughter's cradle.

As she reached in to pick her up, she found her lying unresponsively in her cradle. Billy was still asleep and, sobbing, she awakened him and pointed to the cradle. He leaped out of bed and quickly determined that the baby was dead. Rhoda and Billy were totally shocked by this turn of events. How could this be? Just a few hours ago the babe had little pink cheeks and beautiful blue eyes that were filled with life and happiness. As they stared down at the lifeless baby her parents clung tightly to one another and wept. Why was this happening, and with no warning? They had heard of "cradle death", but it had had little meaning to them. And now here it was.

As they began to recover from their initial shock they thought about their other children. Of course, the loss would be meaningless to Amanda's twin, but how would the other children take this news. How would they tell them that they had lost their baby sister? Would they understand that God had seen fit to reach down from Heaven and take Amanda with him? Blinded by tears they turned to cover the baby's tiny face with a bit of cloth and prayed for the courage that they would need to share this news with the children. As Rhoda clutched Amanda's twin to her bosom, she tried to find solace in Oscar's presence. At least, if God had chosen to take Amanda into His arms, she still had this baby boy to love and care for.

Word of the baby's death spread rapidly. When Orrin summoned her, Rhoda's sister, Abalena, came rushing to her younger sister's side, gathered her into her arms, and the two women wept together. Soon other women began to gather. They left Rhoda and Billy to their grief and one of them gently picked up tiny baby Oscar and caressed him lovingly. Finally, the distraught parents brought their family together and shared the dreadful news with them. Orrin, Nelson, Mortimer, Theresa, and Edgar and Washington could not begin to comprehend the tragedy that had just struck their family. That would take many months, or even years. For now, all that they could feel was numbness and a sense of deep sadness.

Meanwhile, the womenfolk, who had helped Rhoda through the birthing, quietly slipped into the role that was all-too familiar to many of them. They went about the task of bathing the baby and cladding her in the little dress in which she would be buried. After Billy and Orrin had expended their capacity to weep they hurried out to the workshop where they prepared to create a coffin for the tiny infant. At first, they worked silently, each in his own world, as they tried to understand what had just happened. Billy felt spiritually shaken and a bit abandoned by his all-powerful God. He searched his mind trying to ascertain what he could have done that cast him and his family in the Lord's disfavor. They attended church faithfully, they prayed diligently at home, and they read the Bible as best they could. He could not arrive at any easy answers to his questions and felt that his only recourse was to try to be an even better Christian in the future—whatever that might entail.

At the same time, Orrin's thoughts kept creeping back to his own father's disappearance. He had long since given up any hope of seeing his father again, but grieved that there had been no finality, no closing. If only they could have found his body. That would at least have given him the opportunity to say goodbye, even in the tomb. However, all of that had to be left to his imagination. For now, he had to keep his mind on the task at hand. He must step forward and give Billy love and support through this terrible time. Somehow, he knew that this was what God was telling him to do.

By day's end the little coffin was completed, and the women had lined it with linen cloth and laid the babe in its midst. They surrounded the body with sweet herbs and spices. These would ward off the gaseous fumes that rose from a dead body until it could be buried. With this done, Rhoda and Billy bent over the coffin, and gave their baby a final kiss. Then they silently sealed the coffin and scattered more herbs over its top. The devastated parents knelt and said a forlorn prayer together.

The next morning, as the first fingers of light came across the lake Rhoda and Billy rose to greet a beautiful late summer, cloudless day. Billy hastily dressed and Orrin joined him outside. They lifted the tiny coffin, one at each end, and gently carried it out to the waiting grave that lay beneath the beautiful old maple tree. This was where they would lay the babe to rest. The grief-stricken family huddled before the grave as friends and neighbors stood by, most of them also with tears in their eyes. As Billy and Orrin lowered the coffin into the opening before them, they prayed for God's mercy and love for the babe, and for themselves. Then each of the attendees came forward, took a bit of soil in his or her hands, and gently tossed it on top of the coffin below. Next Rhoda and Billy stepped forward and added their handfuls of soil to those of the others while the children clung to them in anguish and sought the warmth and love of their parents. Finally, Orrin and Billy took up their shovels once again and prepared to lay the babe to rest.

Men and women alike wept audibly before turning toward their own homes. As they walked along, they could not help wondering who would be next. Would it be one of them? Rhoda and Billy lingered in silence, with their arms tightly wrapped around one another. Finally, they, too, turned toward home, with the children following close behind. Now they must pull together the threads of their lives, just as so many others had had to do. It was a tragic and sad moment indeed!

CHAPTER TWENTY

LAND DEALINGS

Following the Revolutionary War, in Essex County as elsewhere, common practice was, "When an individual wished to secure a piece of land, he erected upon it a cabin, and repelled others by physical force; if unsuccessful or absent, his cabin was prostrated, and the last aggressor took possession of the coveted premises, and claimed the title."[228] On The Point there had been no aggression or arguing over who owned the land. The settlers simply believed that they had an honorable claim to the place which had once been open, uninhabited and ready for settlement.

When Samuel Adsit and John Crum took up residency on The Point in 1794 , they drew up a rough survey naming the seventeen settlers who lived there at that time.[229] In 1796 they surveyed and made a drawing for the first road on Willsborough Point.[230] It had never occurred to any of these earliest settlers on the Point that they did not have a rightful claim to the land upon which they had taken up residence. They had no idea that they were actually mere "squatters" and they would have been indignant if they had been called by such a name.

In 1801 Samuel Barney, Sr. and his sons Solomon and Samuel Jr. came from Vermont. For seven years Samuel Sr. had served in the Revolutionary War and ultimately attained the rank of Lieutenant Colonel in the Vermont Volunteer. For this, he had received a land grant from the State of New York that included most of Willsborough Point. There were already a few other families living on the same parcel of land and since there was no record of protests of actions one has to assume that they worked things out with future settlers.[231]

Subsequently, John Stroud bought 160 acres from the State of New York for the sum of $200. He had no idea that the Federal Government had already recognized certain other grants for the same land. Now both Barney and Stroud claimed that they had acquired the same parcel of land through the State of New York. It appears that they struck up some sort of peaceful deal and Stroud's son, William, went about clearing the 160 acres of land, building a home and barns planting orchards and crops on The Point. [232]

The year 1818 presented those who lived on The Point with a new and unexpected challenge—one that had nothing to do with the weather which, mercifully, continued to be seasonable. This time it had to do with land ownership. Like most of the early settlers on The Point who had come from a New England state, Billy had retained the independent spirit that was so prominent in that part of the country. In his mind, the land upon which he had settled was his land. He knew that he had no deed, or legal claim, in writing. He was confident that he had claimed it rightfully and he was not going to give it up. After all, he had spent the past twelve years there creating a homestead for himself and his family.

The status quo remained in place until 1818 when Seth Hunt, a land speculator from Keene, New Hampshire, appeared on the scene. John Montresor, the original owner of the Montresor Patent had died in debtor's prison in 1799 and, ultimately, on August 18, 1817 the ownership claim was transferred to his son, Thomas Gage Montresor. [233] Thomas, in turn, sold the entire Patent to Seth Hunt.[234] This was like Charles Kane, of Schenectady, New York, the land and business speculator who joined forces with Daniel Ross to establish the Anchor Shop in Willsborough in 1801. As a land speculator, who had just invested in a sizeable piece of property, Hunt was eager to recoup his financial investment by selling off parcels of land as quickly as possible.

Claims like Hunt's were frequent, especially when a grant, such as the June 6, 1765 Montresor Patent, had been made many years before and lain dormant for a considerable length of time. As we have seen before, all too often there were several people making competing claims for the same piece of property and none of them knew that the other claims existed. After the War of 1812, when settlement claims continued to increase, Essex County set up an association and a system for bringing some order to the situation. This "required a person desiring to occupy a lot, to perfect a survey of the premises, and to file a transcript with the secretary of the society. The title thus established was held sacred, for the purpose of that community".[235]

One day there was a knock on Billy's cabin door. Rhoda was alone with the children and, being a cautious soul when it came to someone she did not know, she peeked through a crack in the door. Seeing that it was two strangers, she sent young Nelson up to the field where Billy and Orrin were working. Billy turned the team over to Orrin, who was fully capable of working them on his own, and proceeded down the hill toward the cabin. As he approached the door, where the strangers waited patiently with their horses, Billy thought that they looked like honorable and honest gentlemen and he invited them to come into the cabin. Once they were all seated at the table in front of the fireplace he inquired as to their business.

Mr. Hunt politely introduced himself and then turned to introduce his lawyer, Noah Webster.[236] Mr. Webster reached into his leather satchel and pulled out a set of papers that he said validated Mr. Hunt's acquisition of the lands included in the Montresor Patent. He added that all of the land on The Point was part of this Patent.

When he had recovered from the shock of what he was hearing Billy asked for an explanation. He had never heard of something called the Montresor Patent. As politely as possible he requested further information. He asked, "What is a Patent? Who was Montresor? Why was all of this suddenly coming to light?" Mr. Hunt explained as much as he could. Then he turned and asked Mr. Webster to produce the papers that gave an answer to Billy's questions.

Billy's reading skills were not very good, especially when the matter before him was as lengthy as these papers appeared to be. He asked Mr. Webster to read the terms to him. As he heard the words that came tumbling forth from the reader, Billy's first response was intense shock. How could this be? It had never occurred to him that what he believed was rightfully his land, was not—at least that is what Mr. Hunt claimed. As a matter of fact, he had always looked, with some disdain, upon people he viewed as irresponsible freeloaders who were living on someone's else's land without their knowledge. He certainly had never seen himself as a "squatter".

In the end, after much continued discussion, Billy was satisfied that the man's claim was legitimate. With great hesitancy and trepidation, he inquired regarding the price that he was being asked to pay for "his" land. He knew that there was no way that he could pay for the property all at once but stated that he could pay a portion of the sum as "honor" money if Mr. Hunt would accept that. He promised to pay the remainder over time, but as quickly as he could. When they had reached a mutually satisfactory agreement, Billy consented to have "his" land surveyed before the final papers were drawn up. As the two men got up to leave, they informed Billy that he was the first person that they had come to call upon. They shook Billy's hand and thanked him for his willingness to work with them to devise a plan that was agreeable to both parties.

After Mr. Hunt and Mr. Webster departed, Billy asked himself over and over whether he should trust these men. Was Mr. Hunt simply out to swindle people into giving him money? Was there really a Montresor Patent? Billy felt very vulnerable because he could not read the documents that they presented for himself. He also wondered if Mr. Hunt would follow through on his promises. Everything seemed legitimate to him, but he still felt cautious and a bit afraid.

Later, as he related the happenings to Rhoda, he wondered why Mr. Hunt had chosen him to be the first person to call upon. Had the man heard that he was an honest and honorable man and so felt comfortable calling upon him first? He hoped that this had been the case. On the other hand, he wondered if Mr. Hunt thought that Billy would be an easy target, so he had decided to start with him? Neither of them could find answers to these questions. However, they felt that it was their duty to forewarn others on The Point. As Billy rode from house to house spreading the word, he did the best he could to explain what had occurred. His friends and neighbors had as many questions as he had, and he left them in a state of turmoil.

Mr. Hunt and Mr. Webster continued to call upon other settlers on The Point while Billy proceeded to have a survey done on the piece of property that, previously, he had thought he owned. When the survey was completed the two men returned and accompanied Billy to Elizabethtown, the Essex County seat that was commonly referred to as "Pleasant Valley" or simply "The Valley". After signing and filing the necessary paperwork the official transfer of ownership from Mr. Hunt to Billy Blinn took place on.[237] The men shook hands and headed back to Willsborough where Hunt and Webster would continue to negotiate with others. Although Billy was concerned about the financial obligation that he had taken on, he could not help feeling relieved that his claim to his property was now totally legal and he was no longer a squatter.

Although residents on The Point had been completely taken aback by the news that they were not the rightful owners of the parcel of land on which they had resided for some years, they had no way of proving that Seth Hunt's claims were not legitimate. Some, like Billy, although surprised by this chain of events, took it well and went about the business of legitimizing their claims. Some arranged payment plans, as Billy had. Others simply did not want to pay for "their" land and pulled up stakes and headed west to settle on the lands that were opening up in the western part of New York.[238]

Seth Hunt was able to sell land to Samuel Barney, but it was not on The Point. Instead, it was in the village not far from the iron shop. That took care of the Barney parcel. However, when Mr. Hunt approached William Stroud he met with an angry man. Stroud was irate that he should be asked to pay for land that he had developed over the past twenty years, especially when he had already paid the New York State government for this same parcel. Unfortunately, he could not produce any documentation that proved that he had actually bought land from the State Government. In the end he was allowed to remain on the land until he could secure another 160-acre parcel west of the village, which he did ultimately.[239]

While Billy's land acquisition was relatively simple, the land acquisitions of Jacob and Samuel Adsit, sons of the original settler Samuel Adsit the 2nd were more complex than most. Their father and his wife, Phebe Purdy, settled on the Point in 1794 and built a small log cabin on the property that they claimed. Unfortunately, Samuel died in 1796 and, within a year, Phebe married James Reynolds. James was a somewhat hapless farmer and Revolutionary War veteran who was missing fingers due to British bullets. He had lived on the edge of poverty most of his life and moved into the Adsit cabin with Phebe. When Seth Hunt came to call upon James and Phebe and demanded payment for the land that they had thought was theirs the almost destitute couple stated that they had no means of entering into such a transaction.

Phebe's sons Jacob and Samuel the 3rd worked out a way to meet their mother's monetary obligation and secure the property. They divided it into two parcels. Jacob purchased the southern parcel of 73 ½ acres, on which the cabin stood. For reasons that are not clear Isaac and Polly Jones purchased the northern portion of 89 acres. Then on June 23, 1818 they sold their parcel to Samuel Adsit the 3rd with the stipulation that Phebe and James, would be able to live on the property until Phebe died.[240] The store that Billy and others used as ready access to supplies, as well as the dock, was on Samuel's portion. The brothers felt that they had arrived at a truly unique way of solving what could have been a very difficult family problem.[241]

Aside from the land ownership issue, 1818 was a good year out on The Point, and in the area in general. With peace having been fully restored, and the year of horrors behind them, everyone had become increasingly confident of the future. Twelve families lived north of Billy's northern property line, which abutted the road that led out to Asa Frisbie's land. Fourteen families lived south of Frisbie's road and as far south as the neck of land that separated The Point from the rest of Willsborough.[242] While mindful that they were part of the larger entity- Willsborough -The Pointers began to think of The Point as their own special and unique place. In many ways theirs was a different lifestyle from the town. Everyone was a farmer and many of them took advantage of the lake for their livelihood. Some, like the Adsit's also had a place of business, but that was not the norm. The new landowners treasured the land that was now legally theirs and worked it with increasing vigor and commitment. They remained a proud bunch, just as they had always been.

Life in the Blinn family went on as usual and, remarkably, with no untoward events—no loss of a child, no failure of crops, no catastrophic storms—the list of possibilities could have gone on endlessly. With the help of Orrin and, lately, Nelson and Mortimer, Billy's farm had prospered. Together they had turned more forest into fields, each of which had proved to be remarkably productive. They had built more structures for storage of their crops and shelter for their animals, including a rather large barn that was proving to be incredibly useful as it could serve in both capacities.[243] Billy and Orrin had even talked about putting yet another, and larger, addition onto the cabin, and turning both the original cabin and the additions into a board and batten structure. With all of Theresa's willing help, Rhoda was feeling more relaxed than during the years when babies kept arriving in such rapid succession. God had been good to them indeed!

Figure 21 Billy's New Barn. Ashley Ahrent

For children growing up on The Point this was a perfect place to live. They could roam the countryside without fear, walk the beach, fish in the lake, climb a tree and, generally, have fun with one another when they were younger. When age and time of year permitted, they would file into the schoolhouse to acquire the rudiments of reading, writing and arithmetic. The older boys quickly learned that life was not all play. As soon as they were able—usually by the time that they were nine or ten—they were expected to become apprentice farmers and to learn the ways of a farming. Nelson, age twelve, and Mortimer age ten, were doing just that, as Orrin had done before them. Edgar, age six, and Washington, age five, were not too far behind. Only year-old Oscar was exempt. Girls were expected to acquire all of the skills of their mothers. As the only daughter, eight-year-old Theresa carried a heavy burden. Every day she worked side-by-side with Rhoda as they cooked meals, washed up, scrubbed clothes, worked in the garden and all of the other duties of a wife and mother. In addition, Theresa continued to be a little mother to the younger children, much to her delight.

Orrin had grown into a fine, strapping, handsome young man of twenty. His parents loved him dearly, and greatly respected him for his humility, honesty, and kind and gentle manner. They were a bit awed by his innate desire to help others in any way that he could. This was not a characteristic that one usually saw in a man his age. They saw this as one of his many gifts. He had been at their sides whenever, and however, they needed him. He was a bright young man who had proved to be an eager learner. No matter what Billy showed him how to do, he always caught on quickly and followed through just as he was told. He loved the land and continued to treasure his time with his father as they worked side by side, day after day. All in all, Orrin had all the promise of being a very successful farmer when he struck out on his own. Rhoda and Billy often stopped to wonder what their lives would have been like if he had not become part of their family. They simply could not fathom the idea.

Upon occasion Orrin would stop to reflect back upon his ten years as a member of the Blinn family. When he did so he could not help musing about what his life would have been like if his father had not disappeared, and he had grown up with his original family. He found this almost impossible to imagine. He would have grown up in the village, gone to a different school, had different friends, maybe helped at the anchor shop, who knew? Would he ever know what happened to his father? He had to accept the fact that his disappearance remained a mystery. How was his mother adapting to her life in Stillwater? Had she and her father forged a good relationship after those years when he seemed to ignore her in her time of great need? What were his siblings doing? Sometimes, when he stopped to think about them, and especially Polly, he experienced a sense of loss. Strange as it seemed, in some ways, he missed his brothers and sisters even more than his mother.

As he jerked himself back to the present he would turn his thoughts to Billy, Rhoda, and the children—the persons who comprised what he viewed as his "real" family. In some ways he saw himself as a Blinn, and not a Clark, but Billy and Rhoda had persuaded him that he must hold onto his paternal name and honor his birth mother and father in this way. Orrin sometimes wondered what his life would have been like if Billy had not come forward and offered to take him under his wing. After all, he might have wound up being bound out to a family that grudgingly accepted him into the household, solely in order to get an extra set of hands. They certainly would not have embraced him as a member of their family. He thanked God that he was where he was. He loved the Blinn family and he loved being a farmer's son. He loved being on the land, he loved spending most of his days outdoors, he loved looking across the lake toward the mountains and, most of all, he loved life. What a blessing had been bestowed upon him!

Two days after 1819 rolled in, Orrin Clark reached his majority at age 21. This meant that he would no longer be legally indentured to Billy, and he was free to go his own way to make a future for himself. Although both Orrin and his parents had always known that this moment would come, the years since Billy and Rhoda had taken him as one their children had passed like the speed of lightning—and now his majority was here. The reality simply had to be faced, and decisions had to be made.

Where will Orrin live out the rest of his life? It was his to choose. Will he remain in Willsborough? If not, where will he go? Will he remain a farmer, as he has been taught? If not, what trade will he select to be his? Will the bonds of loyalty, love and appreciation hold him within the Blinn family, or will they grow distant over time? Can he adjust to being on his own, and making his way on his own? His future was his to create. So many questions remained to be answered!

BIBLIOGRAPHY

ONLINE SOURCES

Bellis, Mary. "History of the Plow." ThoughtCo, Jul. 12, 2018.

Bidwell, Percy Wells. *Rural Economy in New England at the Beginning of the 19th Century*, vol. 20. Augustus m Kelley Pubs, 1972.

Bogan, Dallas. "Early Pioneers Lived in One-Room Log Cabins, Heated by Fireplace in Which Wood Was Cooked". *Tngenweb.Org*, 2019.

Bomberger, Bruce D. "The preservation and repair of historic log buildings." *The Preservation of Historic Architecture: The US Government's Official Guidelines for Preserving Historic Homes*: p. 285, 2004.

Buchanan, Rita. "Herb to Know: Flax". *Motherearthliving.Com*, 1995.

Crews, Ed. "Meet the Tinmen". *History.Org*, 2013.

"Embargo Act United States [1807]". *Encyclopaedia Britannica*, 2019.

Favretti, Rudy J., and Gordon P. DeWolf. "Colonial garden plants." *Arnoldia*, vol. 31, No. 4, pp. 172-255, 1971.

Fisher, Oneita. "Life in a Log Home". *The Annals of Iowa*, vol. 37, no. 7, pp. 561–573. *State Historical Society of Iowa*, 1965.

Glismann, A.H. "History of Ironing and Irons—Flat-Irons, Sad-Irons, Mangles". *Oldandinteresting.com*, 1970.

Harris, Benjamin. "The New England Primer", *Encyclopedia Britannica*.

Horton, Janice. "Out by the Roots: A New Way of Looking at the Forest. Lyme" *NH, Northern Woodlands*, issue 64, spring 2010.

James Smith, Samuel. "The New-England Primer Textbook". *Encyclopaedia Britannica*, 2013.

Kuffner, Trish. "Family Education", *Sandbox Networks, Inc*, 2018.

Le Capitaine, Shane, "A General History of Potash Processing", undated.

Letourneau, Georges and Sames, Jay. "Ash to Cash—the untold Story: Nature's Burnt Offering to 19th Century Settlers", *Les Editions Histoire Quebec and La Federation Histoire Quebec*, vol. 18, no. 3, 2013.

Levins, Sandy, "A Return to the 18th Century. The Herb Garden Then and Now. Plant Life in an 18th Century Mansion." *Historic Camden County*, undated.

Mauro, D. Elizabeth, "The Congregational Christian Tradition, The Art and Practice of the Congregational Way". *Congregational Library and Archives, History Matters.* National Association of Congregational Christian Churches, 2013-2019.

Marrieta, Ellis. "19th Century Soap Making—Its History and Techniques". *Spadét*, 2017.

McAlester, Virginia, and McAlester, Lee, "A Field Guide to American Houses". *National Park Service.*

Nix, Steve, "Identification of the Most Common Hardwoods, a Guide for North American Hardwood Tree Identification". *ThoughtCo*, 2019.

Oplinger, E. S., and Oelke E.S., "Alternative Field Crops Manual". *University of Wisconsin Extension, Cooperative Extension and University of Minnesota, Center for Alternative Plant and Animal Products and Minnesota Extension Service,*

Page, Tom, "The Basics of Planting, Growing, Storing Potatoes". *Peak Prosperity*, 2013.

Ray, Michael, "Embargo Act, United States [1807]", *Encyclopedia Britannica*, 2019.

Riley, M. E., "Clothing of the Ancient Celts", 1997.

State Historical Society of Iowa, "Life in a Log Home—Building a log cabin", *Annals of Iowa*, vol. 37, no 8 (spring 1965).

Sturloson, Thordur. "History of Herbal Medicine", *The Herbal Resource*, 2014.

U.S. Department of Agriculture Forest Service, "Building with Logs". Washington, D.C., 1944.

Washington, D.C. National Park Service, U.S. Department of Interior. "Teaching with Historic Places Lesson Plans, Log Cabins in America, The Finnish Experience", 2016.

Walton, Geri. "Health Remedies, Preventatives, and Cures in the 1700 and 1800s", *Unique Histories from the 18th and 19th Centuries*, 2014.

Weslager C. A., "The Log Cabin in America: From Pioneer Days to the Present", 1969.

White Flower Farm. "Growing Potatoes", *Litchfield CT*, 2019.

Woodman, "Growing Your Own Potatoes. The basics of planting, growing and storing and potatoes". *Growing Your Garden.*

BOOKS

Belden Noble Memorial Library. *Essex New York, An Early History*, Queen City Printers. 2003.

Bellico, Russell P., *Chronicles of Lake Champlain, Journeys in War and Peace*, Fleischmanns, New York, Purples Mountain Press, 1999.

Bellico, Russell P., *Sails and Steam in the Mountains, A Maritime and Military History of Lake Champlain and Lake George*, Purple Mountain Press, Fleischmanns, New York, 1992.

Bidwell, Percy Wells, *Rural Economy in New England at the Beginning of the Nineteenth Century*, London, England, ForgottenBooks.com, 2015.

Christen, Richard S. and Jenkins, John, *The Art of Writing "Handwriting and Identity in the Early American Republic"*, University of Portland Pilot Scholars, Education Faculty Publications and Presentations, School of Education, Portland, Oregon, 2012.

Everest, Allan S., *The War of 1812 in the Champlain Valley*, Syracuse University Press, 1981.

Glenn, Morris F., *The Story of Three Towns*, Westport, Essex and Willsboro, New York, 1977

Hill, Ralph Nading, *Lake Champlain Key to Liberty*, The Countryman Press, Woodstock VT, 1976.

Hill, Ralph Nading, *Yankee Kingdom, Vermont & New Hampshire*, A regions of America Book, Illustrations by George Daly, Harper & Brothers, New York,1960.

Johnson, Clifton, *The Country School in New England*, D. Appleton and Company, New York, 1893.

Johnson, Clifton. *Old-Time Schools and School Books*, The MacMillan Company, New York. 1904.

Klyza, Christopher McGrory and Trombulak, Stephen C., *The Story of Vermont: A Natural and Cultural History*, University Press of New England, Jan. 6, 2015.

Noble, Henry Harmon, *A Sketch of the History of the Town of Essex, New York, with some account of the Mother Town, Willsboro*, Champlain, privately printed, 1940.

Noble, Henry Harmon, *The Battle of the Boquet River,* Reprinted from the Twentieth Annual Report of the American Scenic and Historic Preservation Society, Appendix D J. B. Lyon Company, Printers, Albany, New York, 1915.

Sherman, Gordon C. and Elsie L., *An Illuminating History of the Champlain Valley and Adirondack Mountains, Nine Hundred and Twenty-Nine Years of History*, Volume II, Denton Publications, Inc. Elizabethtown, NY 1977

Shurtleff, Harold R., Samuel Eliot Morison (Editor) *The Log Cabin Myth, A Study of the Early Dwellings of the English Colonists in North America,* Cambridge, Massachusetts, Harvard University Press, 1939

Sloane, Eric. *A Museum of Early American Tools*, American Museum of Natural History, Special Member's Edition, Ballantine Books, New York, 1964

Sloane, Eric. *Diary of an Early American Boy, Noah Blake 1805*, Wilfred Funk, Inc. New York. 1962.

Sloane, Eric. *The Seasons of America's Past*, Wilfred Funk, Inc. New York, 1958

Sloan, Eric. *The Second Barrel*. Funk & Wagnalls, New York. 1969.

Smith, H.P. (editor), *History of Essex County, with Illustrations and Biographical Sketches of Some of its Prominent Men and Pioneers*, D. Mason & Co, Publishers, Syracuse, NY 1885.

Van Wagenen, Jr., Jared. *The Golden Age of Homespun*, Cornell University Press, Ithaca, New York. 1953.

Watson, Winslow C., *The Military and Civil History of the County of Essex, New York and a General Survey Of Its Physical Geography, Its Mines And Minerals, And Industrial Pursuits, Embracing An Account of the Northern Wilderness And Also The Military Annals Of The Fortresses Of Crown Point And Ticonderoga*, J. Munsell, State Street, Albany, NY, 1869

OTHER SOURCES

Adsit, Samuel, "Store Account Book 1811-1836", *Clark Collection*, New York State Library, Albany, New York.

Ancestry.com

Bruno, Ronald [Historian], "Occasional Papers of the Willsboro Heritage Society", Vol. 4, No. 1. Undated.

Bruno, Ronald, "Oral History", Town of Willsborough, Historian

Crum, William [Pathmaster], "Citizens of the Fifth District", May 25, 1796

Clark, Solomon, Orrin Clark and the Bear Cub, Plattsburgh, New York, Plattsburgh Sentinel, March 12, 1880. (Willsboro Heritage Society Collection, Willsboro, NY.)

"Site or Native Boulder and Bronze Tablet Located Near Mouth of Bouquet River", *Elizabethtown Post and Gazette,* June 11, 1914.

"Property conveyed from Seth Hunt to Billy Blinn, May 21, 1818 and recorded Sept. 27, 1842.", *Deed Book V*, p. 169.

"Organizational Diagram of 37th Regiment NYS Militia", *Willsboro Heritage Society Collection*

Plattsburgh Sentinel [Magazine], Plattsburgh, New, York, March 12, 1880

Smith, Milford Hale, "Genealogy of the Adsit Family, 1716-1923", self-published, 1923.

"Stroud Family History", *Willsboro Heritage Society*, 1929.

Tefft, Tim "The 1812 Homestead, Local History, Site History, & Local Statistics". *Educational Foundation,* 1997.

"Town of Willsborough Records 1809, 1810, 1811, 1812, 1813, 1814, 1815, 1816, 1817, and 1818", stored at *Willsboro Heritage Society*.

U.S. Government, *Federal Census*, 1810.

NOTES

1 H.P. Smith (editor), History of Essex County, (Syracuse, New York. D. Mason & Co. Publishers, 1885), 441.

2 Winslow C. Watson, *The Military and Civil History of the County of Essex, New York,* (Albany, New York, J. Munsell, 1869), 121.

3 Ibid., 120.

4 Ibid., 121.

5 Ibid., 31.

6 H. Nicholas Muller III, *Oral History,* June 2019.

7 Watson, *The History,* 123.

8 Ibid., 123.

9 Ibid., 441.

10 Henry Harmon Noble, *A Sketch of the History of the Town of Essex, New York, with some account of the Mother Town, Willsboro,* (Champlain, privately printed, 1940), 5.

11 Ronald Bruno, *Oral History,* Town of Willsboro, NY.

12 Ibid. 2016.

13 *Ancestry.com.*

14 *Ancestry.com.*

15 *U.S. Federal Census,* Shelburne, Vermont, 1790.

16 Dallas Bogan, *Early Pioneers Lived in One-Room Log Cabins, Heated by Fireplace in Which Wood was Cooked,* (Campbell County, Tennessee, THGenWebHost, Copyright 2004, Last modified on 4/28/2019).

17 State Historical Society of Iowa. *Building a log cabin,* (Des Moines, Iowa, Originally published in the Annals of Iowa, Vol. 37, No 8, Spring, 1965.

18 Lyle F. Watts, Chief, U.S. Dept. of Agriculture, Forest Services, *Building with Logs,* (Washington, D.C., 1944) Structures Report, by Clyde P. Fickes and W. Willis Gordon), 2.

19 Eric Sloane, *Diary of an Early American, Noah Blake 1875,* (New York, Wilfred Funk, Inc., 1962), 58.

[22] Eric Sloan, *Diary of*, 47.

[21] Lyle F. Watts, *Building with*, 3.

[22] Ibid., 5.

[23] Ibid., 34.

[24] Ibid., 12.

[25] Ibid., 12.

[26] *C. A.* Weslager, *The Log Cabin in America: From Pioneer Days to the Present* (New Brunswick, N.J., Rutgers University Press, 1969); Virginia and Lee McAlester, A Field Guide to American Houses (New York: Alfred A. Knopf, 1984); National Park Service, Reading 1.

[27] Lyle F. Watts, *Building with Logs*, 12.

[28] Ibid., 25.

[29] Ibid., 23.

[30] Ibid., 3.

[31] Ibid., 15.

[32] Ibid., 19.

[33] Ibid., 28-29.

[34] Ibid., 27.

[35] Dallas Bogan, *Early Pioneers*, 1.

[36] *Town of Willsborough Records, 1806.* (Willsboro Heritage Society, Willsboro, NY.)

[37] *Ancestry.com.*

[38] *Ancestry.com.*

[39] Jared Van Wagenen, Jr., *The Golden Age of Homespun*, (Ithaca, New York, Cornell University Press, 1953), 41.

[40] Ibid., 42.

[41] A. H. Glissman, *The Evolution of the Sad-Iron,* (Published by author,1970), 22.

[42] Winslow C. Watson, *The Military*, 540.

[43] Belden Noble Memorial Library, *Essex New York An Early History*, (Burlington, Vermont, Queen City Printers, 2003),12.

[44] Bruce D Bomberger, *The Preservation and Repair of Historic Log Buildings,* (Washington, D.C., U. S. Dept. of Interior Cultural resources, Preservation Assistance, Preservation Briefs 26, 6.

[45] Eric Sloane, *A Museum of Early American Tools*, (New York, Ballantine Books, 1964), 12,13.

[46] Jared Van Wagenen Jr., *Golden Years*, 29,30.

[47] Eric Sloane, *A Museum*, 16,17

[48] Ibid., 18, 19

[49] Ibid., 86, 87.

[50] The Colonial Williamsburg Foundation. US.

[51] Ibid., 39.

[52] Ibid., 39.

[53] Eric Sloane, *The Seasons of America's Past*, (New York, Wilfred Funk, Inc.,1958), 36.

[54] Eric Sloane, *A Museum*, 72.

[55] Eric Sloane, *The Seasons,* 36.

[56] Ibid., 38.

[57] Ibid., 40.

[58] Ibid., 46, 47.

[59] Janice Horton, *Out by the Roots*, (Lyme, New Hampshire, Northern Woodlands, Spring 2010).

[60] Percy Wells Bidwell, *Rural Economy in New England at the Beginning of the Nineteenth Century*, (London, England, ForgottenBooks.com. 2015), 330.

[61] Eric Sloane, *The Seasons*, 45.

[62] Mary Bellis, *History of the Plow*, (ThoughtCo, 2018).

[63] Percy Wells Bidwell, *Rural Economy*, 322-325.

[64] Tom Page, *Growing Your Own Potatoes. The basics of planting, growing and storing and potatoes. Growing Potatoes in Your Garden,* (March 19, 2013).

[65] Steve Nix. Identification of the most common hardwoods. Thoughtco.com (May 30, 2019)

[66] Ibid.

[67] Marietta Ellis, *19th Century Soap Making—Its History and Techniques,* (The Soap Factory, June 12, 2017).

[68] Ibid.

[69] Eric Sloane, *The Seasons*, 107.

[70] Eric Sloane, *The Seasons*, 51.

[71] Ibid., 63.

[72] Ibid., 63.

[73] Thordur Sturloson, *History of Herbal Medicine*, (The Herbal Resource, Jan. 30, 2014).

[74] Sandy Levins, *A Return to the 18th Century. The Herb Garden Then and Now*. Plant Life in an 18th Century Mansion. Historic Camden County, New Jersey.

[75] Rudy Favretti. 1971. Colonial Gardens. Arnoldia Arboretum pp145-171. p147

[76] E.S. Oplinger, E.A. Oelke, M.A. Brinkman and K.A. Kelling. Buckwheat. Alternative Field Crops Manual.
E.S. Oplinger, *Alternative Crops Manual*, (University of Wisconsin Extension: Cooperative Extension, 1989).

[77] -M. E. Riley. 1997. "Dyes & Dyeing" Clothing of the Ancient Celts

[78] Eric Sloane, *The Seasons*, 63.

[79] Ibid., 63.

[80] *Plattsburgh Sentinel*, March 12, 1880. (Story related by Solomon Clark, Willsboro Heritage Society, Willsboro, NY).

[81] Ibid., 68.

[82] Ibid., 93.

[83] Ibid., 68.

[84] Eric Sloane, *The Second Barrel*, (New York, Funk & Wagnalls, 1969), 69.

[85] Rita Buchanan. Herb to Know: Flax. For beauty, nutrition and flavor, this tenacious plant is hard to beat. motherearhliving.com June/July 1995

[86] *The Congregational Christian Tradition*, (Boston, MA, Congregational Library and Archives, History Matters, The Congregational Christian Tradition, 2013-2019).

[87] Ibid., 1.

[88] Ibid., 1.

[89] Ibid., 1.

[90] Ibid., 2.

[91] Rev. Dr. D Elizabeth Mauro, Dean, *The Art and Practice of the Congregational Way, A Church Guide Undated Center for Congregational Leadership*, (Olivet, MI., National Association of Congregational Christian Churches, 2014), 16.

[92] Ibid., 22.

[93] Ibid., 14.

[94] Ibid., 11,12.

[95] Ibid., 41,42.

[96] Ibid., 17.

[97] Eric Sloane, *Diary of,* 20.

[98] Ronald Bruno, *Oral History*, 2015.

[99] Clifton Johnson, *The Country School in New England*, (New York, D. Appleton and Company, 1893), 3.

[100] Ibid., 12.

[101] Trish Kuffner, *Family Education*, (Sandbox Networks, Inc, 2018).

[102] Clifton Johnson, *The Country*, 6.

[103] Ibid. 9

[104] Richard S.Christen, John Jenkins, *The Art of Writing "Handwriting and Identity in the Early American Republic"*, (Portland, Oregon, University of Portland Pilot Scholars, Education Faculty Publications and Presentations, School of Education, 2012). 491.

[105] Ibid., 492.

[106] Clifton Johnson, *The Country*, 8.

[107] Clifton Johnson, *Old-Time Schools and School Books*, (New York, The MacMillan Company, 1904), 114.

[108] Clifton Johnson, *The Country*, 11.

[109] Benjamin Harris, *A History of its Origin and Development, 1897,* Encyclopedia Britannica.

[110] Ibid., 20.

[111] Ibid., 16.

[112] Ibid., 26—29.

[113] Michael Ray, Associate Editor and Encyclopedia Britannica Editors, *Embargo Act, United States (1807)*, Encyclopedia Britannica, 2019.

[114] Létourneau, G. & Sames, J. (2013). Ash to Cash—The Untold Story: Nature's Burnt Offering to 19th Century Settlers. Histoire Québec, 18, (3), 25–30.

[115] Shane Le Capitaine, A General History of Potash Processing, undated.

[116] Winslow Watson, *The Military*, 446.

[117] Ralph Nading Hill, *Lake Champlain*, 16.

[118] Ibid., 170.

[119] *Town of Willsborough Records, 1809.* Willsboro Heritage Society, Willsboro, NY.

[120] Ibid., 1809.

[121] Winslow Watson, *The Military*, 449.

[122] *Town of Willsborough Records, 1810.* Willsboro Heritage Society, Willsboro, NY.

[123] Ibid.

[124] Ibid.,1809.

[125] Ibid.,1809.

[126] H.P. Smith (editor), *History of Essex County*, 449.

[127] *U.S. Federal Census*, Essex County, 1810.

[128] *U. S. Federal Census,* Essex County, NY, 1810.

[129] Winslow Watson, *The Military,* 449.

[130] Winslow Watson, *The Military,* 451.

[131] Ibid., 449.

[132] Samuel Adsit, *Store Account Book 1811-1836.*

[133] Ancestry.com.

[134] *Town of Willsborough Records 1812,* Willsboro Heritage Society, Willsboro, NY.

[135] Ibid.

[136] Ibid.

[137] H. Nicholas Muller III, *Oral History*, June 2019

[138] Ralph Nading Hill, Lake Champlain, 163.

[139] Ibid., 164.

[140] Ibid., 163.

[141] Ibid., 39.

[142] Ibid., 170.

[143] Ibid., 163.

[144] Ibid., 164.

[145] Ralph Nading Hill, Lake Champlain, 170.

[146] Ibid., 165.

[147] Ibid.

[148] Ibid.

[149] Russell P. Bellico, *Sails and Steam in the Mountains,* (Fleischmann's NY12430, Purple Mountain Press Ltd., 1992), 205.

[150] *U.S. Federal Census 1810,* Essex County, New York

[151] Ralph Nading Hill, *Lake Champlain,* 4.

[152] Ibid., 42.

[153] Allan S. Everest, *The War,* 32.

[154] Russell P. Bellico, *Chronicles,* 206.

[155] Allan Everest, *The War,* 59.

156 Russell P. Bellico, *Chronicles,* 207.

157 Ibid.

158 Allan s. Everest, *The War, 93*

159 Ibid., 93.

160 Ibid., 95.

161 *Town of Willsborough Records, 1813,* Willsboro Heritage Society, Willsboro, NY.

162 Ronald Bruno, *Oral History,* 2018.

163 H.P. Smith, *History of,* 447.

164 Everest, The War, 110.

165 Allan S. Everest, The War, 110.

166 H. Nicholas Muller III, *Oral History*, June 2019.

167 Ralph Nading Hill, Lake Champlain, 172.

168 Allan S. Everest, *The War,* 116-117.

169 Ibid., 118.

170 Ibid., 118.

171 Ibid., 118.

172 *Town of Willsboro Records 1814,* Willsboro Heritage Society, Willsboro, NY.

173 *Organizational Diagram of 37th Regiment NYS Militia,* Willsboro Heritage Society Collection.

174 Allan S. Everest, *The War,* 149.

175 Ralph Nading Hill, *Lake Champlain*, 178.

176 Morris Glenn, *The Story*, 16.

177 Ralph Nading Hill, *Lake Champlain*, 178.

178 *Plattsburg Sentinel*, Feb. 9, 1894.

179 H. P. Smith, *History of.* 547.

180 Ibid., 547.

181 Russell P. Bellico, *Sails and Steam*, 216.

182 Henry Harmon Noble, *The Battle of the Boquet River,* (Albany, J. B. Lyon company, Printers, 1915) Reprinted from the Twentieth Annual Report of the American Scenic and Historic Preservation Society, Appendix D. 591.

183 *Elizabethtown Post and Gazette, June 11, 1914.*

184 Henry Harmon Noble, *The Battle,* 592.

185 Russell P. Bellico, *Sails and Steam*, 218.

186 Henry Harmon Noble, *The Battle,* 593.

187 Russell P. Bellico, *Sails and Steam*, 219.

[188] Russell P. Bellico, *Sails and Steam*, 219.

[189] Ibid., 121

[190] Allan S. Everest, *The War*, 162

[191] Ibid., 163

[192] Ibid., 166.

[193] Ibid., 79.

[194] Ibid.,170.

[195] Ibid.,173.

[196] Ibid.,175.

[197] Ibid.,176.

[198] Ibid.,177.

[199] Ibid.,185.

[200] Ibid.,187.

[201] Ibid.,187.

[202] Ibid.,190.

[203] Ibid.,186.

[204] Ibid.,190.

[205] Allan S. Everest, The *War*, 193.

[206] Ibid.,193.

[207] Ibid., 193.

[208] Ibid., 201.

[209] Eric Sloane, *The Seasons*, 70

[210] Morris Glenn, *The Story*, 285.

[211] Ibid., 289.

[212] Ronald Bruno, *Oral History,* 2016.

[213] Ibid.

[214] Russell P. Bellico, The Treaty, 317

[215] Samuel Adsit, *Store Account Book.*

[216] Morris Glenn, *The Story,* 215.

[217] Eric Sloan, *Seasons of America*, 30.

[218] Ibid., 30.

[219] Morris Glenn, *The Story*, 215.

[220] Winslow C. Watson, *The Military*, 210.

[221] H.P. Smith, *History of Essex*, 447.

[222] Winslow C. Watson, *The Military*, 210.

[223] Robert Evans. Blast from the Past. Smithsonian Magazine. July 2002

[224] H.P. Smith, *History of Essex*, 447.

[225] Winslow C. Watson, *The Military,* 210.

[226] Ibid.

[227] *Town of Willsborough,* 1817.

[228] Winslow C. Watson, *The Military,* 209.

[229] William Crum, Pathmaster, *Citizens of the Fifth District,* May 25, 1796.

[230] Ronald Bruno, Historian, Town of Willsboro

[231] Ronald Bruno, *Occasional Papers of the Willsboro Heritage Society, Volume 4, Number 1. Undated*

[232] Ibid.

[233] Milford Hale Smith, PhD., *Genealogy of the Adsit Family, 1716-1923,* (Rutland, VT, self-published, 1923).

[234] Ibid.

[235] Winslow C. Watson, *The Military,* 209.

[236] Stroud Family History,1929.

[237] *Essex County Real Property Records,* May 21, 1818.

[238] H. Nicholas Muller III, *Oral History,* June 2019.

[239] Ibid.

[240] Milford Hale Smith, PhD. Rutland, VT, *Genealogy of,* Appendix 8.

[241] Narrative compiled by Solomon Clark, 1888.

[242] Town of Willsborough Records, 2018.

[243] Ronald Bruno, *Oral History,* 2018.

INDEX

GLOSSARY OF UNUSUAL TERMS

Morpheus—The god associated with sleep and dreams

Sledge—A general purpose flat wood sled without runners

Peavey—A lever for handling logs

Stone Boat—A flat wood sledge designed to carry heavy loads

Adze—A woodworking tool with a wide iron plate set at right angles to the handle

Chinking—Small stones inserted between logs in a log cabin

Daub—A sticky substance inserted between logs in a log cabin

Shakes—Wood shingles

String Latch—A string through the door that lets the interior latch move up and down

Puncheon Floors—Floors made of wood that has only been smoothed on one side

Broad Axe—Axe similar to an adze used to peel bark away

Trammel—Crane over the fire in a fireplace to hold pots

Settle—Bench with a high back

Gambrel—Roof with sloping ends and sides

Harrow—A farm tool with teeth used to break up soil

Yoke—Wood piece that fits over oxen shoulders and keeps them moving together

Gad—Sapling used as a whip

Tinder Box—Box that holds twigs for starting a fire with a spark-making rock

Sad Iron—Heavy triangular piece of iron with handle used to smooth clothes

Felling Axe—Axe designed primarily for taking down trees

Hatchet—Small axe with short handle

Spiles—Tree tapping spouts for maple sap

Pones—Cross piece that joins uprights to hold pots over a fire

Snath—Handle of a scythe

Sheaths—Bundles of stems that have been put together

Stooks—Cone shaped stacks of flax

Retting—Laying flax outdoors to dry

Scutch—Flat board used to remove flax straw out of the fiber

Heckle—Board with metal teeth to refine flax fibers

Plummet—Rough pencil

Ferule—Ruler used by schoolmasters to keep discipline

Manumitted—Freed from slavery

Swaths—Piles of cut grain

Grain Cradle—Framework for farm implement to cut grain

Fingers—Roots used to make teeth for grain cradle

Sned—Ash wood used to attach the cradle to the fingers

Nib—Piece of wood which the reaper can use to hold onto the cradle

Snath—Handle for holding the cradle

Sheaves—Bundles of grain

Tapes—Shoe and boot laces

ABOUT THE AUTHOR

For Darcey Hale history has been her passion since childhood when, much to her parent's surprise, she asked for a copy of James Breasted's Ancient Times: A History of the Early World for her 9th birthday. This fascination was further reinforced by time spent in The Yucatan during sixth grade where she clambered over ruins and imagined herself as a fair maiden being thrown into a sacred cenote to appease the wrathful gods. Later, by good fortune Vassar College initiated an American Cultural History degree program while she was there. This brought her love of history into focus, especially as it relates to the lives of American people in the 19th century.

After college, by pure dint of circumstance, she found herself teaching in suburban Philadelphia and, much to her complete surprise, she loved it. She received her master's degree from Villanova University and for the next almost 50 years taught practically every grade, founded a school, became an administrator and spent the final years of her career as the head of several schools. More importantly, during those years she and her husband raised four sons, two of whom became teachers themselves. The tradition continues!

Retirement led Darcey to Willsborough Point and her discovery of what became The Clark Collection. Her life came full circle as she became immersed in archiving and caring for the legacy that they had unknowingly entrusted to her. Their story had to be told. It was far too fascinating to lie dormant. Thus, Darcey chose yet another turn in the road and embarked upon a writing career at 85. The rest is its own bit of history that she shares with you, her reader.

THE CLARK COLLECTION

A PORTRAYAL OF NINETEENTH CENTURY INDUSTRY, COMMERCE, AND CULTURE IN THE CHAMPLAIN VALLEY - AT THE NEW YORK STATE LIBRARY

The "Clark Collection" is an extensive and varied assortment of 51,000 paper items and 6,000 photographs that portray the social, cultural, business, financial, economic and political lives of the Clarks of Willsborough Point throughout the 19th century. Together they offer the researcher and historian valuable insights into life in the Champlain Valley of New York during that period. Over the past twenty years Morris Glenn and I discovered these records in remarkably good condition in the Clark family homes, Scragwood (1840) and Old Elm (1842) and in all of their various outbuildings.

The Collection consists of: diaries; personal and business correspondence; printed materials, postcards, invoices and receipts, legal notes, land surveys, newspapers; periodicals, sheet music, farming, quarrying, shipping and shipbuilding business records; employee and company store records, architectural and engineering drawings; Invitations, programs and other ephemera, and photographs dating from the period 1760 to 1902.

Through pictures and words, the family diaries, writings and personal correspondence transport the reader back in time. They invite you to join them in their daily lives, to be part of their life experiences—some good and some tragic—and to develop a true sense and understanding of these individually, and as a group. At times they were incredibly devoted and loyal and upon other occasions they were seriously at odds with one another. In the Collection Orrin is the primary focus until 1850 when his four children—three boys and a girl—enter the spotlight as adults themselves.

After much deliberation and thought the Clark Collection was donated to and Special Collections department of the New York State Library where it is already receiving special curatorial attention. It is being conserved, archived and catalogued according to the Library's standards. The ultimate goal is to scan and digitize both the paper materials and the photographs so that they will be electronically available to a broad audience of researchers, historians and general history buffs.

ABOUT TBR BOOKS

TBR Books is a program of the Center for the Advancement of Languages, Education, and Communities. We publish researchers and practitioners who seek to engage diverse communities on topics related to education, languages, cultural history, and social initiatives. We translate our books in a variety of languages to further expand our impact. Become a member of TBR Books and receive complimentary access to all our books.

Our books are available on our website and on all major online bookstores as paperback and e-book. Some of our books have been translated in Arabic, Chinese, English, French, German, Italian, Japanese, Polish, Russian, Spanish. For a listing of all books published by TBR Books, information on our series, or for our submission guidelines for authors, visit our website at

http://www.tbr-books.org

 **TBR Books**

A Program of The Center for the Advancement of Languages, Education, and Communities (CALEC)

Our Books in English

The Gift of Languages: Paradigm Shift in U.S. Foreign Language Education by Fabrice Jaumont and Kathleen Stein-Smith

Two Centuries of French Education in New York: The Role of Schools in Cultural Diplomacy by Jane Flatau Ross

The Clarks of Willsborough Point: The Long Trek North by Darcey Hale

The Bilingual Revolution: The Future of Education Is in Two Languages by Fabrice Jaumont

Beyond Gibraltar Trilogy, by Maristella de Panizza Lorch

Our Books in Translation

Die bilinguale Revolution: Die Zukunft der Bildung liegt in zwei Sprachen by Fabrice Jaumont

La revolución bilingüe: El futuro de la educación está en dos idiomas by Fabrice Jaumont

ДВУЯЗЫЧНАЯ РЕВОЛЮЦИЯ: БУДУЩЕЕ ОБРАЗОВАНИЯ НА ДВУХ ЯЗЫКАХ by Фабрис Жомон

La Révolution bilingue : Le futur de l'éducation s'écrit en deux langues by Fabrice Jaumont

ABOUT CALEC

The Center for the Advancement of Languages, Education, and Communities is a nonprofit organization with a focus on multilingualism, cross-cultural understanding, and the dissemination of ideas. Our mission is to empower multilingual families and linguistic communities through education, knowledge, and advocacy.

The specific objectives and purpose of this organization are to provide information, coaching, support, and tools to multilingual families seeking to create language programs and advance cross-cultural understanding in their schools; to support diverse communities through education, coaching, advocacy, knowledge sharing and international connections; to publish and distribute research papers, books, resources, and case studies with a focus on innovative ideas for education, language, and culture; to support and promote authors, researchers, and artists engaged in multilingual education, the advancement of languages and linguistic communities, and cultural development; to sponsor, host and/or participate in events and activities that promote language education and cultural development.

We also support parents and educators interested in advancing languages, education, and communities. We participate in events and conferences that promote multilingualism and cultural development. We provide consulting for school leaders and educators who implement multilingual programs in their school. For more information and ways you can support our mission, visit our website,

http://www.calec.org